The Leading *Lady*

DEB MARLOWE

To Christine,
It was lovely to
Meet you at RT!
Best!.
Deb Marlowe

For more information:

www.DebMarlowe.com

HALF MOON HOUSE

Don't miss the other books in the Half Moon House Series

The Love List

An Unexpected Encounter

A Slight Miscalculation

Liberty and the Pursuit of Happiness

A Waltz in the Park

Beyond a Reasonable Duke, found in the 50 Ways to Kill Your Larry anthology

and

Coming Soon:

The Lady's Legacy

With Many Thanks to Mary Ann Landers for her idea to name the inn The Sword and the Sheath

and

To Deb's Debutantes—the nicest group of ladies I know! Thanks for listening, sharing your joys and woes, for being fabulous cheerleaders and just for being there, every day!

Table of Contents

Other books in the Half Moon House Series

Chapter One
Dover, England
1814

You think you can imagine my joy, dear reader, at that first taste of freedom after months of Lord M—'s abuse. You cannot. I could scarcely contain myself. That first glimpse of the half moon and its accompanying stars—that sky was the picture of relief, of hope, of liberty and possibility. It was the brightest light in my life, before or since, and I've long labored to bring the same to others in need.

—from the journal of the infamous Miss Hestia Wright

A man who had lost everything is the most dangerous of all. That's what the old wives said, wasn't it? Well, what the hell did they know, after all? Someone should make them amend it.

Disrespectful, old boy.

He was sorry for it, perhaps. Most old wives had likely lived long enough to know their share of pain and disappointment, betrayal and death. Still, he would correct that common misconception, if he could.

A man with nothing to lose is surely the most *reckless* of all.

Lord Truitt Russell should know.

Except, he hadn't *lost* everything that was important to him. He hadn't *misplaced* his honor or his good name. They'd been stolen from him. And right now he felt reckless indeed, as if he'd do any damned thing to get them back.

He leaned back in his chair as laughter ricocheted about the taproom. Loud, infectious and fueled by endless pints of the hearty local brew, it managed to brighten even the smoke-haunted, weary tone of the Cloak and Dagger Inn.

Contagious, that sort of half-drunken, high good humor. The Inn was the favored post-performance haunt of Dover's theatrical troupes. Tonight, actor, singer and stagehand alike drank deep, celebrating some triumphant performance. Spirits flew high, along with banter, wit and the kind of happy, ribald ribbing that made an onlooker wish to join in.

He might have done so, once. Not long ago he might have bought a round and pulled that buxom seamstress into his lap as he took a chair amongst them. He might have spent his evening laughing hard and holding his own in the barrage of fast-flying barbs. He might have finished out the night with a joyous romp betwixt that pretty girl's curves and between her thighs.

But that was before—before his disgrace, before his own abysmal lack of judgment led him to unwittingly aid a nefarious plot against his own king and country.

Before Marstoke.

He shook off the burning fury that came with the thought of the manipulative marquess and kept his attention fixed on his quarry. Tonight he *meant* to do any damned thing, and he was bound and determined to do something reckless.

He focused, keeping track of his prey even as he pasted a benevolent half-grin on his face and pretended to watch the frolicking actors.

Two men were his real focus, both young and wellborn. They sat hunched, heads together, as if the smoke and the crowd and the shadows at the back of the room were not enough to keep them hidden.

Tru knew them, though they were younger than he by several years. Nick Penrith, Lord Rutherford's fifth son and the other, Lyle Rackham, a nephew of Viscount Beryl. He'd never exchanged words with them or sat across from either of them at dinner, for all that they'd nominally belonged to the *beau monde*. He didn't think they knew him. He was being careful, nonetheless.

Damnation, but it was a chore to keep that idiotic look on his face, to hide the great swath of his resentment. But they were but pawns, these two, and a brace of fools in the bargain. Young and malleable enough to be made into zealots. Old enough to be hung for treason.

The same fate Marstoke and his cohorts had meant for him.

He wanted to haul the pair outside to the cobbled street and beat them within an inch of their lives. He, at least, had been tricked into carrying out his part in the Marquess of Marstoke's dishonorable scheming. These two embraced betrayal with their eyes open. They played at it like children, with obvious excitement and smug, self-important whispers. It seemed a miracle that he had been the only one to discern their connection to the missing Marstoke and their clumsy, continued efforts on his behalf.

But though Tru deplored their actions—and the amateurish way they went about them—he didn't have to question the *why* of it.

He knew.

They were younger sons, extraneous branches on the family tree. Tru knew the difficulties of struggling to thrive in the shadow of a noble older brother. He knew the lost feeling, the bitterness that came from invisibility, from struggling to find an identity even as the family scion was handed his. And those two were a good bit further down their respective lines than he. Sunlight was scarce so far from the top, as was a sense of purpose and value.

Yes, resentment and dissatisfaction could easily flourish in the shade. Marstoke would have seen it—and put it to his own twisted use.

He wiped his mouth with a sleeve. The how, the why, and the wherefores—none of it mattered. Only Marstoke mattered. Where he was hiding, what he was plotting now and how he could be dragged back to justice-- those were the subjects that consumed Tru. And thanks to Penrith's valet, who had a penchant for dice and a willingness to cover his losses by taking a bribe, he knew that these two were even now traveling to join the marquess.

Perhaps the hefty weight of their mission had at last lent them an air of seriousness. He'd had to be more careful tonight in tailing them. Even now one of them swept the room with a searching glance. Tru took another deep swill of ale, pretending to choke with laughter as one of the actors spun about a pillar.

"There once lived a maid, quite busty

Whose thirst could be labeled quite lusty . . ."

Tru called out encouragement along with the rest of the delighted patrons. But the hair on his neck was bristling, his instincts screaming. He hazarded a glance in the pair's direction, and just caught sight of them disappearing into a narrow door set in the wall at the end of the bar.

*"I vow that **this** won't leave ye dusty!"*

The actor finished his limerick with a crude grab at his crotch. Tru stood, intentionally staggering a bit, and shaking with laughter. He hitched up his borrowed, worn breeches and left a thumb tucked into the waistband. A happy drunk in search of a privy could be forgiven many sins.

He stumbled a bit as he made his way to the door, but he turned the latch with silent stealth. It opened onto a short passage, so narrow a heftier man would have difficulty navigating it, and ending just past a lone doorway on the right. It was lit with a single tallow lamp sputtering on a ledge next to the doorframe.

Tru slipped in. He eased up to the door to listen. Murmurs? Perhaps. But they were faint.

He considered. It could be damned difficult to fight free, were he caught in this narrow space. But what if Marstoke was inside that room at this very moment? His pulse quickened at the notion. His gut burned for vengeance, for the chance at redemption. He couldn't leave without knowing.

He eased the door open, just the slightest bit.

Nothing, save darkness. Silence. He tensed. Waited. Not a sound came from the room.

Just a bit further, ever so slowly.

He peered in—and with a filthy curse that echoed loudly in the limited space he threw the door open. Just in time to see the wall panel across from him slide closed. In time for the burly man closing it to catch sight of him. In time for the bastard to grin, his gold tooth shining, and toss Tru a saucy wink as the hidden door slid shut.

"Hell, no," Tru said. "No, no, no." He reached the panel in a rush and thumped it with his fist. Was that an answering laugh, faint and fading away? Frantic he pushed against the wall, trying to make it slide back. It didn't budge. Cursing, he searched with his hands, running them over the dusty plaster, hoping to feel a latch or a trigger. Frustrated, he began to search the shelves nearby, knocking things to the floor in his haste. Nothing. He reached lower and began to shift barrels and sacks of flour.

"The doors into those tunnels open only from the other side," a lethally soft voice said from behind him.

Tru spun about, sinking into a crouch and reaching for the knife in his boot. A form leaned casually against the frame of the door he'd just entered.

He didn't hesitate. Without a sound he sprang, and in an instant he had his knife at the stranger's throat and the man's arm twisted up high and tight behind him. "Open it," he growled.

"Can't be done," his prisoner said easily. "Though I would if I could."

Abruptly, Tru released the man. "Stoneacre," he said in disgust. "That's the second time in our short acquaintance that you've surprised me in such a manner." He stepped back with a scowl. "It's a habit that could easily get you killed."

"Not as quickly as going into these tunnels uninvited will," the earl countered.

"What do you know of it?"

Stoneacre had shown up at the end of last month's debacle with Marstoke, charged by the King's Privy Council to investigate the rumors regarding the treasonous marquess.

"Didn't you look up when you entered this place? The Cloak and Dagger is built right into the chalk cliffs. The castle is up there, nearly directly overhead." Stoneacre grinned. "Just a few short years ago, those tunnels housed two thousand army men, ready to defend us from the French. Now the Coastal Blockade means to use it to fight smuggling—which makes it that much more ironic that parts of it have been blocked off and reconfigured and are run by gangs of smugglers and ruffians."

He frowned. "It cannot be opened from here?"

The earl shook his head. "I'm afraid not."

Tru aimed a savage kick at a wine cask, allowing the violence to serve both as answer and opinion. "What in hell are you doing here, in any case?"

"Watching you watch that pair of wet-behind-the-ears nodcocks, it would seem." He crossed his arms. "We knew that pair have got themselves mixed up with Marstoke's scheming. We've been watching them—and we were somewhat shocked to find you doing the same."

He raised a brow. "Just how did that come about?"

Tru wondered at times if the Privy Council was the true extent of the earl's connections, especially when he spoke so casually of what 'we' thought or 'we' found. But one thing Tru did know, Stoneacre wanted Marstoke almost as much as he did. Moreover, Stoneacre already knew the worst. He could trust him with the rest. He drew a deep, steadying breath. "That night, in London—the evening when the Russian girl was abducted—"

"Ah yes," Stoneacre interrupted with a grin. "The night you so valiantly came to her rescue."

"Yes, that night," he agreed bitterly. "When I stepped in, rescued a girl who didn't truly need saving, got myself trapped in Marstoke's nets, destroyed my reputation and ruined my life."

Stoneacre raised a brow. "Exaggerating just a bit, are you not?"

"Why don't you ask around and discover if it's exaggeration or not? No one knows exactly what happened that night at the theater with the Prince Regent and all the foreign dignitaries. But they know *something* happened. They know Marstoke disappeared that night. They know his house has been searched, his servants questioned, his papers confiscated. And they know that I was working closely with the marquess on some quiet project. They see how the Prince Regent has distanced himself from me." He clenched his fists. "Why don't you question the tradesmen who will no longer extend me credit? Ask them about exaggerations. Ask the hostesses who no longer invite me to their parties. Or the impudent chit who crossed Bond Street the other day to avoid passing within the pavement's width of me?"

And he couldn't even bear to mention the look of doubt in the Prince Regent's eyes. They'd been friends for years, comrades if not exactly confidantes. But now Prinny held himself distant, as if he believed Tru might have participated in the scheme to make him look weak and foolish, unfit to rule.

"It's not tailors, society matrons, or impudent chits that bother you, though, is it?" the other man asked quietly.

"God, no."

Stoneacre had been there, at the end. He'd seen the depth of Tru's folly. He'd helped Tru and his brother avert the disaster Tru had unwittingly helped to set in motion. He understood the political chaos that might have come about, the riots, the social upheaval, the shift in history itself, should Marstoke have succeeded.

But Stoneacre didn't know what had happened inside Tru when he'd fallen for Marstoke's manipulations. He couldn't see the old doubts that came rushing back, the despair at having to face his own uncertainties again. And Tru didn't want him—or anyone else—to suspect.

All he wanted was to go back—back to the time when he could hold his head high and he was the only person who gave a thought to his inadequacies.

"In any case, I got close to a few of those blackguards that night." The abduction might not have been what it appeared, but the fight to keep him from aiding the girl had been real enough. "I thought I recognized Penrith's boy, behind his mask. So I did a little investigating. And I found that he is indeed mixed up in Marstoke's scheming. In fact, I have good reason to believe that he and his nodcock friend, as you so aptly named them, are headed to meet with Marstoke at this very moment." He turned away and stepped away from the wall. "So stop talking and lend me your aid. If you are the expert, tell me how to get inside there."

"You cannot go in there. Some of these passages are ancient. Some are dangerous. The ones that connect here are well and jealously guarded. Those boys entered with advanced arrangements and a good deal of ready coin. If you go in without both, you'll come out a corpse."

Frustration roiled up and out of him. "Damn it,

Stoneacre! Did you hear what I said? They are going to *Marstoke*. I must find him. You know that. This is the best lead I've found since the blighter disappeared. If I can't follow those two, what would you have me do?"

Stoneacre straightened. His grin looked eerie in the dim light. "Come with me instead. There's no need to follow them. I'll take you where they are headed."

Tru stared. "You've found him?"

"We've discovered where's he's been hiding."

A great weight lifted from Tru's chest. Suddenly he could breathe, as he hadn't been able to for weeks. A flare of hunger, of purpose, roared to life in his gut. "Let's go."

"It will mean a lengthy trip," Stoneacre warned.

"I don't care if it means storming the gates of Hell. Let's go get him."

Stoneacre nodded and clapped him on the shoulder. "We're going. We have a stop to make first, though."

***

Callie Grant's temper had stretched to the end of its tether. Even in the dark and the rain, this end of Dover smelled of tidal mud and rotting fish. A light drizzle began to fall, dampening the stink not a whit. It would have to be a deluge to make a difference in this dimly lit, rubbish-filled lane.

"Don't think you can lie to me, Birch." She summoned her best, most effective snarl and tossed it at the huge man. "I know you and your friend accosted Letty Robbins in London last week."

Birch's cohort, an evil-looking cur with a great scar across his forehead, sidled a bit to his right—the better to box her in.

"Stay where you are!" she barked. "The both of you." With deliberate slowness she inched her hand from the folds of her skirt, displaying only the butt end of her pistol.

The cur froze, but Birch only scrubbed a weary hand across his face. A white smear followed in the trail of his fingers. "Weren't no accosting goin' on, Callie Grant. 'Twere just a job. An escort job, like. What is it ye want? I'm gettin' wet, but my throat's still dry." A raucous sailor's song drifted from the tavern the pair had been approaching before she stopped them. He glanced toward the door with clear longing.

"I saw you myself, hustling Letty away," Callie declared. She'd literally dropped everything—abandoning her full market basket in the street—to follow the trio through London's busy streets to a coaching inn in the Strand. The two men had obviously planned ahead—they were handing Letty into a stage when Callie rushed into the courtyard. She'd been forced to jump aside as the coach surged out into the street, but a young ostler had informed her that it was bound for Dover.

"Aye?" Birch asked. "Then you saw that this weren't no abduction. Letty was expectin' us and she come willin' enough."

Callie had to fight off a wave of defeat at his words. She'd suspected as much. But it didn't matter. She squared her shoulders and wiped the rain from her face. She'd been saving Letty from herself since the girl had toddled her first step. This was no different.

"Say what you will," she said with a wave of her hand. "What's important is where she is now."

"We don't need to tell ye nothin'," Birch's cohort spoke up. He had white dust in his hair and white marks smeared across his rough linens. What had the pair of them been into, to be so covered in thick white streaks? He inched closer again. Too close. "We done the job wot we was paid for."

Callie rounded on him. "I don't know you—and I presume that you are too ignorant to know the perils of crossing me. Birch can tell you the folly of getting on my bad side—and that of Hestia Wright."

"Now, Miss Callie," Birch began. "You and Hestia Wright cannot be savin' every wench with rash intentions and bad judgment."

But his friend bristled, throwing his shoulders back and lowering his brow. "See here, Miss Up and Mighty. Your friend give us enough lip. I ain't takin' it from you, too."

"Quiet, Cobb," Birch ordered. "We don't want trouble, Miss Callie." His voice gentled. "Letty's right where she wants to be. You'd best just let 'er go."

Denial surged. Callie drew breath to answer, but Cobb interrupted with a derisive snort. "What's got into ye, Birch? Why in blazes are you dancin' around this girl's skirts? We had orders not to touch the other one. She knew it, too, and I swear she worked to get my blood up, out of pure spite." He shifted position and adjusted his smock. The addition of white smudged fingerprints did nothing to improve the look of it. "And I still ain't had the chance to scratch that itch. Now, there's been no word on this one. She's clean. Smells good. Smart-mouthed, but she's alone. Ain't nothin' that says we can't teach her a better use for that mouth."

"Shut it, Cobb," barked Birch.

"Why?" Cobb leered. "I got a mind to take my ease o' 'er."

Here it was again. A drama played out endlessly over time, in dark lanes like this one, in brighter, wider streets, in hovels, homes and mansions the world over. Was there anything more universal than abuse of the weak? Than a man thinking to use his greater strength, wealth or position to brutalize a woman? Any other woman would have had the sense to be terrified. But Callie had learned the trick of turning her fear into fury. She knew it was possible to fight back—both for herself, and for others.

Cobb was edging closer. He watched her pistol hand, Callie noted with satisfaction. She kept her other hand, the one with the blade, still and ready to strike. She tossed her hair, slowly growing wet enough to drip, out of her eyes. All of her frustration with Letty, her anger at this bully and all of his brethren, flared high, setting her resolve.

She'd learned a few things about his sort over the years, working with Hestia Wright. She'd stood off against men who made Cobb look like a schoolyard bully, against drunkards and vicious pimps, abusive husbands and self-righteous parents. She braced her knees and watched his chest. Always the chest, which messaged intent. She took note of his, saw the instant he meant to move, tightened her grip—and found herself snatched out of the way.

She glared upwards, snarling, ready to flail Birch's hide, only to find that it was another man entirely holding her arm in a vise grip.

Another man—whom she recognized in an instant.

She froze. Her eyes widened and her cheeks heated until she felt they must look like beacons glowing through the misty drizzle. The ground shifted beneath her feet.

Lord Truitt Russell.

Of all the men she never wanted interfering in her business—it was he, pulling her close, growling a warning at Cobb, stealing her breath and her stability.

She hadn't thought twice about confronting Birch and Cobb in a rapidly darkening alley—Birch knew her, knew her work, and understood the incredible heft of Hestia Wright's name backing her. He would allow her to skirmish with Cobb, but he wasn't going to let things get out of hand. She might be on slightly dangerous ground with these two, but at least it was familiar territory.

That had never been the case with Lord Truitt Russell.

She'd beheld him with nothing but scorn when first

he turned up, interviewing prostitutes of every level for his reworking of the old Love List—just another lordling amusing himself in the London's stews and back alleys. Later they had clashed—finding themselves at cross purposes after the Marquess of Marstoke's true intent for the List had been discovered and the extent of his villainy revealed. But disdain and frustration aside, she'd always *noticed* him.

How could she not? His height, his endlessly wide shoulders, all that lean muscle wrapped in masterful tailoring—he'd been crafted to attract feminine attention.

"Move on now." Lord Truitt's voice rumbled with suppressed anger as he tossed the order at Cobb. "Go about your business and leave the woman alone."

His raspy tone vibrated right through her, tickling hidden parts of her anatomy.

She shivered. This was bad. Very bad, indeed.

Cobb, either too frustrated or too stupid to know when to back down, puffed up like a bantam rooster. "Here now, we call first claim on 'er!" He reached for her again. "We don't hold with poachin'. Find yer own—"

A soft snick sounded behind her. Before anyone could react, Cobb found his protest cut short as the point of a blade came to rest perilously close to his dirt-smeared neck.

Callie looked around and groaned. "Not you too, Stoneacre."

She had to put a stop to this. To their actions and her even more unwelcome reactions. She snatched her arm free and glared between the two interfering men. "What do the pair of you think you are doing? I have business here! There's no need for you to interfere."

Lord Truitt frowned down at her—and there it was, clearly visible. The precise instant that he recognized her. That awareness didn't come alone, either. It dragged a dose of shock along, and a less-than-flattering horror that broadcast itself across the handsome lord's face.

"Callie Grant." He let her go and stepped away, as if she carried the plague.

Perhaps in the darkest hours, at her most private moments, Callie might have conjured up a scenario in which the two of them were not sniping and bickering like children. She might have indulged in a vision of a dance, or a conversation conducted in adult harmony. She might even have dreamed of a kiss, of this particular man dragging her name out in a moan—but she hadn't imagined it said with a tone of impatient disdain.

He turned on Stoneacre. "The chit's asked the right question for once. What in hell are we doing? Is this your idea of a jest, Stoneacre? Or is it some warped test? Since I ruined myself rescuing one damsel in distress, do you think I must have a hand in saving them all? Did you think to laugh? Or was I supposed to instantly recognize the most contrary girl in the kingdom and the one least likely to appreciate my help?"

Callie bristled. "Never mind," she snapped. "Don't answer. I don't care why you are here—only that you take your leave. Now."

"Gladly." Lord Truitt turned on his heel.

"Wait," Lord Stoneacre ordered. He bent a kind look on Callie. "Miss Grant, I'm afraid we've come for you."

She blinked. "Excuse me?"

"What was that?" Lord Truitt demanded.

"Well, damn it all," Cobb spat.

Birch stepped up. The white smears across his forehead and on his shoulders had begun to run in the rain. "It looks like you gentlemen can take the lady in hand. We'll jest be goin' to tap a glass, then." The big man jerked his head at his partner and the two of them faded back toward the tavern.

Callie barely noticed. She was staring at Stoneacre's sympathetic expression and greatly fearing she knew what it meant.

"What's this about, Stoneacre?" Lord Truitt asked again. "You said we were going after Marstoke. Miss Grant has made her position on this issue clear already. Repeatedly, in fact, during the social whirl surrounding my brother's marriage to her friend." He folded his arms. "She doesn't want Marstoke found and dragged back to justice—not by me or anyone else."

"I don't think Miss Grant's feelings on the topic are so simple. In fact, I believe her objections arise from her worries about Lord Marstoke exerting undue influence on Letty Robbins."

Her shoulders slumped. "I'm too late, aren't I?"

"I'm afraid so. She's with him even now." Stoneacre nodded toward Lord Truitt. "But we are going after Marstoke—and I need to speak with you before we do."

Stoneacre was a powerful man. Wealthy and titled in his own right, but richer by far in his friends and influence, or so rumor had it. And now this influential man stood dripping rain, regarding her with an unfailing, steady compassion.

Damn.

"You know, don't you?" she clipped.

"I'm afraid so."

She groaned.

Stoneacre offered his arm. "Let's find a dry spot to talk."

She put her arm in his and glanced over her shoulder at Lord Truitt. "Does he have to know as well?"

Stoneacre smiled. "I'm afraid so."

Callie sighed. She stole another glance back. Lord

Truitt smoldered back at her with dark beauty and frowning disapproval.

Damn. And damn again.

Chapter Two

St. Malo, Brittany

Dumped from a carriage, alone, with child and without prospects—yet, still I was filled with determination. I set out along that dusty lane, following the promise of those stars, taking the first steps into what Lord M— expected to be a short life filled with want and misery. I knew better.

—from the journal of the infamous Miss Hestia Wright.

The screams unsettled her.

Letty Robbins had led quite a sheltered early life. Perhaps it wasn't surprising for the illegitimate daughter of a Grand Personage, as she liked to call her eminently uninterested father. She'd left all of that behind as soon as she could, however. She didn't like quiet, had no interest in *sheltered*. She'd wanted to see more, have more, *live* more.

Events had taken an unexpected turn, however, and consequently she'd spent the last year seeing more than she had bargained for—and yet, less than she might have—living as she had amongst London's worst collection of thieves, thugs, bawds and whores. She had learned quite a bit, though—including how to distinguish screams put on for a show from the real thing.

Her heart pounding, she stared at the small house nestled amid a copse of scrub pines, knowing that the pleading cries coming from there were real.

The sun shone, brightly illuminating the pretty little scene. A soft breeze brushed her cheek, smelling of sweet, ripening fruit. It was all so utterly incongruous with whatever terrifying events must be happening in that house.

Abruptly, the screaming stopped. Almost as if someone had heard the direction of her thoughts.

Letty dropped the fragrant branch that had blocked her path, turned on her heel and headed back the way she had come. Back to the dubious safety of the rambling, stone villa. Another lesson lately learned—not to ask questions. She might be in league with the Marquess of Marstoke, but she'd be worse than a fool to think of crossing him. She wanted no part of what might be going on in that cottage—and wanted less for anyone to know she'd discovered it.

She said not a word to anyone and she didn't see the marquess at all that day. By the following day she counted herself safe. She must not have been spotted. Relieved, she spent the afternoon at her lessons, though she grew more irritated by the moment as the young upstart of a maid corrected her again and again.

"No. It's the left leg she always stretches out as she sits to write letters. And don't forget to tilt your head."

Letty complied.

"The other way."

She shot the girl a nasty look and only got a grin in return.

"There it is. That's it, exactly."

Letty rolled her eyes.

"I'm glad to find you doing so well, my dear."

She jumped. That last bit of praise had come from behind her, and in the marquess's smooth, cold tones.

"No, continue," he instructed. "She writes a great many letters. This is an important mannerism to master."

Obedient, she turned to the paper before her once more.

He watched her in silence, perched upon the arm of a padded chair. The minutes stretched out. The silence grew thick with all of the words not being said. Worse, Letty began to run out of nonsense to inscribe with her quill. *When I am the grandest lady in the land*, she wrote, *I will banish that cheeky maid to the scullery.*

"Did you enjoy your walk yesterday?" Abrupt, the question cut into the quiet.

With all of her will she held still, kept her answer casual and unaffected. "Yes, thank you, my lord. The estate is very pretty."

He didn't answer. She glanced up and her nerves suffered a jolt at the intense look of displeasure he bent upon her.

"It was just a short walk," she said. "And uneventful."

He stilled and she knew she'd made a mistake. The quill in her hand began to shake.

"Keep your wanderings to other parts of the estate, my dear," he said softly. "Unless you have a wish to take up permanent residence in that little cottage?"

She shook her head and bent to her writing. *The greatest role in the history of theater and the stage*, she wrote. *In the history of history. It will be worth it.*

He stood. "I've guests arriving soon. A pair of young acolytes. They shall get in very late, in all likelihood. I inform you because I wish you to keep your distance from them, as well. They've no need to know the specific direction of our plans just yet."

Disappointment stilled her hand. She knew the type he recruited for such positions. Young gentlemen of good birth and wealthy families. Exactly the sort of men she'd hoped to meet, when she'd left home so long ago.

The marquess correctly interpreted her silence. "Letty, you will do as you are bid."

Frustration stiffened her spine, fueled by the knowledge that despite the significance of her role, he held not an iota of respect for her. For months—beginning long before her hurried journey to this French backwater—she'd performed every task set before her and done it well. She'd had no word of praise or thanks and she'd been given no idea when her toils would be over and she'd be set upon the path that promised so many rewards. Straightening, she set down the quill. "If this works, there will come a time when it will not be so easy for you to order me about in this fashion."

She had no time to even think what a fool she was, the violence came so swiftly. She never saw him move, only had a second to jump back as the spindly desk before her flew hard through the air and into the wall. Suddenly he was before her, his hand encircling her throat.

"Leave us."

The maid scurried for the door, closing it behind her as she fled.

"On the contrary, my dear. If this works, I will always and absolutely order your every waking moment."

The words were quiet, the tone conversational. It frightened Letty more than the violent outburst.

"Why else would I spend so much time, effort and money on *you*?"

She couldn't answer, could only struggle to swallow past his tightening grip.

"Little fool. You are nothing but a fine nose between correctly shaped eyes. Were it not for your profile, you'd be singing still at the back of that dreary little theater. Or spreading your thighs for some minor baron's son."

He pushed her abruptly away and she stumbled backward, tripping over her chair and landing in a heap upon the floor. She didn't dare take her eyes from him.

"Why could you not be *useful?*" It came out a snarl, causing her to flinch back. But he turned away from her and crossed to gaze out the window, upon the climbing, cultivated hills beyond the woods. He drew in a great breath and let it out slowly. "The game heats up." He shot a look over his shoulder. "Appearance is one thing, but a worthy mind is yet another. You, alas, are but a placeholder, a piece to be moved about as I see fit." He spun around and advanced. "Do you understand? You will play your role but *I* will hold the power. All of it."

Letty pressed her lips together and nodded.

"Good." He walked on past her. "Don't forget this lesson." At the doorway he paused. "And know that if you do, then I won't hesitate to remove you from play altogether."

With soft snick of the closing door, he was gone. She stared at the ceiling overhead, unseeing, for long moments before climbing painfully to her feet.

An eerily high-pitched, deep-throated hum jangled her nerves. She turned to find Anselm, Marstoke's toady, had cracked the door to peek through. His impassive expression was, as usual, completely incongruous with that horrid sound he made. He made her skin crawl.

She kept her expression blank while she wondered if he'd been the one to inform on her.

Moving slowly, she righted the table and chair. Anselm grew bored and took himself off.

Taking her seat, she took up her quill and paper, stretched out her left leg and angling her head, began to write again.

I fear I have made a grievous mistake. It will likely be my last.

Chapter Three

For miles I walked, alone in the dark. But not truly alone, after all. I had a child to protect, and a thousand visions of our future to keep me company.

—from the journal of the infamous Miss Hestia Wright

Tru's fingers danced against his thigh, the only sign of his impatience as he followed Stoneacre and the Grant girl through the damp streets of Dover.

Yet he burned with it. The restless ache that swirled in his gut picked up speed, fueling eagerness and anxiety. At last. After all these weeks—a hint, a promise of action. He didn't want to be tamely trailing the sway of Callie Grant's skirts through an ever-increasing downpour. He hungered to go now, to hire a carriage or hop aboard a ship and head straight to wherever it was Marstoke was hiding.

But his habitual impulsiveness had gotten him into this mess. He would not fall prey to it again. He hoped to God he'd learned at least that much as his life fell to shambles. So he strained, pulled back on the reins of his impatience and allowed his fingers to tap out his angst, when all he really wished to do was to reach out, wrap them about Marstoke's neck and get a firm grip on justice and truth.

Stoneacre led them into a nondescript building not far from the Marine Parade. Fair to bursting with questions, Tru surged forward, only to be held up as a portly man stepped into the entry hall to meet them. He held out a leather packet. Stoneacre examined the papers inside, then pulled him aside. Whispers slid toward Tru in the damp hall, taunting, as Stoneacre asked questions, low and rapid fire. Tru watched, longing to insert himself and find out just what was going on. He sidled closer to Callie Grant instead.

The girl had been a thorn in his side since he first met her, a few weeks ago, just after his brother had struck him free of Marstoke's clutches. She had no love for the damned marquess either, but she'd spent every waking moment since telling anyone who would listen that they should let him lie wherever he'd landed, allow him to wreak havoc elsewhere and leave them in peace.

He could scarcely believe that she was the reason Stoneacre had delayed their immediate departure. Ironic, that.

Yet still, if anything—or anyone—stood a chance of distracting him from this restless impatience, it was she—a walking, talking bundle of startling contrasts. They'd had more than one rancorous confrontation already, so his mind could easily dredge up the memory of her clear, green eyes, offer up an image of them beckoning a man from a sweet, heart-shaped face.

Street gossip named her Hestia Wright's right hand—and she looked the part of companion to the world's most famous ex-courtesan. Callie Grant was a bedroom fantasy come to life, with delicate skin, so pure and light you felt sure you could see through it. The perfect foil for that wealth of unruly hair, darker now with the wet and missing its usual auburn tint. But it was her body that held a man captive, helpless to look away. She was small in stature, yet boasted more curves than the Thames. Her bosom was a thing of wonder even without sodden curls straggling down, pointing the way, and damp clothes clinging tight. In Tru's eye she stood testament, a magnificent temple to womanly bounty.

He knew better than to touch, however. Nearly every bit of the girl crooned a siren's invitation, but her tongue sang another, sharper song altogether. Men in general she held in disdain, but for him she'd nurtured a special contempt. He wasn't surprised, therefore, when she stepped sharply away, keeping her back to him.

"You're standing too close, Lord Truitt." She cast a cross glance over her shoulder. Wrapping her arms tight about herself, she shook her head. "I wish I knew how you do that—and if it is meant to be purposeful or comes entirely naturally."

"How I do what?" True asked absently. Easy to ignore Stoneacre and his friend when he was fully occupied *not* staring at the wet folds of her gown and how they clung tight to the small of her back before smoothing over her hips.

"Irritate me at every turn. It appears effortless on your part, but at times I do wonder if you work at it." She spun about to confront him and he had to avert his eyes. That damp muslin painted a different, far more erotic picture from the front. "Take tonight, for instance, in that alley. Your interference was unnecessary and unwelcome."

Tru frowned. "Timely and essential, I believe are the words you meant to say. That miscreant was about to make a grab for the weapon in your pocket."

She tossed her head. "At which time I would have sunk the knife in my other pocket right into a particular spot in his shoulder—rendering his entire arm useless."

That brought him up short. "Bloodthirsty, are we?"

"And experienced," she agreed. "He had made his intent clear. Should I have played the helpless lady and let him put his filthy hands on me?" She snorted. "No. I've long experience dealing with men of his sort."

He could not have picked a better distraction. Even avoiding the wicked temptation of her wet gown, there was the glint in her eye and the twist of her pretty mouth. "Do you have us all sorted, then, Miss Grant? Alphabetized, perhaps?"

Her gaze lifted to his. "I thought I had."

"Would you care to share your categorizations?"

She held up a hand and ticked off a finger. "Those like Cobb, who like to hurt or dominate women." Another finger ticked down. "Those who merely use them, as if they were a scrap of linen to be thrown away." Another finger. "Then there are those who largely ignore women—after all, we don't often possess power or fortune. Those types do find an occasional use for us, but it rarely lasts long."

The sudden, bleak expression on her face surprised Tru. Their gazes held.

She paused, and the air between them thickened, suddenly ripe with tension and . . . possibility.

She dropped her hand. "There are others," she said quietly. "But you, Lord Truitt? I don't think I know you well enough to know just where you fit."

He opened his mouth to reply, but Stoneacre finally beckoned. "We can talk in here," he called. He gestured to the room his companion opened up.

A parlor, comfortable, but not fine. Nondescript might be the word for it. All done in shades of brown and beige with no family portraits on the wall or personal touches anywhere.

"This is Richards," Stoneacre said. "He'll be our host tonight. If you need something, he'll provide it. Don't hesitate to ask."

The other man bowed. "Please, take advantage of the fire. There is brandy on the sideboard. Tea and sandwiches will arrive shortly."

Stoneacre reached out and touched Callie Grant's arm as she started forward. "Perhaps you'd best go upstairs and change, first?" He waved a hand toward the staircase at the other side of the entryway. "You were out in the wet longer than either of us, and we don't need you taking a chill. We'll wait for you to return before we begin."

"Thank you, sir." She lifted her chin. "But I prefer my own things. I only traveled with one bag, and I left it behind at the Spotted Duck."

"I have it here," said a soft voice from above. Tru and Miss Grant both turned to look up. "And I've brought you some things from home as well."

"Hestia!" The girl's face lit up at the sight of the woman at the top of the staircase. "What are you doing here?"

"Following you."

Hestia Wright, former courtesan, famous philanthropist and easily the most beautiful woman of Tru's acquaintance, started down the stairs.

"Did you think I wouldn't hear of your sudden departure—or the why of it?" She laughed. "The gossip vine at Half Moon House is far too efficient for that. I started out after you at once—and encountered Lord Stoneacre. He, it turns out, was following Lord Truitt to the same spot, and for a similar reason." She paused on the last step and flashed a brilliant smile around the hall. "And now here we all are."

"Yes, with urgent business to discuss," Stoneacre interjected. "So, if you would, Miss Grant?" He gestured toward the second floor.

"I promise I won't allow a single relevant syllable to pass anyone's lips," Hestia said with a smile. "Now go and dry off, dear. Your bags are in the first door to the right."

As Callie Grant acquiesced, the other woman turned and bent the full force of her smile on Tru.

And a formidable weapon it was too. Hestia Wright had been named the Queen of Courtesans in England and on the Continent. She'd been consort to kings, princes and policy makers across Europe. Her wealth was rumored to be immense, her influence was known to be weighty—and all of that paled in comparison to her pale, ethereal beauty.

"Lord Truitt, will you walk me in?"

He gathered himself and held up an obliging arm.

"We shall be good friends, I believe." The touch of her hand felt as light as a feather.

"'Shall we?" he asked, surprised.

"Of course." She blinked. "If the old adage holds true. . ."

Tru stiffened a little. He'd already discarded and disparaged one old wives' tale tonight. "Which adage is that?" he asked, unable to keep a slight edge from his tone.

"Why, the one about the enemy of my enemy, to be sure. Should that one prove itself, then we shall be very good friends indeed."

He smiled, then. He'd heard the rumors about this woman, about her hatred of the Marquess of Marstoke and his for her. His brother had let slip a hint of a battle between them, one that had waged unabated for years. If that were the case, then he would be happy to ally with her—and finish what she'd started. "I shall look forward to it."

"Good. You may call me Hestia, as we are to be friends. And have I heard correctly that you are called Tru?" She smiled at his nod. "A very good name, indeed." She met his gaze with a candid one of her own. "I expect you shall live up to it, sir." She breezed over to a table, then turned. "Oh, Stoneacre, be a dear and hold that door open again, will you? I hear the tea tray coming."

Tru stood back while servants hustled to set up a table and chairs. Hestia took charge and poured them all a cup, adding a healthy dollop of brandy to each. He took it with a nod of thanks, drank deep and let the spreading warmth ease the knot of anxiety in his gut.

"Ah." Hestia poured one more. "Not an ounce of dawdle in that girl," she said with approval as Callie Grant entered with a quick, light step.

She was tidy again, Tru noted, and clad for warmth

in a plain, long-sleeved gown. But no amount of drab clothing could disguise the sweep of those curves or the fresh glow of pearly skin. Nor did it do an effective job of hiding the steel underneath. Tru knew it was there. He braced himself, certain it would manifest soon enough.

His fingers began to tap again, beneath the table. "Hang this delay." He looked pointedly at Stoneacre. "Where's Marstoke?"

Callie Grant accepted the cup from her friend. "Damn Marstoke. More importantly, where's Letty?"

They exchanged a glare.

"Don't start bickering, you two." Stoneacre held up a hand. "As of tonight, they are the same question, with the same answer." He met Tru's eye. "Brittany. We found him at a small estate just off the coast."

Both women stilled. They exchanged a significant glance, but Tru merely filed their reaction away, where he could examine it later. His mind jumped immediately ahead. Brittany. A packet, that meant, to get them across the channel. Tomorrow morning at the latest. He had his passport, his papers. He had money enough. He shifted position, anxious to start making plans—until Stoneacre transferred his gaze to the girl. "And Letty has already joined him there."

This time her response brought Tru tumbling right back. In his experience, Callie Grant was all flash and spitfire. But this news did something to her. Her shoulders drooped, her lips trembled. The look of vibrant challenge drained from her face. It was loss moving in a wave across her expression. Defeat.

He found he didn't like it.

Stoneacre reached for her hand. "Don't despair just yet," he counseled.

She looked up.

"We mean to go after her. But there are extenuating

circumstances. Are you familiar with a girl named Mary Cooper?" he asked her.

"No." Tru saw her pause to mentally review before she looked to Hestia. "We haven't had anyone by that name at Half Moon House."

Hestia shook her head.

"What does she have to do with Marstoke?" Tru asked.

"It's what she might do *for* Marstoke that worries us," Stoneacre sighed.

"Start at the beginning," Hestia interrupted. "They both need to understand it all."

Callie Grant's teacup rattled in its saucer as she set it down. Hestia looked to her with compassion. "I'm sorry darling, but you'll see that I'm right." She cut a gaze to Stoneacre. "Show him the picture."

Nodding, the earl, searched through the stack of files and pulling out a thick sheet of parchment, offered it to Tru. He took it. It was a sketch. A good one, of a young girl in fancy dress and shining jewels.

"Do you recognize her?"

"Should I? She's familiar . . ." He stopped to study the strong nose, the elegant nape and tight rosebud mouth. Suddenly the pieces clicked together. "Oh, yes. Stupid of me. It's the Princess, is it not? I should have known. Princess Charlotte." He handed the sketch back.

Callie Grant groaned aloud and hid her face in her hands.

"No." Stoneacre had gone solemn. "That's Letty Robbins."

"It is?" He stretched out a hand and looked at the sketch again, and nodded when Stoneacre also handed over a rumpled newspaper. "It's true I've never met the Robbins girl, nor yet have I met the Princess in person, but you can see—this looks remarkably like the pictures you see of her in the papers and caricatures." He glanced between the two. "How did that happen?"

"The usual way," Stoneacre replied sardonically. "This group of royals—you could fill a regiment with the children they've bred on the wrong side of the blanket."

"She's a royal ba—" Stoneacre winced and Tru stopped himself. "A natural child? Of which royal?"

Stoneacre glanced at the ladies' side of the table. "Her mother was an opera dancer, it would seem." He looked to Miss Grant as if for confirmation, but she kept her face blank, her eyes focused ahead and not on any one in the room. Still, the unspoken question was telling, all the same. Stoneacre sighed before he continued. "Her father is believed to be Prince Ernest."

Wicked Ernest. Tru had exchanged only a word or two with him, during court functions. He was the one spoken of in hushed voices. The prince, it was whispered, who got a child on his sister, the Princess Sophia. The prince who reportedly murdered his valet and got away with it. The one whose name was used by nannies and weary parents across the kingdom to frighten children into submission.

"Her dedication to Marstoke is perhaps easier to understand, then," Tru mused. "Perhaps he does not look so bad next to such a father."

Stoneacre cleared his throat. "Yes, well, Marstoke's manipulation of Letty Robbins is grievous by itself, but coupled with his relationship with the princess? It becomes a disaster."

Tru frowned. "Marstoke *has* a relationship with the princess?"

"He does according to the letters and papers we found in his secret office—the one discovered by your brother's new bride."

Tru brushed off the twinge brought on by mention of Marstoke's failed conspiracy. Thoughts of his own part in it could not help but follow—and that was precisely the reaction that he meant to erase. Permanently. From his own mind and everyone else's too. "But I thought the general complaint circulates that Charlotte is kept restricted, closely monitored and unseen."

Stoneacre leaned in. "That's just it. Marstoke must have spent years speaking briefly to her at the few court functions she's permitted to attend, arranging accidental meetings during her short jaunts out. He must have worked slowly and for some time to gain her trust. He also found someone in her household to smuggle their correspondence. There are stacks of letters that make it clear that he was her confidante."

"So he's formed a friendship with the Princess Charlotte—and now you believe he means to make use of the other girl's likeness to her?"

"Of course he means to make use of it." Her face tight, Callie Grant leaned forward. "That costume, that part, was her first speaking role." She tapped the sketch of Letty Robbins. "All she ever wanted was to act. She put in her time, performing in the background, but she dreamed of acceptance and the adoration of the audience. She did well, too, in that part. She had her mother's talents, she always told me."

She bit her lip. "Marstoke must have caught the resemblance right away. Letty only played that role a few nights before his lackeys picked her up right out of the theater and deposited her with that pimp in the back stews of the city. Clearly they didn't want anyone else to notice what he had seen right off. They didn't put Letty out on the street or in a brothel like the rest of Hatch's girls. They kept her separate. Alone. Filled her head with dreams and big plans. Hatch wanted something better for her, she used to say. Sometimes her eyes would shine as she talked of it. Nebulous, vague ideas, but grand." Her breath caught. "And sometimes she spoke of it all past a black eye and through a split lip." She ducked her head, rubbed a temple with two fingers. "And now we know just what those plans were."

"I'm sorry for your . . . friend." Tru suspected that he was the only one here who didn't understand Callie Grant's connection to the Robbins girl. Given the color in her cheeks, he hesitated to ask. "But I know the Regent fairly well. Surely he's warned the princess away from Marstoke now."

"Yes, and it didn't sit well, especially in light of the other problems between her and her father. Did any of you read of the incident last week?" Stoneacre asked. "In a fit of temper, the Regent dismissed his daughter's entire household. She ran to her mother and almost created another great scandal."

"They argue over the girl's broken betrothal to the Prince of Orange," Hestia chimed in. "The Regent really must give up this notion. His daughter is not the only one who believes it to be a bad idea."

Stoneacre gave a bitter laugh. "That matter is beyond the scope of my responsibilities. Mary Cooper is not, however. She was a maid in Charlotte's household and was dismissed with the rest. She was the one smuggling letters for Marstoke."

How was any of this getting him closer to a packet bound for Brittany? Tru wanted to fling the question at the other man. Instead he clenched his fist and injected a patience he didn't feel into his tone. "How can you know that? And how does it pertain to this?" He waved a hand.

"We weren't sure it was her. Until several days ago, when we found Marstoke—and Mary Cooper with him."

Callie Grant sucked in a breath—and that tiny whisper of a sound was enough to break down the dam holding the flood of Tru's chafing restlessness.

"What does it *matter*?" he asked, springing to his feet. "So Marstoke has a servant girl and an actress with him. What's important here is that we know where he is!

We must act now—*leave* now!" He left the table, but pacing to the mantel and back didn't help.

Neither did Hestia Wright's raised eyebrows. "Oh, it matters, Lord Truitt," she said softly. "Only stop to think a moment. Yes, Marstoke appears to know the Princess, but now he has a servant girl who can speak of intimacies. She can describe Charlotte's habits, her patterns of speech and mannerisms, the schedule of her days, her friendships and rivalries inside her own house as well as out." She paused and Tru noted a tiny, telltale clench of her lovely jaw. "Don't you see what mischief he could do with the pair of them?"

Callie Grant's tone rang hollow. "He's training Letty to be a substitute for Charlotte."

For a long moment only the faint crackle of the fire sounded in the room. "Surely he would not . . ." Tru's mind tried to wrap itself around all the implications.

Abruptly Hestia too pushed herself away from the table. "You underestimate the sheer breadth and depth of evil in him," she said accusingly. "Even you, with more cause than many to understand what he is." She turned her back on them all for a moment.

"Look at what he did with a simple list of London's lightskirts," Stoneacre reminded them. "Revenge, assault, abduction. He nearly destroyed Hestia, her work with Half Moon House, and your new sister-in-law with it. He came within a hair's breadth of igniting an international incident that would have put the Prince Regent in a very bad light." He took up the brandy and poured a healthy dollop in his teacup. "Imagine the mischief he could get up to with a doppelganger to the Princess. As you said, Charlotte is not seen out much. Letty could easily be taken for her—and then she could discredit the princess just by being seen in inappropriate company or getting up to some public misbehavior."

"It could be far worse than that." Callie Grant's voice had gone flat. "What if the princess was invited abroad, perhaps to meet some other eligible prince?"

Stoneacre looked aghast. "Her mother is even now making preparations to leave the country."

"Exactly. What if she went to visit her mother— and a different Charlotte came back?" She met Tru's gaze directly. "You have firsthand experience with how easily Marstoke can lie and manipulate. How he can twist the truth and make something feel logical and right. Even after we took Letty in at Half Moon House, she was in contact with him, taking orders through Hatch for months. Now he's got her close. He knows what to say, what will coerce her. He's likely got her convinced that this is the role of a lifetime, a grand adventure, a service to her country."

Tru sank into a chair by the fire. "Charlotte will wear the crown one day—and knowing Prinny and his excesses, it may be sooner rather than later."

Hestia Wright turned around. "And there might be a false Princess, waiting in the wings, with Marstoke at her side and a full pardon in her fist."

Tru stared. The full horror of what Marstoke could accomplish opened up before him. It was a mad scheme— and just exactly the sort Marstoke might dream of pulling off. The enormity of it, the mental image of a triumphant Marstoke taking back all he'd lost, and more, hit him hard in the gut. He absorbed the blow without a sound, his hands tightening into fists. "We'll stop him," he said low. "Long before it gets to that point."

"We will," Stoneacre agreed. "The groundwork is already laid. Richards is purchasing our passage as we speak. We'll leave in a few hours time." He reached across to take Callie Grant's hand. They were alone at the table now. "I'd like you to come with us."

Tru started. Something surged to life in his chest. He could clearly recall the girl arguing fiercely against the very idea of this trip. He could just as clearly imagine Marstoke making mincemeat of her, should she end up in his way. Denial swelled, given energy and form by the shock in her face.

No. He wanted to forbid it. But the look on Hestia Wright's face stalled him—that, and the recollection of his earlier resolve. *Any damned thing. Something reckless.*

This surely qualified as both. He pushed back the protective surge in his gut and swallowed all of those worthy, instinctive objections. "Why?" he asked instead. "What does everyone else know that I do not?" He looked Callie Grant in the eye. "What exactly is your relationship to the Robbins girl?"

***

There it was. The question she feared most— coming from the last person she wished to answer.

Pain, fury and loss assaulted Callie, as merciless as they'd ever been in the last few weeks. Damn Marstoke to hell and back, for ripping her world apart with his scheming. And now Lord Stoneacre knew the truth. All of it. She'd seen it reflected in his gaze. But to think of the same knowledge in Lord Truitt Russell's face?

No. Her shoulders hunched against the idea. She knew that Lord Truitt, though he'd let Marstoke convince him to pen the revised Love List, had never had an inkling how the marquess meant to use it. He'd had no part in the plan to destroy Hestia or to incite the populace against the Prince Regent. She knew he'd tried to stop Marstoke, in the end, and that he was wild to find the man and bring him back to justice, to make amends for his part in the debacle.

And yet. She couldn't bear the thought of him knowing all of her secrets.

It wasn't shame that held her back. Neither did her reluctance have anything to do with Lord Truitt's wickedly dark eyes. Less still did it have to do with his tall, strong frame and capably broad shoulders. Certainly it was nothing to do with her fascination with that wicked-looking scar, a crescent someone had carved into the edge of his cheekbone.

Not. One. Thing.

It was just . . . the thought of seeing pity soften the hard angles of his face . . . it made her shiver. And it wouldn't stop there. After pity would come curiosity, speculation, maybe even scorn.

No.

Instinctively she turned to Hestia and beseeched her help with a silent plea.

Hestia frowned in response. Callie understood that Hestia believed she should tell Lord Truitt everything. But she wasn't ready. Might never be ready. She pressed her lips together and silently asked again.

And, at last, Hestia relented. "Callie and Letty have been close since they were girls," she said. "The burden of Letty's welfare was put into Callie's hands long ago."

She's alone now. We must be her family. Watch out for her.

Lord Truitt knew when he was being fobbed off. "That's no real answer," he accused.

"It's all the answer you need," Callie bit out.

"What matters is that you are the one that Letty will listen to," Stoneacre interrupted, still holding her hand. "She'll fight us if *we* try to convince her to come back."

"She likely will," Callie agreed with a sigh.

"And we'll be forced to take her into custody. She'll be set against us, when what we need is for her to cooperate, to tell us what she knows of Marstoke's plans." His grip on her hand tightened. "You are the only one who can convince her to come away freely, to thwart Marstoke and help us take him back to justice. Please. Will you come along?"

Watch out for her.

Rebellion flared, vivid and bright. Everything Lord Stoneacre said was right. Callie knew she was Letty's best chance. Her help would likely bring about a better outcome for everyone.

But denial stabbed deep and a full dose of resentment pumped in behind it. She was exhausted, worn out from the worry and fear of the last weeks, heart sore from losing her close friend, Brynne, even if it was to Lord Truitt's handsome, ducal brother. Lord Truitt's mere presence set her on edge, but most of all, she was tired— weary of being the strong one, the steady one, the one who cleaned up the messes left by the rest of the world.

When? When would someone look at her and notice her pain and weariness? When would someone move heaven and earth to make things right for her?

She felt the press of Hestia's gaze upon her, knew exactly the secret grief that had added the weight to her mentor's soul. "I have to ask, my dear," her friend whispered. "You know I do, if there's even a chance—" Hestia's look conveyed her private fear, one that no one else here would understand. She fell silent for a moment. "But I would ask in any case," she continued more smoothly. "Because you know you would not be able to live with yourself, did you not go." Hestia paused. "But, Callie?"

She turned her head.

"Let this be the end of it. You've carried your burden long enough. You've done your best—and no one knows better than I do, what a formidable thing that is." She hardened her expression. "Should Letty return with you, then all well and good. You can set her loose to live her own life and make her own, hopefully smaller, mistakes. But should she not return, despite your best efforts?" Her eyes narrowed. "Then it will be no fault of yours." She turned her glare toward the gentlemen. "Is that understood here, between all of us? In this room or out of it, no one lays the burden of Letty's sins on Callie."

Lord Stoneacre sat upright, an arrested look on his face. Something moved behind his expression, beyond his open gaze, but it was too fleeting for Callie to identify.

"Understood," he said, standing. "And agreed."

Hestia nodded. "One last fight," she said, nodding encouragement at Callie. "I'll miss you terribly, but I know Stoneacre will take good care of you." She tried to smile. "Watch and listen for me. Finish this for yourself, as well, Callie dear, and you'll be free."

Free. She heard the reverence Hestia placed on the word, but she couldn't quite understand it. It sounded unattainable. And empty.

But she nodded. "I'll go."

"Good." The earl looked relieved. "And thank you." His smile was true, if brief. "There will be a few hours before we can leave. You should try to rest. The rooms upstairs are yours to make use of. Get a couple of hours of sleep, at least, but we'll be ready to leave before daybreak." He beckoned. "Tru, let's head out. We've some arrangements to make."

Callie's gaze fixed once more on the breadth of Lord Truitt's shoulders as he rose to follow the earl out. He carried burdens too, though she doubted he was as accustomed to the load as she. Now they would share this one.

She only hoped that this time Letty's antics would not cost them all more than they wished to pay.

Chapter Four

All night I traveled, and into the dawn of the next morning, without ever seeing a soul. My feet grew tired, but my spirits were buoyant. It wasn't until I saw a trace of chimney smoke over distant trees that I had a hint of trouble.

—from the journal of the infamous Miss Hestia Wright

The waterfront buzzed with activity, even at this ungodly hour, just before dawn. It felt subdued, though, all the hustle of swarming sailors and busy fishermen muffled by the gloom.

England mourns my departure, Callie thought facetiously.

But it felt true. Everything loomed crotchety and grey, from the low hanging clouds, to the light drizzle dampening the air, to the sea birds fighting over a pile of fish guts just a few feet down the dock.

Still, it was a delusional thought. Not quite wishful thinking. Yes, Hestia would miss her. The truth of that was in her mentor's face as she gathered Callie's cloak tighter and smoothed the fastenings. The girls at Half Moon House might miss the crusty breads and rich stews she offered when she took a turn covering for cook's weekly free day—and the old woman's occasional slide into a bottle of blue ruin. They might miss her good knife hand the next time a thwarted pimp or violent husband came looking for his woman. But beyond that?

"Men," said Hestia with a roll of her eyes. She stared down the docks, where Lord Truitt and Lord Stoneacre huddled with the supercargo of the *Spanish Lady*. The earl had booked them passage on a merchant schooner rather than a regular packet, hoping to avoid the notice of Marstoke's spies. Now the pitch of their conversation rose and fell as they discussed wind, hull design, and course and speed records. "They are like excited schoolchildren." With a solemn look, Hestia held up a heavy bag of coins and tucked it into the pocket sewn in Cassie's cloak, next to her breast. "But you understand this is not child's play." She stopped suddenly, and swallowed. "Callie . . ." Her hand trembled as her words trailed away.

Callie grasped her hands tight. "I will listen closely, Hestia, and find out what I can. It could be a coincidence, though. Brittany is merely out of England, but close enough for Marstoke to keep an ear to what's happening. I feel sure it is nothing more."

"But if it is not . . . If he's looking . . . or if he's found . . ." Callie suspected she was the only one alive who knew Hestia's deepest secret and her greatest fear. They'd known each other years before the older woman had shared the truth and her worries about it, and it remained the one subject that could spread uneasy ripples across her usually flawless confidence.

"If it looks like Brittany is anything more than a convenient hideaway for Marstoke, then I will get word to you right away. I promise."

"Thank you, my dear." Hestia swallowed and pulled close her usual veil of dignity and competence. "I regret the need for secrecy on this matter. On all other accounts, though, you must trust these two. Truly, I would not let you go were they not good men. I believe they will do everything in their power to keep you safe." She stared after the group of them again. "I think you should go easier on that one, though."

"Easier?" She let go of Hestia's hands. "I've dropped everything to travel abroad at a moment's notice. I've pledged to do all I can to persuade Letty. I can't think Lord Stoneacre has cause to complain."

"I'm not talking about Stoneacre and you know it." Hestia raised a brow. "I know you are tempted to classify Lord Truitt as just another selfish and spoiled young nobleman, but I don't think you can. Recall if you will—he got into this whole mess because he tried to help a woman in trouble. He had no way to know that Marstoke would not have harmed that Russian chit. And consider what he knew and when he knew it—and you find he's conducted himself honorably at every turn since." Her mouth twitched. "He's different, this one. He watches you."

Callie let out a huff. "He's a man. They *all* watch me."

"Not like this one. He's not focused on that fabulous bosom of yours. He watches your face when you aren't looking." She paused a moment. "I think he's interested. Or he might be, if he would allow himself."

"Well, I am not interested." But she didn't look away as he removed his hat. Leaning back against the wind, he lifted his head and breathed deep. The sea breeze toyed with his hair, mussing it a bit as the sun, fighting its way past fast-moving clouds, searched out lighter, chestnut strands to catch her eye.

"I know you've been unsettled lately." Hestia's beautiful face showed signs of worry, of strain and little sleep. "I fear a good deal of that is my fault. I've relied too heavily on you, my dear."

"Don't be ridiculous." A chord of panic twanged in her breast. She couldn't lose Hestia too.

"You've been a wonder. Such a prop to my spirits, and I've never had a more reliable arm to lean upon." Her face brightened. "Just look at all we've accomplished together, my dear."

"It's nothing next to what we have yet to do," Callie said, fighting unease. "You're talking as if I'm traveling around the world. It's to be a short trip. Lord Stoneacre has assured me so. A few weeks and I'll be back at Half Moon House."

"Yes." Hestia nodded. "But I know you've been

restless since Brynne left us to marry Lord Truitt's brother. I've seen the wheels spinning in your head. That's as it should be. I want you to keep thinking, my darling. Every day you do so much—for me, for Letty, for all the women and children we seek to help. But on this trip, there will be time to yourself. Quiet time, perfect for reflection. I wish you would use it. Think about what you want and need out of your life. Imagine the changes that might bring you joy, peace, contentment."

Very deliberately Callie did not allow herself to glance in the direction of the gentlemen. Hestia did, however, as the group broke apart and they began to move toward them.

"So many solemn reasons for a journey, I know, but I hope you will also enjoy the new places and people." Mischief suddenly brightened her manner. "Make new friends."

"I've friends enough," Callie said, reproving.

"None with shoulders like that." With a smile Hestia turned to greet the three men.

She could not argue the point. Lord Truitt's hat was back in place. The morning sun, bereft of his thick mane to play in, had snuck a few bright rays through the clouds and aimed them unerringly at the impressively narrowing taper of his frame. Callie looked away. She didn't want to notice such things about him. She didn't want to associate him with sunshine and broad shoulders, with principle and honorable intent. Everything would be so much easier if she could dismiss him as another nobleman who took what he wanted, used whomever he wanted and gave nothing back.

Lord Stoneacre stepped close. "Miss Wright, Miss Grant, may I introduce Mr. Perlott?"

The niceties were exchanged and then the supercargo waved a hand. "Miss Grant, the wind and tide are finally both coming up favorable. If you'll come quickly aboard, we need to be on our way."

"Of course."

She turned to Hestia, but Lord Stoneacre beat her, moving in and taking her friend's hand. "I cannot express my thanks for your help in this matter," he said warmly. "When we return I will do my best to find a suitable way to repay you."

Callie stared. The earl sounded utterly sincere, but also . . . interested. And just a tad too intimate. She watched Hestia's face harden.

"Bring Callie back safe. That will be thanks enough for me."

Lord Truitt stepped forward. "We shall keep her safe, you have my word. And we'll bring Marstoke back as well, bound, chained and ready to meet justice."

Hestia bestowed one of her dazzling smiles on him, warm and approving. "Keep those promises, my lord, and it shall be just as I predicted—we will be very good friends indeed."

A trivial exchange, light and flirtatious, and yet for some reason Lord Stoneacre suddenly looked as uncomfortable as Callie felt.

Then there was time only for a quick hug and a whispered farewell, and she was hustled across to a longboat and being rowed out to the waiting ship. Mr. Perlott escorted them to their cabins. Callie's was last in the short passage and farthest from the ladder that continued on and led down to the crew quarters. The gentlemen, tired from a long night's planning, wished to rest, but she took one look at her tiny, stark quarters, felt the sway of the ship as it picked up the current and asked Perlott to find her a spot on deck where she would be out of the way.

He found her a place at the stern rail and returned to his duties, which suited her fine. Here she could feel the wind and spray and watch England recede into the distance. She waved to Hestia's tiny, disappearing figure and gripped the rail with white-knuckled fingers. Events were moving quickly and dragging her right along with them. She'd been comfortable at Half Moon House for a long while now, had forgotten the rush of fear and tension that came with being on her own. She could adjust, though. She'd been alone before, with the care of young Letty an additional burden to bear.

Slowly, she began to relax. She caught the rhythm of the dance between the ship and the white-capped sea and let it soothe her. Coming back to her more normal self, she also fell back on habit and extended her senses and awareness, trying to read the mood and cadence of her surroundings.

Presumably the crew was used to passengers, but as the only woman aboard, caution wouldn't come amiss. She moved her position slightly so she could see and hear more from amidships. No one objected and she came to see that the crewmen appeared a cheerful lot, singing as they worked, and making jests at each other as the *Spanish Lady* left the tidal harbor and the captain called for fore and aft sails.

Only one man gave her pause. She'd thought him merely curious at first. But the same short canvas pants and long, dark pigtail kept crossing her line of vision and she noticed the seaman begin to glance her way, speculation in his eye. Her jaw tightened.

Ignoring him worked for a short while. She deliberately kept her gaze turned outward, toward the horizon. Until he dropped from the rigging with a thud, just a few feet away from her. She jumped and recoiled, and he met her gaze as he straightened and deliberately adjusted his manly parts before he turned away.

Callie sighed. Why was there always one?

She waited and watched. He moved closer again as the minutes passed. As if it were natural, just his tasks drawing him nearer to her spot on the rail. It wasn't. They both knew the steps of the dance, both were aware of the music. No matter. He was a snake, weaving about his prey, thinking to catch a mouse. He would be the one surprised when he bared his fangs to strike and found his head trapped beneath a lioness's paw.

She tensed when he moved behind her, disappearing from her line of sight. Trying for nonchalance, she turned back, facing the stern again—but there was no sign of him. She looked up, cursing herself for leaving her blade tucked into her portmanteau.

She swore silently again when the soft step sounded right behind her. She was ready in an instant, however. She spun on her heel and threw out a low, forceful punch. Her tone loud and meant to carry, she demanded, "Just what is it that you think you want?"

Her elbow jarred painfully when her fist was caught mid-strike. For the second time in as many days she frowned as she looked up into Lord Truitt Russell's baleful visage.

Sheer instinct prompted Tru to catch Callie Grant's fist in mid-swing. The hard look of determined bravado on her face had him catching her other elbow too.

"Good God, are you all right?"

She blinked up at him. Tried to tug away. "Lord Truitt! Please forgive me. I'm sorry—I thought you were—"

Tru's every muscle went on alert. She'd looked palpably dark. Dangerous. It was fading now, but for a moment the unspoken message on her face had been clear—and familiar. She'd been ready—prepared to do any damned thing at all to get away.

"Thought I was what? What's happened? Has somebody frightened you?"

She laughed but it was entirely unconvincing. "Frightened? Me? Have your attics gone to let?"

She tugged harder and he let go. "What is it, then?" *Don't lie to me.* The message lived in his expression and in the protective tilt of his body, loud and clear.

"It's nothing." She tried for a smile and failed. She waved a hand toward the empty sea. "I was watching England disappear and I felt . . ."

He watched her carefully. "Homesick?"

She shook her head. "No."

"You did seem uncommonly tense," he pressed.

She frowned suddenly. "And you've appeared uncommonly at ease this morning. It's certainly a vast difference from the intensity I've come to expect from you, sir." She raised a brow.

He shrugged. "We're on our way. It's happening, finally. We're going to get him." He took a step back and let that happy truth roll over him again.

"Yes, you can regain your all important honor."

"My honor is important." He cast a glance at her. "Do you think that I don't worry for the larger mischief Marstoke might get up to? I do."

"Of course you do. I'm sorry." She did sound a bit apologetic. "I know he's already entangled you in his bigger schemes—and you thwarted him. Your efforts saved the Prince Regent—the whole country—more than just embarrassment. He might have started an international incident had you not helped stop the Love List from going out as he planned."

Bitterness rose up. Yes, he'd been tricked, kidnapped and held captive for foiling Marstoke's plans, and in the end he'd only been reviled for it, because the marquess had escaped and the whole truth was too embarrassing for the Regent to admit to. Damned right, his honor was important. This had become a personal battle.

And he was—at last—about to engage in it. He pushed his dark thoughts away. "I can afford to relax for a few hours." He tilted his head. "Though it does seem as if you and I have traded places, in the emotional sense."

She looked back over the water again. "It's nothing. I was just feeling . . . adrift."

He nodded. "That's because you are in the wrong spot. Come? There's something I'd like to show you."

She hesitated and he held his breath. He wouldn't insist.

She glanced around again, as if looking for something. A reason to refuse? But at last her shoulders relaxed and she relented and let him lead her across the deck. With a wave to the captain, he helped her down a ladder, across the midship deck and up another few steps to the forward deck. "I've found it's always better here, in the bow of the ship," he confided. "Especially when you are feeling blue-deviled. Here you are going toward something, not away. I don't know why it makes a difference, but it does."

"It does make sense, I suppose," she mused. She cocked her head at him. "You are consistent at least."

"In what way?" he asked, mystified.

"You seem to be attached to the state of moving forward, making progress."

He loosed a bitter laugh. "Perhaps because I've experienced so little of it before now." He knew at least part of their past antagonism had arisen because she'd seen him as useless, just another aimless young nobleman. Her dismissal had hurt that much more for the sting of truth it carried.

"I'm beginning to doubt that," she said quietly. She moved ahead of him and he gestured for her to approach the rail. "But as this is my first sea voyage, I shall bow to your judgment regarding the decks."

"First time at sea?" Deliberately he released some of the tension he always felt in her presence. Pleasure, simple and expectant, ran through him. "Then you are in for a treat." He motioned her forward again. "Grab hold of the rail, then lean over and look down."

She cast him a doubtful look, but did as he bid. And he drank in her sudden gasp of delight. "Oh, how lovely! What are they?"

"Porpoises," Tru told her. "Perlott says they often play like that, in the wake of the bow."

"Oh, look at them leaping!" Enchantment colored her tone and softened her expression. For some reason it made Tru's chest swell, as if he'd recovered the missing crown jewels, not just made a solemn girl smile.

"How smoothly they slip into and out of the water," she said in wonder.

"Watch that one, right at the front." Tru pointed. "Yes, him . . . wait . . . There!" He laughed as one of the animals slipped just ahead of the ship and indulged itself in a continuous loop of barrel rolls.

"How does he do that? He barely moves, just the smallest circle of his tail and he's rolling endlessly."

"The water is distorted around the moving bow of the ship. He's taking advantage of the endless wave, Perlott says."

For nearly a quarter of an hour they stayed, watching the impromptu show, until eventually the porpoises began to drift away.

"Oh, how wonderful that was," Miss Grant said, turning around and leaning on the rail. Sobriety had slipped back onto her face. She glanced up at him. "What do you suppose the purpose of it is?"

He chuckled, willing to share in the joke—and then realized that she was entirely serious. "Purpose? I rather think there isn't one, is there? It's as Perlott said. They are frolicking. Having fun."

Surprise shone evident in her gaze. "Oh?" She

peered over the rail again but the last of the animals had dropped away.

Tru stared. "Miss Grant, do you know how to have fun?" He snapped his mouth shut, too late to cut off the words. It was too personal, and quite the rudest question he'd ever asked.

She didn't seem to be offended, however. In fact, she appeared to be considering the matter. Quite seriously.

Well. That only made him wish for an answer. "Miss Grant?"

"I am familiar with the concept," she said defensively. "I'm just thinking."

"Tell me one single thing in your life—something that you've done purely for the enjoyment of it," he demanded.

Several quiet moments passed. A tense, almost stimulating span of time in which they eyed each other and Tru felt as if he was taking her measure again—and yet for the first time.

"Well . . ." She deflated suddenly. "I'm awfully good at the marketing. I can get the best prices out of most every carter."

"No." He waved a dismissive hand. "That is a chore, a necessity. I mean something frivolous and fun."

Her lips pursed. "I bake sometimes, when I want to distract myself or when I'm feeling . . . unsettled."

"Ah . . . macaroons, is it? Pastries? Tiny iced cakes?"

She frowned. "No. Loaves of bread to go along with dinner at Half Moon House. Or breakfast rolls, occasionally."

"That hardly counts, then."

"You'd be surprised how much tension you can get out, pounding at dough," she insisted.

He snorted. "That just means the baking serves two purposes." He gestured toward the ocean below. "Think of those animals. How joyously they leaped. Couldn't you sense how free and happy they felt, leaping from one world to the next, reveling in the waves and the wind and the sun?"

She pressed her lips together and nodded.

"That's what I mean."

She shook her head, a little helplessly. "Just for fun?" She sighed. "I don't think I've ever done something like that."

A brave and sobering thing to admit out loud. But Tru could not pity her. Perhaps that was her secret, after all. Was it merely purpose that made her different from every other young miss he knew? She had a vision, important work to be done, beyond attending the next society ball and snagging the most eligible catch on the marriage mart. Well, he supposed those were purposes, as well, if not really unique or admirable ones.

Certainly something set her apart. Given their previous encounters he might be forgiven for thinking it her fiery temper or her willingness to go toe to toe and bosom to magnificent bosom to argue her point.

It was more than that, he knew now, and he suspected her purpose was a large part of her appeal. After all, he could attest to the wrack and ruin that came of an aimless life.

Except that he had a purpose now, too—and the sudden mischief setting her alight was making him forget it. She stared up at him, expectant and looking as if she was on the verge of saying something slightly risqué.

"Yes?" he asked with caution.

"Oh, never mind!" She gave a sheepish laugh. "I was willing to make the attempt, at least. I was trying very hard to come up with a joke about a porpoise with a purpose. I know there must be one, but I can't quite get it to come to my tongue."

Tru laughed anyway. She looked almost unfamiliar without her usual mask of disdain. The hard set of her jaw and the tight line of her shoulders had relaxed a bit. Sea winds had teased loose a few strands of that mahogany hair and thrown back the folds of her cloak. She looked altogether *softer*. He felt, suddenly, that he could grow to like this version of her.

The odd thought brought him up short. It hardly mattered how he felt about her, did it? Not when she'd transmitted her scorn for him often enough in their squabbles. Not while the world believed in its own version of him—that of a traitor, or a fool.

"You are right, though," he said, suddenly brisk. "I have grown inordinately fond of moving forward. We can do just that right now, too. Stoneacre was setting some things up in the captain's day cabin. He should be ready for us."

Retreating into stiff formality again, he motioned for her to precede him.

Chapter Five

*The cramping struck quickly and without mercy.
By the time I stumbled into the dusty yard of the country
inn, I knew the awful truth. A plump and kindly lady
came out to greet me, but I collapsed, sobbing, at her feet.*

*—from the journal of the infamous Miss Hestia
Wright*

Tru tried to hold on to resentment as he escorted Callie Grant to the captain's day cabin. It proved surprisingly difficult. The afternoon sun caught her as she paused before the darker passage, outlining her voluptuous curves, throwing her hourglass shape into high relief. Tru noted the hitch in the ceaseless activity about them as more than one seaman stopped in his work and let his gaze linger upon her.

Resentment and rising violence stiffened his spine. Deliberately, though, he pushed it away. With careful movements, Tru closed the door behind her. Let the poor buggers look. They could scarcely help it, after all. What man could? And she was not only well protected, but formidable in her own right.

He followed her into the cabin.

Sunlight sparkled from the windows banked across the stern galley. In the center of the room, Stoneacre had commandeered the captain's navigational table. Charts and tools had been carefully shifted to one side, and the earl was busily unrolling and anchoring maps across the bared space. A large, leather dispatch bag sat at one corner, spilling parchment.

"Come in, come in!"

The earl didn't look as if he was functioning on just a few hours sleep, but then again, neither did Callie Grant. Stoneacre beckoned to her. "Come around to this side.

We've at least four hours until we stop at Calais, and another day after that until we disembark. We might as well put all that time to good use."

Tru ran a finger along a detailed chart of the French coast. "Are you going to share our destination, then? I understand the need for circumspection, but surely now we can speak freely."

Stoneacre tossed a chart across the table. "Here."

Callie Grant strained to look as well. "A walled city?" she asked.

Tru frowned and dredged through old, half-forgotten geography lessons. "St. Malo?"

"Yes, that famed breeding ground for pirates and privateers. What better place for Marstoke to hole up in, eh?" Stoneacre narrowed his gaze in the girl's direction. "I know that Tru's French is impeccable. His brother assures me that if it were not, then he wasted a small fortune in tutors." He grinned at Tru then contemplated Callie Grant again. "And Hestia Wright tells me that you speak French like a native? And that you are also familiar with Breton?"

She nodded.

"And that you are quite an accomplished cook?"

She flushed. "That's an exaggeration of my abilities, I'd say—"

The earl interrupted her. "Also that you might be familiar with some regional Breton dishes?"

She drew herself up. "Lord Stoneacre, are you saying that you wish me to *cook* on this expedition?"

Familiar impatience came flooding back. "Come, Stoneacre, explain. We're tired of being kept in the dark."

The earl gestured for him to pull up a chair. "This is not going to be a case of snatch and grab, however tempting that idea might be. We need to give Miss Grant the time and ability to persuade Letty Robbins to cooperate and return with us. We need to gather what information we can on Marstoke's activities and what he might be planning next. It's going to take some finesse to pull it all off."

He pulled the map of the walled city close and jabbed a finger at a spot outside the walls. "The marquess has been holed up in a villa well outside the town. He's got a pretty stone manor centered in the low point of a valley. Crops and vineyards cover the surrounding hillsides. No trees in the sightline of the house. A few wooded areas, but all away from the main house, centered around a few other buildings and the edges of the estate. There's no cover at all on the road in to the main villa." Tru caught the warning glance Stoneacre tossed at him. "As I said, there will be no snatch and grab."

Callie Grant frowned. "It sounds hopeless. How are we to accomplish any of it?"

"With deception," Stoneacre answered simply.

"Taking a page from Marstoke's own damned book," Tru growled.

"Exactly. And I won't feel a single qualm about it, either," the earl agreed. Frowning, he pulled a chair up and sat next to the girl. "There are a few added complications. There is news that will force us to make some adjustments."

Callie Grant radiated the same tension that he felt. Taut, they waited.

"I've had word that Marstoke has left St. Malo."

"What?" Tru stood, denial rumbling like thunder in his gut.

"It's not the first time, it would seem," Stoneacre said soothingly. "Our source has scrounged about for information and found that there have been several other trips further into the Breton countryside, and that they seldom last more than a week or so. Gaubert managed to send his boy after Marstoke, to keep track of his movements and find out as much as he can about what he's about."

Tru relaxed a little. "If he can send back word, then this might be a good thing." He leaned on the chair he'd just vacated. "When we arrive I'll leave you two to your work in the town, and I'll follow after them. If we're lucky I can learn a good bit more about what Marstoke's scheming."

"I'll have to turn that around on you, though I know you won't much care for it." Stoneacre spoke bluntly. "Gaubert is a valuable resource, but he's a damned prickly handful, too. It takes experience and a set of kid gloves to handle him. He's spent the last week setting up our cover, but when we arrive he'll insist on heading after his boy— and I'll be the one to go with him."

Tru's jaw clenched. The earl nodded to acknowledge his frustration even as he held up a hand. "I'm sorry, he's too valuable to risk losing. He won't wish to take someone green. It's no good anyway, Tru. Marstoke would spot you a mile off. He won't be looking for me, and in any case, I have experience wearing someone else's skin."

Stoneacre left off impaling Tru with his dagger-sharp gaze and sent it shafting toward the girl. "That's something both of you will have to learn." Pulling out another closed leather packet, he opened it and tossed the divided contents between the two of them. "Your new identities. Gaubert has found a way into the fabric of the town for you. He's acted as your man of business and purchased a vacant tavern on the edge of town. He and his boy have labored for days getting it ready for you."

"For us? A tavern?" Callie Grant stared up at him. "I don't understand. How will this get me close to Letty?"

"There's no way for us to insert you into the house at the moment," Stoneacre explained. "Though we tried. Marstoke brought along a few of his own people, it seems, and the servants attached to the house have their backs up. So there are no openings in the household, but we've begun a longer ranging plan." Tru frowned as the earl's mouth quirked. "Gaubert has reason to complain this time, I'm afraid. He's been busy getting the inn and tavern ready for you, and also making Marstoke's villa as uncomfortable as possible. He's hooked up with a disgruntled under-butler, who has agreed to trade a bit of sabotage for a position in a nice English household."

"What sort of sabotage?" Callie sounded fascinated.

Stoneacre shrugged. "It's all very mysterious. Bedroom fires are smoking. Strange smells have begun to come from behind walls. The cook has had a series of extremely unfortunate incidents in the last few days. Spoiled milk, bad eggs, late deliveries, fires left too hot overnight and cool rooms left open to the heat, that sort of thing. It's left the staff and the guests at the manor uncomfortable—and uncomfortably hungry. Including, it is to be hoped, Marstoke's two newest guests."

Tru's head shot up. "Penrith and Rackham, you mean?"

"The very same. Younger sons they may be, but they are used to a certain level of comfort. Certainly they will not be used to going days without a decent meal."

Understanding dawned in Callie Grant's face, although Tru still didn't see how all of this connected to Letty Robbins. "You are diabolically clever, Lord Stoneacre," she said with a shake of her head. "They do say that the way to a man's heart is through his stomach." She looked up. "So we're supposed to tempt those two young men to become comfortable in 'our' tavern?"

"That's well under way, if everything goes according to plan. They left a day before we did and had no need of a stop in Calais. With luck they have begun to hang about the taproom now, enjoying free samples of some very fine French brandy and hearing Gaubert sing the praises of your hearty roasts and rich sauces."

"I'm surprised we cannot hear their stomachs growling now," she laughed.

"As I said, with luck you'll be asked to feed them before long."

"And we are to make them comfortable enough—or drunk enough—to talk of what is going on in Marstoke's household?" Tru asked doubtfully.

"I doubt Marstoke is recruiting men so foolish. No, we'll play a little deeper than that." Stoneacre pulled out a sheet of paper from the small stack before the girl. "You'll be Chloe Chaput. It's close enough to Callie." Stoneacre's slight grin grew wider as he met Tru's gaze. "I'd meant to pass the two of you off as brother and sister." He raised a brow. "I've had to rethink that, however."

Sliding papers in Tru's direction, he continued. "You are the husband, Tousseau Chaput."

Charged silence fell over the room.

The earl continued, his smile gone now. "If someone slips and calls you Tru," he glanced significantly in Callie Grant's direction, "then it will sound similar enough. But there can be no 'my lording.' The two of you will have to practice your new identities."

He tapped the sheaf of paper. "We'll need a bit of a disguise for you, though, Tru. That scar is too distinctive. We'll have to cover it up." He smiled. "I meant to fashion you a padded waist, but you'll likely be doing some physical work. And in any case, I want you able to move quickly if the need arises."

He tapped the city map. "The story that Gaubert has spread is this: Tousseau Chaput is experienced, having run his family's inn in Franche-Comté. Unfortunately, he had to turn it over to his elder brother when that prodigal returned from the wars. His wife is widely noted for her cooking, and is accounted responsible for much of his success." The earl leaned closer to Miss Grant. "I hope Hestia was correct about your abilities, for we need you to win these two over fairly quickly—for once you've established your prowess, and have them eating from the palm of your hand, the villa is going to become even more uncomfortable."

She frowned. "You will not put Letty in danger?"

"Of course not. But we'll make sure the house is uninhabitable for a few days."

She looked up and Tru could see the pieces connecting behind that lovely, dark gaze. "And they'll wish to come and stay with us? Including Letty."

"That is the plan." Stoneacre sat back.

"This all sounds a heavy burden for Miss Grant." Tru said, straightening. "Not that I doubt for a second that you could handle it," he told the girl. No one who spent any time with her could doubt her extreme competency. He eyed the earl. "And you'll be busy enough tracking Marstoke. But my role in this scenario sounds damned insubstantial."

"On the contrary," Stoneacre disagreed. "I need you to lend Miss Grant authenticity, and provide for her safety."

Tru started to interrupt, but the earl held up a hand. "We'll have to work a bit on your appearance. I know you've never run in the same circles as they have, but it wouldn't do for those two young miscreants to recognize you. You'll be responsible for maintaining your disguises and new identities. You'll have to help manipulate those young bloods and help plant the seed of the idea, welcome them to your establishment. But most importantly, you'll need to do a good bit of scouting, discovering the lay of the land and searching out a safe hiding spot and a feasible escape route, should things go wrong."

Tru held in an instinctive protest and pressed his lips together. The mission—that's what mattered. Marstoke's capture, not his own burning desire to put his hands around the man's neck. The mission, he repeated to himself. The world's view of him as a fool and a traitor must rate a distant second—even if he sometimes believed it too.

"You've done so much work already, Lord Stoneacre," Callie Grant said haltingly. "And yet . . . I worry if what you ask can be done. There is so much to be accomplished, so many things that could go wrong." For perhaps the first time, Tru heard the tenor of doubt in her voice.

Perversely, her uncertainty strengthened Tru's resolve. "It won't be easy, but we'll manage it." He stepped close and laid a hand on her shoulder in an attempt to reassure them both.

It didn't. Instead it sent a bolt of fire up his arm and brought a rush of heat to her cheeks. She caught her breath and he felt the lack of air in his own lungs. At the curved base of her lovely nape, her pulse began to visibly dance.

He took his hand from her, stepped away again. "We'll manage," he said again, and ignored the sudden rough rasp in his tone. Taking up the map of the walled city again, he sat at the far corner of the table and hoped like hell that he was right.

***

The seas grew steadily rougher the next morning as Callie scrunched in her bunk, trying to both write legibly and balance an inkwell between the wall and a brace of books. Memories swamped her as the stack of her mother's recipes steadily grew at her side.

A woman of few words, her mother, but many skills. All the best moments of her childhood had taken place at her mother's side, often early in the morning, while the house was quiet.

The stillroom had been a sanctuary. Together they had worked, barely speaking at times, to mix the simple medicines every household needed, and also the sweet smelling soaps, waxes and cleansers that her mother insisted her staff use to keep his grace's home immaculate. But the kitchen had been their special retreat, where they would take a corner out of the cook's way and Callie would help as her mother prepared moist, delicious *Gallettes de*

Sarrasin, or the Breton butter cake that her father loved, or even one of the many savory seafood dishes of her mother's lost homeland.

She sighed. She'd always meant to make a pilgrimage to the place her mother had left. She'd heard so many stories, and had often thought she would find her there, experience some sort of connection again to her strong, stubborn spirit.

She'd certainly never expected the trip to take place under such circumstances as this. Though her mother would absolutely approve of her mission to haul Letty out of trouble . . . again.

A knock on the door interrupted her downward spiraling thoughts. She should be grateful, perhaps, but felt only a sudden, sharp irritation. "Yes?"

"Miss Grant?"

Lord Truitt. Or Tousseau Chaput, rather. *Her husband.* She stiffened as her pulse jumped into a gallop. "Yes?"

"Are you well?"

"Of course I am," she snapped. Why did he always make her feel so . . . She bit her lip. The real problem, she suspected, was that he made her *feel*.

"May I come in?"

He didn't wait for her refusal. The door opened and he quick-stepped through on the momentum of a sudden swell. He did stop short just past the threshold, but in the tiny cabin that put him right at the end of her bunk. The frown he wore, the one that always bisected that crescent scar with a crease, turned to an expression of surprise as he took in the sight of her unusual position.

"What is it?" Perhaps that came out a bit too testily, but she couldn't seem to stop herself. He brought something out in her, some competitive spirit that had to best him, that couldn't let him get away with anything.

Or perhaps, just didn't wish him to get away.

"I thought perhaps you weren't feeling well, what with the heavier seas." He pointed a finger. "But you are *working*."

It was an accusation.

She bristled. "Well, perhaps you are not the only one who likes progress and forward motion."

"Clearly not." Unfazed, he motioned toward her stack of papers. "What has you so busy?"

She took a breath. They were going to be in proximity to each other for some time. She needed to learn how to deal with the thrum of charged tension and the shivery promise that gripped her when he came close.

"My mother taught me some regional Breton dishes. I'm trying to remember as many as I can—both to cement our aliases and to tempt our targets. Lord Stoneacre wishes me to begin in the kitchens straightaway once we arrive." She shot him a look of apology. "I'm afraid that you will be left alone to see to the taproom and the rented rooms, at least at first."

"I'll handle it." He waved a dismissive hand. "But right now, I thought you'd like to take the chance to get on deck for some fresh air."

She would love to leave the cabin. And the thought of doing so at his side set her pulse to thumping again. Which was why she had to refuse. "Thank you, but I really must finish while I can."

But instead of taking her hint and taking his leave, the irritating man threw himself down on the foot of her bed. "*Moules Marinières*," he said, picking up the topmost sheet. "Sounds delicious." He leaned back against the wall and looked her over benignly. "You continue to surprise me."

"Because I know how to work?" she asked, snatching the paper back.

"Because you know so very many things, actually."

"For a woman?" She lifted her chin.

"For anyone," he said, deliberately mild. Frowning, he sat up. "I'm no misogynist, Miss Grant. I'm not sure where you might have picked up such an idea."

Her temper flared higher at the challenge. "I—" She paused. She didn't hold that opinion, not really. It was just reflex for her to bristle up and push a man away, especially a nobleman. Perhaps most especially, this nobleman. She swallowed. "I'm sorry."

He lifted a shoulder in absolution. "In any case, my dear *Chloe*, I don't know how any man could hold you in disregard."

Her head swam with the sound of her new name— and with all the implications that went with it. All the treacherous, intoxicating possibilities from which she'd been trying to hide.

He cocked his head. "On the other hand, a weaker man might feel inadequate in your presence. You are quite intimidating."

She laughed. Or perhaps her reaction might be more accurately described as an inelegant snort.

"Is it so funny?"

"It is when I think of all the things I *have* been called. Interfering. Busybody. Whore." She raised a brow. "But never intimidating."

"Well, I'll add hardworking, to help balance that dreadful list—and then I'll ruin it by inviting you once again to take a turn on deck. It may be your last chance for a while, and you might wish to see the why of it."

She eyed him, at a loss. Usually she was excellently skilled at rebuffing a man's attention, driving him away. But this one—he wouldn't be rebuffed. He wasn't looking at her with irritation and exasperation any longer. Instead, he insisted on being . . . friendly.

Interesting. Almost charming.

Damn him.

She bit her lip, thinking. It *had* been reflex, her bid to push him away, but perhaps a bit of self-preservation too. And now she must decide. Did she really wish to act this way? Did she only mean to show him her prickly, defensive side?

It sounded exhausting, in all honesty. And lonely. But prickly was also *safe*.

"Oh, very well," she grumped, shifting to the side of the bed. She stacked her papers, stowed her inkwell and shook out her skirts. "Let's see what there is to be seen."

And try to find a balance between abrasive and safe.

Chapter Six

Blood and pain. So much of both. I'd endured such horrors at the hands of Lord M--- and only just escaped. Why had fate decided to torture me further?

—from the journal of the infamous Miss Hestia Wright

She'd forgotten her hat, Tru noticed, as soon as her head emerged from the passageway below. He bent to assist her to the deck. Yesterday the sea breeze had toyed with her curls. Today, a great deal more aggressive, the wind tussled with her very proper coiffure, attempting to tug her dark locks free.

He felt entirely sympathetic with the wind's designs.

She didn't appear to notice, however. Neither did she take note of the approaching storm. It had grown a little closer while he was below, no longer a dark smudge on the horizon but a bank of immense clouds swallowing one corner of the horizon off the *Spanish Lady's* port side.

Impossible to miss—unless one's attention remained fixed upon a smaller space and closer area. Before she'd even fully gained purchase on the deck she'd cast her gaze about, pinpointing the location of every man amidships.

His hackles rose. Suspicion had earlier stirred in his gut, the idea that someone on board had bothered her. Her caution now served as confirmation. Instinctive anger rose up, demanded that he step close and glare a warning at every male in the vicinity.

He did not. Instead he released her as soon as she was steady on her feet and grinned when she finally caught sight of the thunderclouds bearing down on them.

"Now you see why you'll have plenty of time for your work, my dear Chloe." His grin widened as she winced at the name. "The captain says she shows all the signs of being a graver."

"A graver?" She shivered.

"Yes, and I gather it is every bit as bad as it sounds."

She raised a brow. "How far back will that put our arrival?"

"Perlott says the captain has decided we'll never make Cherbourg. He's angling for Le Havre and the protection of the peninsula instead."

They made their way to the port side rail. "It is frightening," she said, holding on against the rising swell. "I wouldn't like to think of sailing into it."

Tru was glad enough to avoid it as well. Even at this distance, great, jagged lightning strikes could be seen striking the water's surface and arching amongst the roiling clouds.

"But it's beautiful too," she said on a sigh. "Isn't it?"

Tru eyed her where she stood, caught rapt as the gusting wind whipped her skirts and alternately tugged at the bodice of her loose gown and pressed it tight against her. "Indeed."

She shot him a chiding glance and he shifted to face the storm. "Apparently it will lose strength and speed when it crosses land. We'll be safer in Le Havre than we would be trying to ride this out."

"Lord Stoneacre must be upset at the delay?"

He snorted. "Lord Stoneacre's constitution turned upset at the first sign of choppy seas. I think he'll be glad enough to reach a port in the storm."

She pressed her lips together then, though her dark eyes shone with appreciation and amusement. And yet, not at poor Stoneacre's expense, he thought.

He mimicked her earlier expression and raised a brow at her.

"Forgive me. I don't mean to disparage the earl." She gave up and let loose a grin that held him rapt. "It's just that—it's a name we often call Hestia, back at Half Moon House. Port in a storm. Because no matter what kerfuffle comes up or what degree of chaos erupts, she's always so calm and unflappable."

Tru nodded. "I can easily see that." He glanced again between her and the roiling horizon. "And if she is the port, then I'd lay money that you are often the storm— or that you at least find yourself in the midst of it."

She laughed out loud. And about them all the ceaseless activity paused, just for a fraction of a moment, as the husky, rough-edged sound carried delight and shared camaraderie about the deck and out into the wind-tossed sea. There it was—the siren's call. Irresistible and designed to send a shiver down a man's spine and a jolt straight through to his cock.

"I have to laugh—because it's true." She sucked in a breath of restless sea air and lifted a shoulder.

"Well, I know I've been unwise enough to stir you up into a tempest in the past. I have to confess, though, that part of me enjoyed it." The part that appreciated passion, intelligence, flashing eyes and the rapid rise and fall of a magnificent bosom.

Her mouth quirked. "Most people don't."

"That fearsome, are you?"

"I'm afraid I can be quite merciless."

He considered his own roiling temper of late, the anger, frustration and impatience set off by the situation with Marstoke. "It begs the question, what gets you stirred up?" He grinned. "Besides me endlessly disagreeing with you, I mean."

The question sobered her a little. "There is so much

injustice in the world we deal with every day. It builds up, sometimes, and I get frustrated."

"There's a truth I can relate to."

"Sometimes it's because someone will refuse to be helped. Or because they make strides in bettering their lives, and then slip back to the old ways." Darkness crept across her expression. "The worst, however, is usually due to Letty."

"That's an encouraging thought." He made a face.

She laughed a little, as she was supposed to. "The worst was when Hestia first discovered Letty had been taken up by Hatch, a notoriously brutal pimp. She had a hint that it wasn't the usual relationship, that Hatch was working with bigger fish and they had something special planned for Letty." She might have been in the confessional, her tone had grown so quiet and dispassionate. "She didn't tell me right away because she wanted to learn more. I was furious when I found out. I didn't want Letty in there for a second longer than necessary."

The wind teased her hair while she stared out at the white caps.

"I quite lost my mind for a bit, I believe. It still frightens me, the memory of my anger. I was white hot and reckless with it. I caused quite a ruckus." She ducked her head. "I almost got people hurt."

"Almost?"

"Thanks to Hestia. She calmed me, eventually, and defused the situation." Turning, she raised her chin. "I'll take the opportunity to tell you now what I told her then. Letty is mine. My responsibility. Then—and most especially now, on this mission—she is my focus. You and Stoneacre can do what you wish with Marstoke. Kill him, drag him back to face justice, whichever. But managing Letty and getting her to England is my task and I'll thank you not to interfere with it."

He wondered if that unwise girl knew what a champion she had in Callie Grant. "Understood."

"Good."

He endured a few moments of her cryptic, contemplative gaze before she must have decided he measured up. "Since I'm being bold and shocking today, I shall ask something of you."

He held up his hands. "Might as well go for broke."

"I shall ask you to keep watch for me. Hestia says my mere presence can set a pot of trouble to boiling." Turning, she faced him fully. "I do get swept up in my own temper at times, and need to be pulled back from the brink. For a long time only Hestia would challenge me. Then Brynne Wilmott came along. She never scurried away when I began to blow hard. Instead she told me to stop stirring the scandalbroth or she would take my own spoon and brain me with it." Her mouth quirked. "That was the moment I knew we would be friends."

Tru stilled. Her words brought them instantly to mind—all the images of their terse confrontations over the last weeks. They rustled in his head, one by one, a slowly turning picture book of frustration—and other feelings too, all ruthlessly suppressed and unacknowledged.

"No one else has stood toe to toe with me. No one else showed the courage to face me with hard truths." She gestured toward the horizon. "Or label me the tempest that I can sometimes be." Their eyes met, gazes direct and unshuttered. "Until now."

Between them the air thickened with tension. It hung heavy with a certain solidifying fascination, and sparkled with potential—until Tru remembered that he had a goal to accomplish, and that they had a job to do.

"So, all I had to do was compare you to a dark and deadly squall and you decided to trust me?"

The edges of her mouth turned up. "Perhaps just a little."

"Well and good. Perhaps you'll share a thing or two with me, then?"

Her humor vanished. "What things?"

The ugly vision of her facing those two thugs in the alley raised again, enough to make him slightly queasy. "That alley fight we interrupted when we found you—how often do you find yourself in situations like that?"

Her shoulders fell a little, and sighing, she turned to face the rail again. The rolling swell had lessened a bit as the ship raced out of the path of the storm and into more sheltered waters. "It happens occasionally. I should think you'd know the sort of thing we see every day. Children abandoned and growing up in packs. Servant girls accosted, then tossed out when there are consequences. Women beaten to within an inch of their lives by their husbands or their pimps, with no recourse and no one to help. Sometimes it gets physical." She frowned. "Do I need to go on?"

"No." That was the ugliness that she faced every day, with nothing more than a pocket pistol, a knife, her temper, and the resolution to make things better. "But I will say that when one is facing such horrors on a regular basis, then a cleansing storm might occasionally be just what's called for."

He ignored her suddenly arrested expression and continued. "And now I'll ask you to show me something— that technique you mentioned. Do you remember? Something about immobilizing an opponent's arm?"

"Yes, of course. But I didn't think you were serious."

He sighed. "I thought we'd covered this ground. If you'll share that nugget, I'll show you some tricks of my own."

"Here, in front of everyone?"

"There's space for us to move in the stern, where we'll be out of the way, and we can call it work, if it will ease your conscience."

She narrowed her eyes for a moment. Suddenly he reached out and covered her hand where it rested on the railing. "I'm not judgmental, Callie, or high in the instep. Remember, I've spent some time in the world you just described. For months I collected the data for the Love List, and moved about many of London's stews and back alleys. I saw some of the unattractive things you mentioned—but it isn't entirely ugly, just as the world of higher society is not all pretty. I've learned not to judge people before you begin to know them."

He looked out at over the rail, but saw the worn and tired streets around Covent Garden instead of the swollen seas. "I met a woman once. A prostitute, cultivating my acquaintance so she could get a spot on the List, like so many others. But she wasn't like anyone else. She was young, yes, and she'd never had much formal schooling, yet she had a head for figures and percentages like no one I've ever met. She far outclassed most of the men I knew at university. And she'd turned that talent toward her business, had calculated her best chances at raising enough blunt to buy a stake in a coaching inn." He shook his head. "If I'd had the money, I'd have handed it over to her. She'd end up owning half of the East side within a decade."

"Margaret Fee," she said quietly.

"Yes!" He grinned. "You know her?"

She nodded.

"And what of Simon, the old tapster at the Three Peacocks, the one with the fingers so arthritic he can barely pour?"

"Yes, you've heard him sing?"

He shook his head in wonder at the memory. "That gnarled and dusty old character, almost permanently bent over that tap, and he opens his mouth and the songs of angels pour out. I've never heard anything so beautiful in my life."

"I know," she breathed.

He met her gaze squarely. "So you see what I mean, do you not? We've had our differences, and I think we've both misjudged each other. Why do we not clean the slate and move forward with more open minds?"

Perhaps he could not change the world's opinion of him. His greatest fear, the one that he'd been pushing relentlessly away, was that even Marstoke's capture would not do the job. But he had the sudden notion that his salvation could begin if he could but sweeten just one person's view—hers.

She stared a long, assessing moment. But then she straightened her spine, adopted a business-like demeanor and led the way astern.

He took that as a good sign and settled to the task at hand. First he asked her to move about the slight open space for several moments. He nodded approval as she began to grow accustomed to the occasional, irregular sharp pitch of the deck and he tried not to focus on the quick flash of an ankle or calf as the wind snatched at her skirts. A few times she sent swift, searching glances towards the crewmen, but she appeared to be relaxed enough to focus on what they had to learn from each other.

Tru listened intently as she illustrated the spot where one could slip a knife in under a man's clavicle and leave his arm hanging unresponsive. He showed her how, if a man had a hold of her, she could put him down with a well-aimed thrust of her blade to his kidney.

"You use your left hand?" she asked once. "I could have sworn I've seen you write with your right hand."

"A necessary evil, beat into me by tutors and at school. But I shoot and fence and fight with my left hand."

She shrugged and they went back to it. Gradually, as they discussed scenarios and practiced mock blows, the winds grew steadier and the seas grew calmer. The watch bell rang, a new set of crewmen took up duties on deck, and they picked up a few spectators.

One of the men quickly roped a short plank to the stern railing and Callie and Tru took turns throwing knives at the target. She was damned good, too. His respect for her grew. Again.

"I'll show you something else," she said, "if you'd care to see a trick."

He raised a brow.

"First thing—throw your blade at the board a few times. Aim for this spot." She indicated a spot low on the target.

He did, and she stood to the side about midway between him and the board, watching his preparation, his technique, and the spin of his knife in the air.

Then she stepped forward. "Now throw it at me."

"What? No."

"Yes. You won't hurt me. I promise."

He shook his head.

"Listen, I've been watching you. I know what I'm doing. Trust me."

"I can't throw a knife at you!"

"If you don't do it, I'll get one of the crew to throw, and I'm not as familiar with them. Trust in me. I can dodge if I need to."

He felt like he was being put to some test. And they would have to trust each other if they were going to make this mission work. Slowly, he nodded.

She stood halfway to the target, but off to the side. She met his gaze and nodded.

He threw it. Just as he'd done before, because that seemed to be part of whatever this was going to be.

His mouth dropped when she snatched the blade out of the air, turned in one swift motion, threw it again and sunk it nearly hilt deep into the board.

The crew roared in approval. Tru shut his mouth and then opened it again to ask what they all wanted to know. "Where in seven hells did you learn to do that?"

"My mother believed that a girl should know how to defend herself. We knew a footman who used to be part of a traveling troupe of performers. We had lessons."

The crew gathered around then, offering Callie advice, teasing Tru and calling out slightly ribald suggestions. An atmosphere of light-hearted fun and camaraderie spread as evening set in, making it obvious when only one of the watching men failed to take part in the hilarity. Short and swarthy, he held silent and kept a brazenly intent gaze fixed upon the girl.

Tru longed to pitch his arrogant arse right over the rail. Even the man's crewmates cast curious and warning glances in his direction. Callie betrayed herself completely by never looking in his direction at all.

"I've another useful thing to show you," Tru told her eventually. "Women have greater strength in their lower limbs, as a general rule, than they do in their upper. Learning to use it can give you an advantage."

"To run?" she scoffed.

"If you can, it is often the smartest defense. But in point of fact, I meant in close quarters." He beckoned. "Step this way." Looking out over the gathered crewmen, he smiled. "This one needs a demonstration, lads. The lady will need a partner. Though I'll promise we'll have no permanent injuries at risk, you might get a bruise or two. Do we have any volunteers?"

Callie blushed as men surged forward and a great chorus of offers rang out. Tru, however, stopped in front of the sullen sailor. "You look a likely candidate. What's your name?"

"Frederico," the man answered reluctantly.

"Come on up, will you?" He took up a stance beside Callie and waited for the man to comply. "There. Now, when I give the order, you attempt to put your hands on the lady."

"Attempt?" The word emerged along with a sneer. He said nothing else, just watched her hotly as Tru fought the urge to knock the dark promise off his face and looked to Callie.

"Now, you've some experience, and if I know Hestia, she's taught you where a man's most vulnerable, yes?"

Lips pinched together, she nodded.

"Good. Now, at this distance, you should aim there. Watch." He demonstrated. "Turn slightly to the side, with your feet apart. Bend one knee. Keeping your balance, point your knee at your target and kick out hard with your foot. More than once if you have time and opportunity."

"Not fair, yer lordship, givin' 'er such a small target!" someone yelled from the crowd.

His fellows hooted, laughing while Frederico flushed. "I would not be so foolish as to stop here," he insisted belligerently. "I would be much closer." He reached for Callie and she stepped back.

"In that case, if he's moved that close, but not close enough for the strike to his kidney," Tru instructed, "then you use the same technique I just demonstrated, but you aim for his shin. Better yet, you steel yourself for a really hard blow and take out his knee."

She heard the command in his voice. Startled, she met his eyes. Frederico took advantage of her distraction to move in again. Tru nodded and pointed.

And she balanced, aimed, and threw a wicked, thrusting kick right square into the dastard's kneecap. It went out from beneath him. With a small, shocked sound, he toppled.

A great, resounding cheer rang out.

Callie flushed.

Frederico groaned and began to curse low in Italian.

Tru leaned down to clap him—hard—upon the shoulder. "A big wallop she packs, for such a little girl, yes? And that's just what she can do unarmed." He smiled darkly. "And I do make sure she is never unarmed. Ah, but you've been a good sport, Frederico." He tossed the man a coin. "For your trouble. And your good nature."

And your distance in the future, he let his expression send the clear warning.

The man understood. He glared a moment, but then nodded and picked up the coin. One of his mates helped him to his feet and he limped off.

Callie wouldn't have any sort of trouble from him now.

She stood, nodding and smiling slightly, as the rest of the sailors commented or congratulated her before trailing back to work or their bunks. Silent, Tru held out his arm. Biting her lip, she took it and allowed him to escort her back to the passenger quarters.

The snap of canvas was muffled down here, but the creak of timbers sounded long and loud. Callie held her silence until they stood outside the closed door of her cabin.

"How did you know?"

Tru shrugged. "I see what's in front of me. And he is a fool. He was becoming more obvious by the instant."

"But was it wise? He may feel the need to retaliate."

He snorted. "Let him try." Earnest, he touched a finger to her chin. He ignored the hot zing of sensation that shot up his arm at the contact, a shock that must be either thrilling or appalling, except that he had a point to make and no time to lend to the debate. "You knew you could stand against him. I knew it. Now he knows it. And all of his crewmates stood witness to his inappropriate behavior as well. He won't bother you again."

"And perhaps he'll think again before bothering another woman," she said, understanding dawning.

"Exactly."

They stared again at each other, the silence filled with that strange rapport and with honesty—and beginning to feel entirely too . . . comfortable.

"That was useful," she said suddenly. "But do you know, my lord? It was also fun."

Tru was saved from a reply by the captain's steward, emerging from Lord Stoneacre's cabin.

"Excuse me? Miss?" Sir?" He bobbed his head. "Beggin' your pardons, but I'm to tell you that the captain's busy this evening with new calculations and schedules, and won't be hosting dinner in his cabin." He nodded toward the earl's closed door. "His lordship isn't interested in more than tea, but if you'd like, I could bring a tray to your cabins." He looked from one to the other. "Or perhaps set up a table for the both of you?"

Tru shook his head. Too much fun was likely not a good thing. It was perhaps not wise of him to spend so much time alone with Callie Grant. Soon enough he was going to have to come to grips with the idea of her as his temporary wife.

"That would be lovely, thank you," Callie said. Firmly.

The steward bowed and went to make his preparations.

Tru frowned. "Is it wise?"

She bit back a grin as he used her own words against her. "Well, the last I heard, it was considered quite common for a husband to dine with his wife."

He rolled his eyes.

"We can leave the door open if you are concerned for your reputation."

Helpless, he laughed. "You never do or say anything expected."

She spun on her heel and entered the cabin. Holding the door for him, she answered, "I daresay that's why you might like me."

You have no idea how right you are.

Wisely, he kept the thought to himself and followed her in.

Callie wasn't doing anything she'd expected, either. In point of fact, she barely had a notion what it was she was doing. Or thinking. Or feeling.

She felt disconnected, as if the ocean's waters had cut her off from her old self as surely as it had removed her from the reach of England. The old Callie—the *real* Callie—would only wish to be left to her work and her isolation. This person—Callie, Chloe, whoever she was now—wanted nothing of the sort. She most vehemently did not want Lord Truitt to leave.

She moved past him, but he stood, hovering in the doorway, taking up half the space in the tiny cabin and a great deal of the air too. She breathed deep, fighting for her share and fighting the urge to reach out and grab that muscular arm and refuse to let go—to keep him here until she puzzled out just who they both were.

For she greatly feared she'd misjudged the man.

Somehow he'd discovered the trouble she'd had with that crewman. Minor trouble only, to be sure, nothing she could not have handled, but when it became clear he knew, she'd expected him to take it over—to treat them all to a display of male posturing, perhaps to throw the weight of his title and social standing at the swarthy upstart. Instead he'd manipulated the situation so that she would be the one to take the insolent sailor down. Yes, there had been a bit of masculine preening at the end, but she could forgive him that, because all in all, he'd shown admirable restraint. And a measure of respect for her and her abilities.

Unheard of, that. And unexpected. But appreciated.

A clatter rose in the passageway and she did reach a hand out to him at last. She was unsure of a great many things, but she knew she'd liked spending time with him today, that sharing knowledge and laughter had created an unexpected intimacy that tugged at her. Like the feel of crisp, fresh linen on a bed or the taste of crusty bread warm from the oven, it was a pleasure she could surely survive without, but had no wish to abandon.

She was also suddenly afraid that she owed him both her thanks—and the truth.

"Would you mind moving my trunk over to the far wall, Lord Truitt? Otherwise I'm afraid we'll be reduced to a picnic upon the bunk."

Obliging, he stepped forward. He'd removed his coat and waistcoat earlier, looking for more freedom of movement as they threw their knives. She tried not to stare at several inches of exposed throat and chest as he leaned over. "Tousseau," he reminded her. "We'd best start getting used to using the new names now." He lifted the heavy trunk, and paused in surprise. "What have you got in here, *Chloe*? Rocks?"

"Worse," she said with a grin.

"Worse than rocks?" He said, disbelieving.

"Cast-iron pans. Lord Stoneacre is of the belief that no decent cook would travel to a new position without her own."

"The man thinks of everything." Grunting, he settled it into its new position.

"He does indeed." Callie frowned. "It worries me,

though. I'm not used to subterfuge. I'm afraid I will be the one to give us all away."

"We'll practice. It will all start to feel normal soon enough."

She was afraid it would not. She'd been carrying thoughts of Lord Truitt—as Lord Truitt—about in her head for far longer and more often than she cared to admit, even to herself.

"I'd rather adjust it a bit to make a slip-up less likely," she mused. She pursed her lips and watched him turn away from the trunk. "That's it!" she said triumphantly, suddenly inspired. "Chloe shall have a pet name for you." She flicked a hand towards the trunk. "Chloe expected to gain an inn when she married you, but had it snatched away. Now you, yourself, are all that you bring to the marriage. You are your own *Trousseau*. It's a good play on Tousseau. Then I can call you Tru and no one will know the difference."

"Very good." He lifted a brow. "And what was that about you not being well-acquainted with subterfuge?"

She laughed just as the steward knocked upon the door. "You may use an equally mocking name for me," she said, moving to open it, "if you can come up with one."

He snorted and went to the steward's assistance as he moved a small table into the room. The man set up quickly and left them to a dinner of stew and a rich plum duff to finish. Tru spoke of the hiring of servants, cleaning schedules, taprooms, stables, all of the tasks and issues they might expect to encounter in their venture and the problems that could hopefully avoid. Callie listened with half an ear and wondered how she was going to go about sharing a secret that she had worked so hard to protect.

The conversation wound down. Tru stood. "I'll take my leave of you, but I'll send the steward down to clear, so that you may return to your work for the evening."

"Wait!" She held out a hand. "I wonder if perhaps we might talk?"

He sank back into his chair. "Is that not what we have been doing?" he asked, sardonic.

Her heart was in her throat. She could not respond with the same levity.

'Perhaps you'll just listen, then."

She saw the moment he decided to go along with the shift in mood. "What is it?"

"There are some things you might . . . things you perhaps should know before we arrive in Brittany."

He waited.

She swallowed. It took effort even to contemplate exposing so much of herself. Especially after she'd judged him so harshly. Her eyes drifted closed. It was only fair, perhaps, that now he would have the chance to find her wanting.

He stood again, after a moment. "I will be at your service, when you are ready, Callie."

"No." A whisper only, not very convincing. She stiffened her spine. "It's about Letty. You should know about our connection before we arrive in St. Malo."

He came suddenly and completely alert.

She breathed deep and looked him in the eye. "She's my sister."

He sat again. His face remained blank.

"Half-sister," she clarified.

He frowned. "That's not what I expected you to say."

She could echo that sentiment, only more irritably. "What did you expect?"

"A debt owed, maybe? A commitment to a longtime friend or valued colleague at Half Moon House?"

His frown deepened, his eyes darted. "When I think back on those endless arguments . . . I thought you a loyal friend, but I did my damned level best to change your thinking, anyway. And all along you were fighting to protect your sister!"

She cocked her head at him. "You would have done the same, had you known."

She could see that he was casting back, going over all the endless strategic discussions they'd both taken part in, reliving all of their private battles. His jaw clenched. "I'm afraid you are right—and I'm not sure I like what that reveals about me."

Callie was far more worried about what the dawning truth about her would mean to him.

"I don't understand. Why would you be so reluctant to have me know the truth?" He stiffened. "You expected that I would turn up my nose? That my regard for you would lower if I knew that your mother was an actress?"

Heat blanched her face. "You have it wrong. My mother was not an actress."

"Did I misunderstand? When you spoke of Letty's theatrical ambitions you said that her talent had come from . . ." He stopped.

She nodded. "That's right. Letty and I don't share a mother, but a father."

His jaw worked. "But that makes you—"

"A bastard?" she said bitterly.

"Royal," he answered bluntly.

"A royal by-blow," she bit out, "which is the same as saying a diamond-encrusted pig. A creature fit for none of the worlds it might live in."

"And yet, still royal." He had begun to look as angry as she felt. "The royal family is practically bursting with natural children. The Duke of Clarence had ten with

Mrs. Jordan alone, for God's sake. They all take their place in court or move, even marry in Society. They have standing, allowances." He gestured around them, then toward her gown. She looked down at the unadorned wool. "None of the rest of them lives in a home for troubled women."

"I am perfectly happy where I am."

"But you should be offered the same courtesies, the same—"

She cut him off with a sharp wave of her hand. "It's of no concern. I've made my decisions."

"But your father . . ."

"Is reliably less interested in me than I am in him." She shifted, uncomfortable and excited, afraid to go on but even more fearful of going back. "Please. None of that is why I wished to tell you the truth."

He sensed the change in the air. His posture shifted ever so slightly. He'd gone alert, a predator tasting, testing his surroundings with all of the senses available to him. Pique still blazed in his expression. On her behalf. A hidden part of her marveled—no, reveled—in the newness of such a thing.

She squashed it. She was not to play the part of nervous, excited prey. Not for anyone. She'd vowed long ago never to take up such a role. No, this would be something altogether different.

But it was there, in his gaze. Interest. Speculation. Even a little wariness.

Smart man.

"Why then, Callie?" he rasped. "Why tell me now?"

"For several reasons. First, because Letty *is* my sister. And like many siblings, our history is long, complicated and not always amiable."

He snorted. "You don't have to lecture me on the

complexities of sibling relationships."

"I thought you should know, I will likely have to labor hard to convince her to come along with our plans."

"Understood." His gaze darkened. She could almost feel the heat coming off of him as he smoldered at her. "Was there another reason to tell me?"

She swallowed past the sudden lump in her throat and moved restlessly in her seat again. "Yes. I gave you a bit of information that might help you in our mission. I wanted to ask something of you in return." She could not keep her toes from curling inside her slippers. "A bit of a trade."

He waited.

"What is it that you want, Callie?"

"A kiss."

It came out a whisper. No. That wouldn't do. She lifted her head. "I want you to kiss me," she said distinctly.

He exhaled. Had he been holding his breath?

"Why?" he asked.

Because his cheekbones were chiseled perfection. Because she'd been dreaming for weeks about putting her hands on those broad shoulders—and longer than that about tracing that crescent shaped scar with her fingers and smoothing away that crease that his frown gave it. Because the fine linen of his shirt couldn't completely hide the hard, masculine beauty of his chest.

She said none of those things, of course.

"Because I want to know, finally, what it is all about," she said with a shrug.

"What it is all about," he repeated slowly. "What *what* is all about?"

She merely waved her hand in the air, gesturing between them.

He frowned.

She blew out an frustrated breath. "Kissing! And . . . you know . . . all of it."

"Kissing is not all of it," he stated flatly. "Are you telling me that you've been living in Half Moon House with a goodly number of current or former prostitutes—and you've never been kissed?"

She bristled. "Yes! I live in a house full of women, many who've been beaten, abandoned or abused. One way or another, most of them have had their lives ruined by men. It doesn't exactly inspire girlish dreams or the urge to go about chasing kisses."

He paused, clearly taken aback. "I hadn't considered it from that point." He frowned, suddenly uncomfortable. "But why me?"

She glanced away from the appeal of those dark eyes and the temptation of his tall, broad frame.

"Because you understand things—many things that are important to me. Because I wish, for once, to do something just for me." She pinched her lips. "Something that might be fun."

He didn't smile. She appreciated it. Perhaps he knew that she did not take this lightly. "Because I trust you," she said at last, low.

He reared back. "Why?"

Did he know how much that simple question gave away? "Tru—you are stubborn and exasperating. But you are also utterly honorable. I know that if I ask you for this, then you will not press me for anything more."

"So that's to be it, then? A taste? A kiss and no more?" He stared, unblinking.

"Yes. No." She shrugged. "I don't know." She leaned forward over the forgotten remains of their dinner. "Are you going to make me ask you again?"

His mouth twisted as if he were considering it. He

sat there silent long enough that she knew he *was* considering it. Her heart sank. He was likely considering how to get out of her cabin and locked safely behind the door to his.

"Hell, no," he said at last. He stood and extended an imperious hand. "On your feet," he said roughly. "Your first kiss should not be on a hard, narrow ship's bunk."

She took his hand, let him pull her to her feet. Relief sent shivers down her spine, so strong it banished any mortification she might have felt that he had read between the lines and arrived at that particularly embarrassing truth. His fingertips left hers and dragged lightly up her arm, sending shivers through her.

He stepped closer. "Just a taste?"

Her eyes slid closed as she nodded. He continued, exploring her jaw, the corner of her mouth, her temple. The shivering stopped—likely because she was growing so warm. He cupped her jaw with one hand, slid the other over her hip and to the small of her back. Pulling her tight against him, he pressed his lips to hers.

A kiss. A simple thing, the soft touch of one mouth to another—and yet. And yet she felt it, instantly everywhere, lighting her up from within, waking all the dormant parts of her, from the top of her head to the tip of her toes.

Gently, he instructed her. Lightly, he brushed her with his mouth. No rushing or insistence. He was inviting her to come along with him. Willingly, she followed him to a place where *lush*, *rich* and *more* were the only words that mattered.

He listened, this one, and somehow that was as erotic as the straining press of their bodies.

Because the rest of her wished to go along with him, as well. Her hands crept upward, enjoying the contrast of soft linen and hard, curving chest as her arm slipped around until she was—incredibly—closer. She dug her fingers into those gloriously broad shoulders and finally reached up with one finger to softly touch that intriguing scar. Her nipples went hard as they rubbed where her hands had just wandered. When he reached down to her bottom and urged her tighter against him she gasped her surprise and approval.

He took the advantage and pressed his tongue to hers. She'd known it was coming, and yet she tensed. He slowed immediately, but did not retreat. Instead he coaxed, played, tempted, until her objections were gone and nearly all of her breath with it.

He grew hungrier, asked for more. The powerful beat of his heart twined with hers.

This. She'd never understood, before now. She'd seen women in thrall before—women glassy-eyed for days on opium, others selling themselves for a pint of gin, countless others throwing themselves away on men who mistreated them. She'd never understood.

But this—he surrounded her, big and masculine and hard. Demanding. It was utterly impossible not to respond.

He moaned. She could feel the rising wildness in him. His mouth seared its way down to her throat and his hand crept up to cup her breast. Her nipple rolled beneath the palm of his hand and all her muscles tightened against the incredible jolt of passion arcing suddenly through her.

He towered over her. She should be wary of the complete control he held over the situation, over her body and its reactions. Instead, she wanted more.

So dangerous, this feeling of being frantically wanted and desperately needed—and also safe, protected, cherished. Free to desperately want in return. This was her opium—she recognized it at once. The heat and taste and smell of him shut down all rational thinking, stole her determination and will power, replaced it with a deep, aching need that settled low and deep in her churning belly.

It should have been a warning. It wasn't. It wasn't even deterrent enough to keep her from thrusting her breast further into his hand.

A clatter sounded. The steward, entering the passage with his cart. Another clash, closer. Finally the noise was enough to blow a distracting breeze through the honeyed fog they'd wrapped themselves in.

They stilled. Disengaged. She fought a moan of protest. He pulled away. Blowing like a set of matching, heaving bellows, they faced each other across inches, breathing each other's air.

A quick knock and the door latch rattled.

He stepped back again. Away.

The steward entered, muttering apologies.

Callie forced a smile, grasped frantically for a semblance of composure, the illusion of control. "Thank you, Tru. For all that you've taught me today." Callie, Chloe, new or old, she could never let him know just how thoroughly he'd unhinged her.

He lifted his coat and gave a short bow. "Of course." Irony invaded his tone. "It would appear that we both still have much to learn." He stepped around the servant, but paused at the door long enough to raise a brow in her direction. "I hope you pass a restful night."

"Thank you."

Alone. She needed time and isolation to face the blows dealt by that kiss. To shore up the barriers that she'd thought were unassailable. Under no circumstances could he know that, however. She rallied, tried for just a hint of mockery. "I'm sure it will be as peaceful as your own." With a nod, she bid him a good night and watched him go.

Chapter Seven

A woman owned the little country inn. A woman with no claims to birth or education. But she had the gentlest touch and the biggest heart I've ever known. Her name was Pearl.

--from the Journal of the infamous Miss Hestia Wright

The *Spanish Lady* weathered the storm very well in the shelter of Le Havre. Anxious about his schedule, the captain would not allow anyone to disembark. They passed a restless, choppy night aboard and were off with the morning tide. The winds were against them, though, setting the captain to swearing and the crew to scrambling. As the morning dawned clear and fresh after the storm, the ship was tacking north toward the Cotentin Peninsula.

Tru spent the long day heckling Stoneacre about his tender sensibilities, consulting with the earl on his disguise and making notes on the order and precedence of the jobs that would need tackling once he took over the running of the inn and tavern.

In truth, it seemed a straightforward enough task to him, but he was hard put to find another way to avoid Callie Grant.

He caught a glimpse or two of her, as she took the air on deck. That was close enough. He watched her, lifting her face to catch the sea breeze, interacting easily with the crew now, and he remembered the words she'd spoken to him, that first night in Dover. She knew enough about men to categorize them, she'd said. Stuff them safely into their respective boxes, he'd interpreted.

He suffered a pang of envy. He wished like hell he could categorize *her*.

Everything about the girl defied such a thing. No wonder the royal side of her family ignored her. She didn't fit with the women of that class, all playing the same game, following the rules and filling their spot in the play. But neither did she resemble the women he'd met in London's harsher, darker haunts. Women were ambitious players there, too, though they fought all the harder for outcomes that put their very lives at stake.

Callie, with her zeal, her concern for others—and with her damned tempting kisses—was different from them all. Not hedged in by rules or prodded by the dark necessity of survival. Not defined by others' view of her.

Who defined her, then?

He supposed she defined herself.

Hell and damnation. Imagine that.

He couldn't. The thought both called him and repelled him. It made him uncomfortable, just as she did.

God, yes. That he could define. She set him on edge. Made him feel like a schoolboy being handed his first set of algebraic equations, a halfling with his first wench dropped in his lap. Interested, willing, but unsure of the direction to take.

He didn't like it. Preventing that precise feeling of uncertainty was the reason he was here. He *hated* being unsure of himself. It took him back, far back to the days after the death of his parents. They'd been dark days, filled with anger and grief even before his brother had been swept away to fulfill his new destiny as Duke of Aldmere. Darker still, afterwards, when Tru had been left alone, lost and bewildered, shuffled aside and shipped off to school as if he'd become extraneous.

He shook his head to dispel such wayward thoughts. None of it mattered, in any case. He could not touch the girl again. No matter how sweetly she asked. No matter how he dreamed of the soft touch of her skin, the hot, sweet taste of her, or the feel of that wondrous bosom in his hands.

For one thing—she was under Hestia Wright's

protection. And though he may have proved himself several kinds of careless, he wasn't idiot enough to incur that lady's wrath.

For another—Hestia had placed the girl under his protection—and while Marstoke might have made him a fool, despoiling innocents was the marquess's failing, not his. Tru would never let that man—or any situation he found himself forced into—turn him into such a villain.

A moment's distraction was one thing, but he could not let her ruin his focus.

Marstoke—that was the focus. The urgency was back in his blood. *Hurry*, it sang to him. He had to find the marquess and bring him back to justice. He had to close this unfortunate chapter of his life so that he could move forward. Or back, he might say. All he wanted was to go back to that simpler time when no dark cloud of suspicion lived over his head, when no man hesitated to take his hand, when laughter came easily and it was a simple thing to look in the mirror.

"It's ready." Stoneacre had found him lurking amidships, behind a coil of rope and beneath the bow rail. The man still looked a little green about the edges. "Come on down and we'll finish up your disguise."

Tru tromped below behind the earl. All of their gear—and a few extras procured by Stoneacre—had been packed and stacked and stood ready to be off loaded. All save a smaller trunk sitting on the bed.

Stoneacre opened it. "Here we are." He held up a jar full of black paste. "Over by the wash basin, if you please. This can be messy. You'll have to reapply every day or so—make sure you do so with plenty of water at hand."

He set to work, showing Tru how to rub a bit of the stuff up from the root of his hair. It didn't take long. Tru surveyed the effect in a looking glass, surprised by the difference. Besides being darker, the stuff made his hair feel thicker and helped it hold a slightly messier, more casual style.

"Not bad," Stoneacre remarked, watching him critically as he wiped his hands. "Now, these." He reached in and pulled out two long, twin strips of short, dark hair. "Facial hair might not be fashionable, but it will hide that scar."

Tru paid close attention as the earl taught him to apply his new sideburns. To finish it off, he added subtle cosmetics that would emphasize his few lines and creases and add age to his countenance.

"Easy enough," he remarked. "How do I look?"

"Dashing. Perhaps you'll start a new fashion." Stoneacre held up another piece, a flimsy patch, rough textured and painted to look like reddened flesh. "Also, because we're covering one identifying physical mark, it would be wise to give you another. One covered scar might not give pause to the curious, but add another in a different spot and they'll start to doubt themselves."

He took Tru's hand and flattened it on the bunk. "Place it here, on the back of your hand, visible but disappearing upward beneath your cuffs. No one will know it doesn't extend up your arm." He raised a brow. "A burn scar—from a stable fire at your family's inn. You heroically saved the livestock, of course."

"Of course," Tru agreed.

"You'll have to keep a coat on, but that's as befits the owner of the place. And be careful to place your pieces correctly and in the exact same spot every day. Consistency is the key to a good disguise." Stoneacre bent over the box again and tossed something at him.

Automatically, Tru reached out to catch the bag. He hefted it. "Money?" And no small amount either. "What am I to do with this?"

"Keep back enough to purchase passage back home—for three." The earl waved off the start of Tru's question. "It never hurts to be prepared." He shrugged one shoulder. "As for the rest, hire staff, buy supplies, use it for all of the expenses a man would have as he sets up his own enterprise."

"Damn Marstoke for making this so convoluted. It's a damned lot of money and work." Tru took his own turn at cutting Stoneacre off. "I know, I understand how important it is to make it all utterly real. But what of the innocent people I'm about to involve? What happens to them when we grab Marstoke and head home?"

"We'll do what we can to take care of them. Compensate them for their lost prospects, at the very least."

It seemed like the very least to Tru.

He said no more, and they both turned as a noise sounded at the door. It opened enough to allow Callie Grant to peek around it.

"We're nearly there," she informed them. She stepped inside. "But the captain says we'll have to wait until morning before we can have our papers processed."

Tru tried not to stare. He knew her high-necked, form fitting gown of sturdy blue wool was meant to make her look staid and respectable—but with that figure it only served to make a man imagine himself peeling the layers away.

Her eyes widened as she looked Tru's way. "Oh! You do look different! Almost piratical." She blushed a little.

He bowed. Damned if he wasn't afraid he'd match her blush. "Now that sounds like a role I'd relish," he said with a grin. "Alas, I am merely to play host to pirates, sailors, spies and other assorted scalawags."

"And I'm to feed them. As quickly as possible, according to Lord Stoneacre." She gave the earl a nod. "I'm ready to get started."

"We are all ready." Stoneacre closed his trunk and stowed it with the rest. Stepping close, he took her hand.

"Remember—Chloe Chaput has had experience with this type of venture. Don't hesitate to enter the situation with authority."

She laughed, a husky, ironic rasp—and Tru tightened. Everywhere.

"Oh, ask anyone at Half Moon House and they'll tell you I have no problem asserting my authority." Her mouth quirked. "If anyone questions me, I'll just tell them that that's how it is done in Franche-Comté."

"Perfect." The earl nodded. "Now I'll disembark separately. Watch for me later in the day, though. I'll stop by and we'll find a way for us to keep in touch."

Tru met the earl's direct gaze as he clapped him on the shoulder. "The victory will be ours this time, Tru. Between the two of us—and your lovely wife—we'll have Marstoke in no time."

Tru squeezed his arm. "I damned well don't intend to go back without him," he vowed.

"Nor do I." The earl nodded at them both. "Just a few more hours, and we'll make it happen."

* * *

It didn't happen right away. Tru's impatience was on display the next morning, making him fidget at the delay while the harbor men checked their documents and sent them on through customs.

Currently, they were waiting. Again. As someone checked some small item on their forged papers. Again. He paced while Callie adopted a stance of bored patience— and together they struck just the right note, he thought.

They stood at a window of the small, cluttered office. His heart beat a little faster as he pressed near, playing the attentive husband, while she looked calm and collected and damned beautiful as she watched the ceaseless activity on the docks.

He wasn't alone in his awareness, however. It lived

in the air between them, dancing through the dust motes, connecting them in some undefined way. He put it to the test, edging back a bit, then again, with a shift away from her.

And there it was. A slight, graceful turn of her shoulder. She rotated toward him, like a cat following warm rays of sun. He would have been smug about it, perhaps, had he not been equally as struck by the auburn streaks lifting from her dark hair to meet the light, or had he not been fighting to ignore the close fit of her spencer as it molded her long arms and generous curves before it nipped in at her waist.

He told himself that now was not the time to ogle her—or to recall that kiss—or to imagine what might have happened, had that porter not interrupted. He might have kissed her soft lips again and laid her back upon the bunk and—

"You are free to go now," the clerk told them, approaching from behind. "Welcome to France."

"Our thanks," Tru gave the man a nod and slipped him a coin. "If you will not mind, I shall leave my wife safely here for a few moments while I find us transportation?"

The clerk agreed.

Tru straightened his coat and leaned close to speak in Callie's ear. "Stay here. You'll be safe enough. I'll find us a hack and a cart for our things and return shortly."

On impulse he took her hand and pressed it to his lips, thinking it might be a gesture a man would make toward his wife as they set out upon a new path together. But her pulse jumped so rapidly beneath his fingers and such a sweet flush rose up over her cheeks that he decided on he spot that Tousseau Chaput would adopt it as a habit.

With a nod to the clerk as he departed, Tru stepped into the bustle of the busy wharf. The din assaulted his ears. He passed a group of sailors, set free on leave. They roared with laughter, drunk with rotgut and freedom. Stevedores chanted as they shifted loads, clerks shouted instructions and numbers, and as he moved further in, doxies flirted and called out invitations.

He ignored it all, asked for directions, and set off, moving steadily and ducking once as a wizened old woman, cleaning fish over a flat board, threw the guts to a hovering flock of screaming gulls. He weaved amongst crates, cases and barrels until he found the lanes that led to the city proper.

He stifled a curse. He'd been expecting a stack of vehicles for hire, but the space loomed nearly empty instead. At the distant corner he caught sight of the last few of a line of wagons, all laden with distinctively branded casks, pulling away. Only a couple of small gigs were left, the sort that could carry a passenger or two—and one lone wagon, also stacked high with casks, rapidly falling behind.

Not for lack of trying, it would seem. In fact, the red-faced driver had abandoned his seat. He stood now before the handsome draft horse, pulling hard and trying to coax the animal into action.

The horse stretched out his head to accommodate him, but refused to pick up his feet.

The other drivers guffawed. "Going to let that nag best you, Ludo?" one called.

The florid driver cursed in colorful Breton. Tru heard something that sounded like "stubborn, bone-knackered nag," before the unfortunate Ludo climbed back up onto the driver's box and slashed the reins viciously. "*Move*, damn you!"

No response.

His color climbing alarmingly higher, the driver stood on the box and faced a large pile of crushed crates across the lane. "Edgar! Get out here now and do something with this bag of bones!"

Without waiting for a reply, he dropped down onto his seat, reached beneath it and brought out a long-handled whip. He cracked it once, hard and fast across the horse's back. The animal flinched, but stood its stubborn ground.

"I. Am. So. Tired. Of. This!" With each syllable, the red-faced, wild-eyed man cracked the horse another blow.

Tru had had enough. He stepped forward, intent on putting on a stop to it, when a low roaring "No!" echoed from the pile of broken crates.

He paused, craning his neck to see a figure crawling backwards from the mess, still hunched over close to the ground. "Don't hit her." The words rumbled like thunder from a big man who slowly stood up. Over his shoulder he said, "I asked you not to hit her. She'll move when I ask her. I told you to wait. I'm almost finished."

"I don't want to wait!" Ludo shouted back. "I want to make this delivery, pocket a *sou* or two and then get back here to make some more!" He punctuated this speech with another blow.

Tru stepped forward again. "That's enough of that now!"

Ludo ignored him.

The horse shuddered.

The other drivers laughed once more.

Tru's eyes widened as the big man—Edgar, he presumed—rumbled again and turned about. He was massive. Large brown eyes hung beneath a prominent brow and an almost bulging forehead. Straight blonde hair swept off of his face and ended in a blunt fall at his nape. In his hands he cradled a—

Tru blinked. A cat. He held a young cat in his hands, one leg bandaged with what looked like a kerchief and pieces of broken crate. As Tru watched, the big man maneuvered it carefully into the outer pocket of his long frock coat.

"Do not hit the mare," the big man told Ludo.

The driver had clearly reached the end of his endurance. He stood again, chest swelling. Pointing a shaky finger he rasped, "Get that nag moving, Edgar. *Now!*"

Edgar crossed to the horse's head. She greeted him with a nicker of obvious relief. But instead of coaxing her forward, the big man moved alongside her and began to unhook her from the traces.

"What are you doing?" Tru thought Ludo might have an apoplexy right there in front of them. "Stop it! Stop it! We have to go!"

"I asked you not to hit the mare. You didn't listen." Edgar spoke with utter complacency. "Now we don't listen to you any longer."

Ludo's mouth hung open. It worked noiselessly for several seconds. Then he started to move, nearly dancing in his inability to contain his rage. Suddenly he lifted the whip again and with a whistling sound as it sang through the air, he laid it across Edgar's shoulders.

Edgar appeared to be just as unaffected as the horse had been, which only spurred Ludo on. He began to strike the horse's broad back again, even as Edgar's hands flew to free her.

Tru took a last step closer. Watching closely, timing it smoothly, he reached out and snatched the dangling whip as Ludo pulled it back for another blow.

"As I said, that's quite enough." Tru adopted his brother's finest ducal manner and threw plenty of hauteur into it. "What is all of this about? Whose animal is this?"

"Mine. The mare is mine." Edgar looked down when the cat in his pocket mewled a protest. "And the cat." He had got the horse free and pulled her a few steps away from the wagon. She went willingly enough now. "I'm

Edgar. Rose is my mare. I'm a carter."

Ludo snorted. "Well the cart is mine, you dim-witted fool. Ridiculous to call yourself a carter if you have no cart!"

"Indeed," Tru agreed. "In much the same way as it to expect to move a load with no horse."

"I had a cart," Edgar said, his expression and tone both still flat. "I was busy. I delivered goods all over the city and across the countryside." He soothed the mare's flank with one hand while the other rested between the cat's ears. "It's eight hundred and twenty-four cart lengths from the docks to the brewery. That's three thousand, two hundred and ninety six steps."

"What happened to your cart?" Tru asked with sympathy.

"Stolen. And wrecked at the bottom of a ravine."

Ludo laughed. And Tru made a decision.

"I never lost a parcel or forgot an address, when I had a cart," Edgar continued. His tone remained even, his expression flat. "I made money and we lived well."

"You didn't live well once it was gone, did you?" Ludo sneered. "Lucky you were that I took you in. Now I've lost all patience. I want you, your nag and your things out of my barn. Today."

His hand on the mare's bridle, Edgar turned to go.

"Wait!" Tru followed and looked at the big man over the back of the horse. "How would you like a job with me? I need a stable manager in my new place."

Edgar blinked. "But I'm a carter."

"And you'll need money for a new cart, will you not? Come and manage my stables for a time, you'd have a place to keep your mare—and your cat. All while you earn a decent salary."

"A new cart," the big man repeated.

"What do you say?"

Edgar eyed the whip Tru had forgotten he still held. "Will you strike your horses? Or mine?"

Tru looked down in surprise, then tossed the thing back toward Ludo. "No."

Edgar nodded. "Then I accept. Until I can buy a cart."

Tru nodded. "Good, then. Glad to have you." He looked about, impatient once more. "I'll hire one of the gigs to carry my wife, but I'll have to wait for one of the wagons to come back to transport our luggage."

"How much luggage?" Edgar asked.

"Not much. A couple of trunks and portmanteaus. Though one of them is heavy," he said, remembering the pots.

"Hold her?" Handing the mare over to Tru, Edgar walked back to the cart and fished a folded tarpaulin out of the back. "This is mine as well." He ignored Ludo's protests. "I remember something that might help."

Chapter Eight

Pearl had experience in these matters. She nursed me well, but I was left so weak. Drained and lethargic, I cried for days. I could barely dress myself at first. Pearl took me in, waited on me herself, let me stay for weeks as I recovered.

--from the Journal of the infamous Miss Hestia Wright.

Callie shivered in the damp air seeping from the window. She was watching for Tru—and chiding herself for that kiss. Part of her knew it for a mistake. He'd been avoiding her ever since—no small feat on a ship as small as the *Spanish Lady*. She'd spooked him—and given him tangible evidence that she wasn't . . . normal. He would never kiss a woman of his own social class with so much heat and passion and *want*. And a woman of the lower layers of society? Well—he'd likely not have stopped at such a kiss.

So she'd once again proved herself an anomaly— but some part of her still couldn't regret it. In fact, she was beginning to think that Hestia had been right. This trip was good for her. She could feel herself relaxing, opening up. She blushed. Blossoming.

More than that—at last she knew. Finally she could understand the temptation, the sheer addictive pull of heat and desire. So much more than just physical yearning— more than the surprising clash of straight-edged jaw and soft, thick hair, of tender lips and hardened chest—though that was delicious enough. She'd never before grasped how seductive the heady feeling of being wanted could be. How it acted as a balm to a wounded soul, could steal in and soothe aches that had become a part of you.

She pushed the thought aside as she caught sight of Tru returning. He opened the door and beckoned her, wearing an odd expression. "I've arranged transportation."

She shot him a questioning look, but he brushed it aside. "You'll just have to see for yourself."

She took his arm and followed him out.

"Chloe," he said as they rounded the corner of the building. "I'd like you to meet our first employee."

She stopped short—and stared. "Our first—" She didn't go on. She was too caught up in the sight before her.

A man, holding a horse. He made her a respectable bow.

She swallowed. The horse was large and handsome. The man was large and . . . not. Across the horse's withers crossed a set of makeshift poles. They extended behind the animal where a tarpaulin covered them.

"This is Edgar. The mare belongs to him." Tru pointed to a pocket in the man's enormous and outdated frock coat. "As well as the cat."

From the pocket a kitten mewed agreement. Tru raised his brows at her in a silent signal for . . . assistance? Understanding?

"Edgar has a gift, a way with animals. I've just borne witness to it myself. I've asked him to manage the stables for us at the new inn." Tru waved a hand. "Edgar, my wife. Madame Chaput."

Edgar bowed again. Callie glanced at the animals, met his direct gaze—and nodded. "I'm so pleased to meet you, Edgar. How wonderful to have found our first employee so soon."

He watched her without blinking. "Only until I have the money for a cart. I'm a carter," he said, in the manner of an explanation.

"Oh?" She looked to Tru.

"Edgar's cart was stolen. He needs a new one. I offered him the chance to earn the money working in our stables."

"That sounds like a good idea all around." She eyed the contraption attached to the horse.

"Edgar rigged that up so he could transport our baggage."

"It's a travois," the big man said. He had a curious, even way of speaking, without inflection or a change in tone. "An old way to move things. The red Indians in the Americas use them."

"Have you traveled to the Americas?" Callie asked, impressed.

"No. I read about it in a book when I was a boy."

"And you recall it well enough to reconstruct one? After so long?"

"I remember everything." Turning, he indicated the luggage the clerk's men were stacking nearby. "Is that all of your baggage?"

"That's it," Tru answered. "Will it fit?"

Edgar studied the pile for a moment. "Just." He beckoned the men forward. "Bring me the heaviest first."

He had their luggage secured soon enough, and Tru gestured. "We'll walk this way a bit before we'll find the gigs for hire."

"Is it so far?" she asked, looking to Edgar. "To the inn?"

"Not so far. I'll have to come behind, going slow to navigate the travois."

"Why do we not all walk?" Callie suggested. "I'd like to see something of our new city."

"Then walk, we shall." Tru offered his arm and she took it, and together they moved off. She stayed close at first, through the first press of the congested wharf. She'd been in the London docks before, working with Hestia, so she was familiar with the stink and the noise and the unrelenting ebb and surge of many curses and orders in as many languages. These were not so extensive, of course, but still loud, coarse and frantic. The chaotic background here, though, carried on in flamboyant French—and the further they went away from the harbor and into the city, the more she was surrounded by the familiar lilt of the Breton language.

She wanted to close her eyes and drink that homey sound in through her pores, to wallow in the warmth that washed over her. Her mother's language. Just the sound of the words meant calm strength, solid support, comfort.

She did close her eyes, for just a moment, as they waited to cross a traffic-filled street, and let it ease her. Then she opened them and found Tru watching her, the corners of his mouth lifted, just the slightest bit.

She stared back at him a moment. Bright and blue, his gaze shone from the frame of his newly dark hair and thin, framing sideburns, and suddenly she realized how much had changed in a short time. Looking at him weeks ago, her wayward mind would have summoned words like *spoiled*, *annoying* and *obstacle*. Now, instead, she was struck by such descriptors as *generous* and *friend*.

Let's not forget *kiss*, a part of her whispered slyly.

She glanced away, let her attention wander over their new and odd companions—and then she turned deliberately back and gave him a great, happy, hopeful smile.

His jaw slackened.

Callie tilted her head, listening again, and thought that this scheme might work, after all.

* * *

That confidence faded a bit when they reached their destination. The *Sword and Sheath*, the sign proclaimed, with an unfortunately phallic rendition carved into the hanging wooden sign.

"That will have to change," she murmured.

Her equilibrium returned however, as she spun about, taking in the situation. The inn was decently sized, taking up one entire side of a slanted, cobblestoned square near the walled border of the city. It appeared to lie along a major route, judging by the traffic bustling by. The foot traffic was brisk too. People passing stared at their arrival, a few smiled and nodded. Callie took it all in and leaned over to Tru. "I think we can make this work."

He tucked her arm into his as the double doors opened. Smiling widely, an older man bustled out to greet them. "Madame! Monsieur! You are come! Welcome to your new home!"

Tru let her go and clasped the man's hand, smiling and nodding as if greeting an old friend. "Gaubert, you old dog. A bit late, eh? But we are here at last and after all of your reports, we are eager to see what you have done with the place."

"What haven't I done? That would be easier to tell!" The grizzled old Frenchman cast her a comic grimace. "Scrubbed, polished and hammered until my fingers bled! But all is in readiness for you. You may take your first customer now, should you wish it."

Tru laughed. "Let's see the place first, shall we?"

Gaubert directed Edgar around to the stables and assured him there would be a boy to help him unload. Then he bowed low in front of Callie and offered her an arm. "If I might, Madame?"

She smiled. "As gallant as ever, Gaubert." She laid her hand on his. "Please, lead on."

She exhaled on a long, low breath as he led her into the entry hall. It was small, but paneled in rich carved wood, with a high desk to the left and an open doorway leading into the taproom on the right.

Two women stood at anxious attention and both bobbed nervous curtsies as she entered.

"This is Marie," Gaubert waved toward the sturdy,

middle-aged woman. "She worked here a bit, for the previous owners."

"I filled in, Madame, when the place grew busy. But I learned enough to know how things go on."

"That will be helpful," Callie said candidly. "I'm sure I'll have questions for you." She gave her a polite nod and then turned to the other waiting servant—a young girl, likely no older than thirteen. "Hello," she offered. "I am Madame Chaput."

"This is Victoire. She's the scullery," Gaubert said a bit roughly.

The girl kept her eyes down as she bobbed again, clutching her cap.

"What a lovely name." Callie eyed the girl closely. "Have you worked in a kitchen before, Victoire?"

Mute, she nodded vigorously.

"How nice. And have you learned to cook any dishes?"

"No, *Madame*." It was barely a whisper.

"Would you like to?" Callie asked.

Her head rose, her eyes huge as she nodded.

"Good. We shall be spending a great deal of time together and I shall need an assistant."

"Yes, *Madame*."

Callie's gaze was drawn away as Tru moved into the taproom. The chairs were drawn up onto the tables, and she could see that it was a good-sized room, with a hearth and a lovely, battered bar.

Gaubert nodded dismissal to the servants and led Callie in after him.

Tru's hand ran along the bar's edge. The false scar looked raw and realistic in the dim light. "I know you've been acting as tapster, Gaubert, but I'll have to take over from you. I've important papers that need to go back to the family straight away."

Callie caught the old man's grudging look of approval. "Aye, of course. I'll head out first thing in the morning."

"Would you like to see the upstairs rooms, Madame?" Marie still hovered in the doorway. "I'd be happy to show you."

"We'll both go along." Tru left the bar and came over to claim Callie from Gaubert. Her heart tripped, then raced into a gallop as he pulled her close and draped an arm across her shoulders. "Chloe and I are very excited to start this new business and this new phase of our lives. We'll greet it together."

They all trooped up the stairs together in the end, and Callie made all the appropriate noises and comments as they toured the guest rooms, galleries and even the servants' rooms at the top of the house.

Yet Tru remained the real center of her focus. He'd dropped very naturally into his role as Monsieur Chaput, innkeeper. And he'd picked up Edgar and his animals. She strongly suspected there was a story there—and that Edgar had been more in need of their aid than he might understand. And Tru had given it as easily as Hestia had ever taken in an abandoned, abused or starving woman.

She didn't know why she was surprised. Here it was, another instance proving that he was not the selfish lordling she'd supposed him to be. Disturbing—how time kept proving them both to be so different than she'd thought. He was more observant and caring than she'd ever credited and she was—

In a world of trouble.

He'd taken her hand as they'd come downstairs to explore the private parlors—small, but well appointed, she noted. But Tru paused as Marie opened the door to another set of rooms at the back of the main floor. Callie was pressed close to his side as he stopped on the threshold to examine the features of the apartment.

"This is our best room—saved for the wealthier guests due to its size and the attached sitting room." Marie crossed and opened a door on the far side. "There's a smaller room adjoined to the bedroom—not much bigger than the size of a bed itself, but it works well for an accompanying servant to sleep in."

Tru's gaze searched out her own. He tugged her inside and to the doorway Marie held open. A large bed took up a great deal of room beyond. The east wall held the door to the servant's sleeping quarters. Letting her go, Tru went to throw open the window sash. Soft sunlight came in the southern facing window, and past that Callie could see the kitchen garden. Further beyond stood a brick wall that must surely be part of the stable block.

Tru spun about. He rested on the windowsill a moment, then strode to her and lifted both of her hands. "No," he said. "I think that the Madame and I will claim these rooms."

Their gazes met. She refused to let hers waver, yet her head had grown suddenly busy, imagining the two of them here, alone and intimate—and not. Images flooded in, Tru in shirtsleeves, shaving. Tru watching her as she huddled in the bed, sheets to her chin. Tru indulging in a hot bath, chest bare and head thrown back against the tub . . .

"But, sir," Marie gaped at them. "As I showed you, the master's rooms are at the top of the stairs, just off the first landing. The wealthier clientele will expect—"

He cut her off with a shrug. "Should we manage to attract some wealthier clientele, I am sure we can arrange something suitable upstairs. But my wife spends long hours in the kitchens. She needs a place to get away from the hustle and bustle, a quiet spot to relax." Letting go of Callie's hands, he crossed behind her, pulled her up against him and nuzzled her hair as they faced the rooms together.

"These should do nicely."

He was after the extra bedroom. She understood and applauded his motives. But a part of her could not help but react to the casual touching, the consideration. More dangerous than even her vivid imaginings, it touched her, tempted her, set off a dangerous yearning that it would be more than part of their charade.

He released her, stepping back and taking a hold of her shoulders. She had to fight to keep from backing into his embrace once more. Oh, but this mission was going to be more difficult than she'd expected—and in entirely different ways.

Careful. Not pushing him away was one thing. She couldn't hold him in contempt any longer or even at a distance, yet she was going to have to be so careful. Not to give these sudden yearnings away. Not to *blossom* into one of those women who threw everything away to chase this glorious heat and flow of passion in their blood.

She summoned a smile, forced herself to step away from the comforting weight of his hands on her, and walked a slow circuit of the room. "Thank you, my dear. You are generous and I think we'll be happy indeed here." She turned her smile on Marie. "Thank you for the tour, but you have saved the best for last, have you not?" She rubbed her hands together. "Please, lead on. I am longing to see the kitchens."

Chapter Nine

*When I could finally get out of bed on my own, I
wrote to my family, asking for permission to come home.
I told them everything, left nothing out, detailed every
abuse I'd suffered at the hands of Lord M---*

*--from the Journal of the infamous Miss Hestia
Wright*

Tru set two pints of ale down with a flourish.
Channeling the restlessness that surged in his veins, he used
it to summon up a good-natured smile. "Drink up,
gentlemen! The rain has not let up, and now the fog and
the damp grow thicker. Dinner is nearly ready and my wife
has crafted a meal guaranteed to warm the fires of your
heart."

"Damned if I don't think your wife could hold off
the North Wind itself, Chaput." Penrith toasted him with
the new pint. "And all with just the sweat of her brow and
the fruits of her ovens."

Rackham tossed down the book he'd been poring
over. "What does she have for us tonight?"

"Oh, a rare treat. A baked seafood pie with a white
sauce and a tender, flaky crust. Braised sweetmeats and a
handsome brûlée to finish." Tru swept up their empty
tankards, making sure to flash the scar on his hand.
"Would you like me to set up the nearest table or would
you care to dine here by the fire?"

"Let's have the table." Penrith shivered. "Though I
vow I'll be right back after to soak up the heat before I
head out. You'd scarce know it was July with that chill
wind off the sea."

"Very good." Tru nodded and moved off a short
way. He'd held his doubts about Stoneacre's plans, but he
had to give the man credit—they were working a treat so
far. The pair of young traitors had drifted in the first

evening, complaining bitterly of the poor fare at their absent host's table. They'd taken ready comfort in the taproom's free-flowing ale, and even more in the large platter of freshly made *galettes* that was all Callie had been able to pull together so quickly.

They'd raved about the savory pancakes and since then, they'd been back regularly and at all hours and she'd made it a point to send them out a basket of warm, crusty rolls or sweet biscuits when they arrived before dinner.

"You're a damned lucky bloke, Chaput, even if you are a bit of a grinning fool." Rackham, who'd spoken in English, watched him closely.

"Eh?" Tru looked up from smoothing out a cloth over the selected table. He and Callie had both taken care to speak only French since their arrival and they'd invented a Breton aunt to explain her knowledge of the local language and customs.

"Nothing, Chaput," Penrith assured him in French. "Rackham only says that you are a fortunate man."

"Ah," Tru nodded. "Well I know it." He aimed a big, deliberate smile at Rackham. "It's a wise man who knows his blessings." He let the grin fade. "And one wiser still, who will fight to protect them."

Rackham rolled his eyes. If he meant to test Tru, he'd been apparently satisfied. He picked up his book, but with a sigh, tossed it down again. "God's truth, you are the lucky one, Penrith."

The blighter spoke English again, and Tru let his attention visibly wander. He carried on with the setting of the table, careful to betray no interest.

"We're in the same coil, Rackham. No difference," Penrith sighed.

"I beg to differ, but there's a damned big difference! Yours is horse mad and a bruising rider. Easy enough. Why does mine have to be enamored of the Romantics?" Rackham threw back his head and pinched the bridge of his nose.

"What? You think I have it easy? I've memorized racing bloodlines back to the Byerly Turk!"

"Yes, but that's not *poetry!*" Rackham's lip curled in disgust. "I have to learn reams of the stuff—and all to heart. You could actually put your work to good use later, at the track or when you set up your stables. At what other point in my life am I going to need to be able to discuss the Lake Poets?"

Penrith snorted. "Well, yours is likely to be pretty, at least. I live in dread that mine will be horse-faced as well as horse-mad."

"At least you'll be able to turn off the lights, should it prove true. Am I to be expected to spout Goethe and Wordsworth every time I wish to bed my German princess?" He waved a hand at his companion. "Laugh if you must, but that's if I even manage to win her. Marstoke doubts whether my family's money will make up for my lack of a title. He says I must work all the harder. Do you know," he leaned in, "he wishes me to write an epic poem about a *river siren*? And be ready to spout it at a moment's notice?"

But Penrith's expression had grown serious. "It's little enough to ask. He rescued your hide when your family's money fell short once again, did he not? After the aid he's rendered us in the past, we've neither of us room to complain." He lowered his tone. "Not to mention that doing as he asks will see both our futures set higher than we've right to expect."

"I know you're right. But I'd rather be off traveling with him now than sitting around here, rhyming *breeze* and *leaves* and *please*." He sighed. "What do you suppose he's doing out there in the countryside, in any case?"

"Anselm hinted that he's looking for something. Or someone."

"And that's another thing—why does he take that

slimy weasel and leave us here? I've a mind to—"

Tru couldn't stretch out the setting of the table any longer. Reluctantly he moved off toward the kitchens, his mind awhirl. A pair of German princesses? And these two young pups groomed specifically to their taste. His fist clenched. He'd been of the mind that Stoneacre and the rest of them were overly fearful of what Marstoke could accomplish with Letty Robbins, but hearing these two set him to rethinking. It sounded as if the man was lining up future European allies. For himself? Or for a puppet of an English monarch?

He pushed through the green baize door to the kitchens—and paused on the threshold as Callie looked up, mid-stir.

He swallowed. It had been easy enough, these last days, to carry on with his original plan of avoiding her. He'd had plenty of work to do, preparing the inn, hiring job horses and an extra servant or two, and making contacts with vintners, vendors and prospective customers.

Callie, too, had been busy. That first day she'd stepped in the main kitchen, looked up to see cobwebs in the corners—and rolled up her sleeves. Gaubert, Marie and Victoire spent their first day in their employment scrubbing all the kitchens with boiling water, top to bottom. Callie had scarcely stopped cooking since. She'd also forged relationships in the markets and put homey touches throughout the inn using bits of local lace and hand painted pottery.

Tru had been careful. He kept busy working about the stables and the areas of the inn where she was not. He filled his days with business and his thoughts with plans for Marstoke. He stayed away from their private rooms until she was in bed and asleep. He'd refused to indulge in more than a glimpse of her there, soft and vulnerable, with all that mahogany hair in a loose braid.

But then there were moments like this. Moments of unexpected confrontation when he was caught unawares and struck hard by the sheer, unavoidable appeal of her.

It made not a lick of sense. She was shrouded in a voluminous apron, with a bowl propped on one hip and a smear of flour across her chin—and he was beset with conflicting desires.

He wanted to go to her, to toss the bowl aside and kiss her senseless, push her against the table and lick that flour off of her porcelain skin, then send his lips and tongue foraging south, exploring all of her hills and valleys.

But he would not. His respect and admiration for her had continued to grow—but so had his determination to resist her many temptations. He was staying focused and here was his reward—the game was truly beginning.

"Do they stay for dinner?" She waited, bright-eyed with interest.

"After I told them of your menu? Of course." He stepped all the way in. "I think it's time we introduced you."

He felt strangely resistant to the idea, although that was just foolishness. It was time to get this plot moving. The quicker they got Letty Robbins in tow, the quicker he could join Stoneacre in the hunt for Marstoke, and the quicker he'd be able to hold his head up in England again.

"I'm ready."

She was already unwrapping herself from the depths of the oversized apron. She smoothed a lace trimmed replacement on in its stead and Tru tried not to stare at that tempting expanse of bosom, contrasted so nicely with her nipped in waist and softly flaring hips. "No cook I know of ever looked like that," he murmured.

"What's that?" Callie was supervising as Victoire dished out dinner plates and placed them on a large tray. Looking it over, she gave a tweak here and there, placed a small vase with a single, long poppy stem on one side and gave him a nod.

"Nothing. Let me take that." He led the way out. "And if they speak English amongst themselves, just look polite and puzzled."

He used his larger frame and the tray to block her from view at first, but she moved from behind him as they grew closer to the fire. True clenched his teeth as the men, catching sight of her, stood.

Penrith recovered first, closing his mouth and summoning a smile. "Chaput, is this your wife?"

Tru made the introductions and began to transfer plates to the table.

Penrith gave Callie a nod. "Madame, how happy I am to meet you at last and thank you for all the delicious meals you've provided us."

Callie lowered her gaze and dipped a curtsy.

Rackham let his gaze travel the length of her. "A pleasure, Madame." He raised a brow at Tru. "No wonder you hide her away in the kitchens." He gave Callie an oily smile. "You must not allow it, Ma'am, but come and visit us in the taproom."

Callie gave him a bob. "You are very kind, sir, but my duties in the kitchens and with the rest of the house keep me busy."

"To great advantage," Penrith replied. "The place is much improved by those feminine touches that must surely have come by your hand."

Rackham said something under his breath and in English. Something about touches and hands.

Penrith ignored him. "We spoke truer than we knew when we called you a lucky man, Chaput."

"But not truer than I knew, sir." He struggled to keep the anger from his tone. "It is an honor to provide for and protect a woman like my Chloe."

"Indeed." Penrith stepped back. "We will not keep you from your duties, and I confess I'm anxious to sit down at your table again."

Tru pulled her away. He handed her the empty tray and began to gather up empty tankards.

"Food be damned," Rackham grumbled as his friend urged him to sit. He was still watching Callie. "It's the forbidden fruit in this country that is getting to me."

"Don't be an arse," Penrith scolded. He'd already seated himself, but he stopped with a forkful of pie halfway to his mouth. "I hope you aren't also referencing that pretty girl Marstoke has tucked away back at the manor."

"Who else? Her and now this voluptuous vixen of an innkeeper's wife." He shot Tru a look of disgust. "I suppose I've been warned off both of them." He sighed. "What do you think Marstoke means to do with that chit he's housing?"

"I'm not fool enough to ask."

"Well, neither am I, but it doesn't keep me from wondering. Maybe he's training her up to be his wife? After all, the last one ran out on him."

"You are a fool indeed, if you think to mention that within a hundred miles of the man."

Tru caught sight of Callie's face as she swept a table with a towel as she walked by. She'd lit up with interest and suppressed excitement. Regretfully, he tugged her away. Her lips pressed thin, but she went willingly enough back to the kitchens.

"They spoke of Letty!" she hissed as they entered. "She's there. At least we know she's still there."

He nodded significantly toward the little servant girl. "We'll talk of it later."

Stalking across to the scullery, he dumped his armful of tankards. He was fuming. His father, a wise and gentle man, had always said a man's character could be read by how he treated those supposed to be beneath him. Such a measure left Rackham lacking. Tru wanted to pound that smug look from his face. But a tradesman couldn't readily respond to such—and he had to play his role.

"Stay in the kitchens until they are gone," he told Callie curtly. "And if you must step out, take Marie or Edgar with you." He slapped on the slouched hat that Gaubert had given him.

She nodded. Bless her, of all women, she knew well enough what a snake like Rackham could get up to. "Where are you going?" she asked.

"To the stables. The frustration of it all is eating into my gut. I mean to take a pitchfork to that newly delivered pile of hay—as a means of keeping me from taking it to Rackham."

He thought she might scold, but instead she picked up a meat cleaver and waved toward a stretched out side of pork. "I'll be doing the same."

Chapter Ten

While I waited for a reply, I did my best to pay
Pearl back for her generosity. I moved slowly, but I
worked hard. I must have taken a bucket and scrub
brush to every inch of that lovely old place before I was
done.

--from the Journal of the infamous Miss Hestia
Wright

"Do you think the master is happy, married to the mistress?"

Victoire spoke low, but loud enough for the worry in her tone—and the subject matter—to capture Callie's attention.

"Why should you think to ask such a thing? Have ye gone sweet on him, girl?" Marie teased.

Callie froze where she was, crouched behind the door in the long pantry that ran like a passage between the kitchen and the back entry hall. She stopped loading parsnips into her apron and listened.

"No!" the young girl exclaimed. "But he doesn't act like he's married to her. Papa is always stealing a kiss or sneaking up to Mama for a squeeze. Even my old master liked to kiss his lady's hand in public but press up behind her when he thought no one could see."

"Well, all marriages are different, my girl. Maybe the mistress don't like such things."

"But she ain't cold-hearted or high-browed. And Master Chaput does *not* like it when those other men look her over. Why doesn't he—"

"Just you never mind, young one. Maybe they like to keep such things private. Don't matter in any case. We got a good situation here and you don't want to go stirring anything up."

Callie stood up carefully and slowly, her mind awhirl. Moving as silently as she could, she exited out the other door. In the back hall she grabbed a basket, dumped her parsnips inside and slipped out the door.

Half an hour later she was back, the parsnips buried under several pints of summer berries. She bustled into the kitchen and handed them over to Victoire. "Wash and dry these well, will you, my dear?"

The girl's face lit up. "Oh, lovely. What will you make with them, Madame?"

"Tarts. They are a particular favorite of my husband's. We've been so busy with the setting up and ordering of everything, I feel as if we haven't exchanged a word that was not about horse feed or cleaning schedules." She laid the parsnips out on the chopping board. "I've a mind to fix him something special so we can celebrate how smoothly it has all come together."

She pretended not to see the significant look that Marie shot the younger girl. "Speaking of cleaning schedules . . . Marie, is the Crescent Room all scrubbed and ready for linens?"

The day passed, but Callie's thoughts were not fixed on braised root vegetables or pastry crust. Their plans were moving forward now. Yesterday a messenger from Stoneacre had arrived with word that the earl had found something of Marstoke. The marquess had taken rooms at an inn and was traveling about nearby smaller towns. Almost as if he were looking for something, she thought privately. Or someone. Stoneacre was going to investigate further, and the messenger, Nardes, was to stay in St. Malo and continue the process of clearing out everyone out of Marstoke's villa.

And if they'd done their job well, it wouldn't be difficult to convince Penrith and Rackham to come straight here, with Letty in tow.

"Have you got a place for me to store this for the night?" the man had asked, indicating a medium sized wooden box. "A room in the stables or a storage shed preferably."

"What's in it?" Tru had asked.

"Take a look," he'd invited.

Tru had opened the lid cautiously, then clapped it back closed. "Bugs. Big ones," he'd told her. "And a lot of them."

"They're to go into the butler's pantry and the dining room tomorrow," Nardes told them. "Our unhappy under-butler says the cook's watching the kitchens with an eagle eye now. The next day it's to be rats coming down from the attic."

"Rats?" Callie had shuddered. "Couldn't that be dangerous? What if they are diseased?"

"Nobody's died yet," Nardes answered with a shrug. "As long as the folks clear out quick, they'll be fine." He handed Tru an invoice with a rat catcher's stamp on it. "Your job will be to recommend me to the swells. Tell them I come reasonable. Once they're out of the house, I'll round the critters up again."

So things were moving quickly. Nardes was infecting Marstoke's house with insects today and Tru was searching out a good hiding spot, in case they needed one. Preferably one on the shoreline where they could meet a ship, if necessary. It all meant that Letty might be under her roof within a matter of days.

Her roof. Callie had been enjoying herself, playing this role, pretending to be something that she was not. She reminded herself now of the real reason she was here. For Tru it would always be Marstoke, but for her, it was Letty. Letty again. And Letty for the last time.

But even that was not what occupied her all day as she peeled and chopped and rolled out dough. No, what circled in her mind endlessly were Hestia's words—about taking something for herself from this adventure.

She was running out of time, if she meant to follow that advice.

"The dining room is filling up, ma'am," Victoire came in, a little breathless.

"Good." Callie began to unwrap her oversized apron. "Perhaps our reputation has begun to spread, my dear." She grinned at the girl. "Now you start filling plates while I go take orders."

They had a busy evening. Penrith and Rackham did not arrive, a fact for which Callie was grateful, as Tru was still out as well. She and the servants did well enough on their own, though, and as the hour grew late, Callie fixed a plate and set it to warm—and sent everyone else off to bed.

"You worked hard today," she told Victoire. "I'll finish the last of the pans. You go on up and get some rest."

"Thank you, *Madame*." The girl bobbed a curtsy, and gave her a shy smile before running up the servant's stairs.

When the kitchen was pristine again, Callie sat and wrote to Hestia. That bit about Marstoke was worrying, especially after Nardes mentioned that the marquess had made Rennes the base for his searching. She readied the note for the post, then took a bit of mending with her and sat before the fire.

She was tired as well, and dozed a bit in her chair. The soft creak of the stair woke her when Victoire came back for a snack. She fed the girl some bread and cheese and a tart before sending her back upstairs.

The hour grew late. It must have been midnight when she awoke with a start to find Tru staring down at her, his smile warm, but his gaze hotter by a measurable amount.

That grin struck her, forced her to remain in the chair when she wished to leap to her feet. Why hadn't she known that a single dimple could become such a great weakness? That the crease of tiny wrinkles at the corners of his eyes could steal her breath away?

"There you are," she said, yawning, to hide how the shock of it had scrambled her reactions. The old excitement hit her, setting her pulse to racing and her nerves to jumping. But the old irritation he'd used to dredge up was long gone. There was a grudging respect there now, still a bit of impatience, and a great, burning curiosity that whispered to her with Hestia's voice. "Take off that disreputable hat and I'll get your dinner."

"You shouldn't have waited up," he chided. "You rise so early."

"Victoire is worried that we are not properly married," she said with a shrug. "I thought to reassure her by waiting up for you with your favorite dish."

"Why should the girl think we aren't properly married?" he demanded.

"Because we don't sneak caresses in the corners, I gather," she said wryly, standing at last.

"Well. If that is what it takes," Tru said with a laugh.

"Come and sit at the table. I saved your dinner." She paused. "Unless you ate elsewhere?"

"When I could come home to your cuisine?" he scoffed. "Not a chance."

She flushed a little. It was ridiculous how much that pleased her. She puttered about, fetching food and utensils. She poured him ale and took his hat to hang it on a hook by the door. "Why do you wear this thing, anyway?" It was broad brimmed and unkempt looking.

"Gaubert gave it to me. Beyond hiding my features a bit, he said a hat like that becomes a part of you. When people see it again and again, they cease to look past it." He shrugged. "I figured it was worth a try."

She sat across from him as he ate. "I fear we'll

have to try harder for Victoire's sake. The poor dear. She lost her last position when the owner's wife ran off with a traveling book salesman. He sold out and the new buyer divided the inn into offices. I think she fears losing another if we are not getting along and decide that working to get this place up and running is too much trouble."

Tru made a face. "I'll follow your lead on this one. The workings of a young girl's mind are beyond me." He sighed over a bit of roasted beef. "I don't see how she could doubt you, in any case." He raised his fork in salute. "You slid so seamlessly into this role, I'd think you were born to it, did I not know better."

Callie colored. He didn't know how close to the truth he'd hit. She paused. Perhaps it would not be so bad if he did know. He already knew the worst, after all. What harm could come from the rest?

"Not born," she corrected. "But definitely raised to it."

"How is that? I thought—"

"Yes, yes. Prince Ernest. All true," she interrupted. "But my mother acted as housekeeper and cook in one of his residences."

His face tightening, Tru set down his fork. "Do you mean to say that he abused a woman in his service?"

"No! Not at all. I'm sure the old devil has a multitude of sins laid at his door, but that isn't one of them, that I'm aware of." She grinned. "It's almost the opposite, in fact."

He started eating again. "Now this is a story I want to hear."

She laughed. "My mother was born in this part of the world. I don't know much about her early life. I wouldn't be surprised if she grew up in a situation similar to this, though." She looked around. "She traveled to Flanders, though, as a young woman. All the excitement was there, she said once. She met my father when he was stationed there with the Hussars. She became his mistress. Willingly, she always told me."

"An odd conversation to have with one's daughter, to be sure."

"It was an odd life. Apparently, Ernest was injured and recalled home, and thought nothing more of her. He bid her farewell and left. But Mother had discovered she was with child and would have none of his casual goodbyes. She insisted on coming with him, and when he refused to bring her along, she packed her things and followed him to England."

Tru stared. "She just showed up at his door?"

Callie nodded. "He tried to turn her away, but she would not back down. Eventually he deposited her in one of his residences and left."

"What did she do?" Tru looked fascinated.

"She rolled up her sleeves and took over the running of the place."

His jaw dropped. "He allowed it?"

"I don't think she gave him a choice. She wasn't having her baby in the streets and that was that."

"I'm suddenly even more frightened of your stubborn streak."

She laughed. "As well you should be. Although I don't hold a candle to her, in that department. She had a will of iron."

"And so you learned to run a household at her knee."

Her head tilted. "That sums it up."

"No wonder you seem a natural fit here."

She stood, took his empty plate and slid a tart in front of him. "These are your undying favorites, by the way, in case Victoire asks."

She bit back a grin as he took a bite and rolled his eyes in appreciation. They did say that a way to a man's heart was through his stomach. She was beginning to suspect that the way to hers might be through appreciating her efforts in the kitchen. Certainly she enjoyed watching him relish her food. He threw himself into it, as he did with most things. And watching him taste and savor with closed eyes and a tilted head sent tight little tremors off in her lower abdomen. She felt his soft moan vibrate in the hollows behind her ears.

"I hope you don't mind my saying it," she began carefully, "but you've adapted to this role far more easily and thoroughly than I expected you might."

He lifted a shoulder. "The impatience is still there, but I'm burying it under the work. If I'm only to have a minor role, at least I'll play it well. And it does feel good to be doing something. I'm finding, too, that I rather enjoy the organizational aspects of the thing. I find myself thinking too, of the improvements I'd make around here, were this place really mine."

"If only the Prince Regent could see you now," she joked.

He stiffened.

"Oh, I'm sorry," she rushed to say. "I only meant it as a joke. I'd understood that you are one of his highness's cronies."

"I was, once." There it was again, the rush of urgency to be done with this thing. To strike back at Marstoke, keep him from doing any further harm, and ease his own doubts in the process. To have the protection of his facade firmly back between him and the world.

He pushed it all away. He was having a good meal with a lovely girl. This was not the time to indulge his impatience or worry about his flaws. He searched instead for a way to distract her from such a line of thinking, as well.

"You know, I like making connections as well. Finding the best vintner, the most reputable coal dealer, striking a bargain that benefits all." He shrugged. "Perhaps I can find a way to use those skills when we go back."

"If you enjoy it, you most definitely should. Your brother has any number of estates, I'd wager. You should talk him into turning the running of one over to you. You'd do a bang-up job."

"Would I?" He weighed the idea in his mind. "How do you know?"

"Because I've seen what you've done here in the last few days. I daresay you look as much at ease here as I do."

"Well, I thought we were doing well, but if we haven't convinced the scullery . . ." He fell silent for a moment. "And actually, I'm feeling a bit guilty. As much as I'm enjoying the feeling of being needed, this is all still pretend for me. But it's not for these people."

"Yes, I know what you mean." He heard the sound of relief in her tone. "We need to make sure they will all be taken care of when this is over."

"Precisely." He eyed her with approval. "I'm glad you share my concerns."

Callie was still turning over what he'd just said. "You enjoy being needed? Is that why you rescued that Russian girl from Marstoke's bullies that night, and got yourself embroiled in all of this at the start?"

He straightened in his chair, his gaze narrowed at her. She didn't think he was going to answer at all for a moment, the way he glared. But he relented after a moment, pushing his empty plate away and leaning an elbow on the table. "I suppose so," he said gruffly. The distance in his eyes convinced her he was seeing something far removed from her cozy kitchen.

"You know," he said eventually. "I do have a

spot—just a spot, mind you—of empathy for Penrith and Rackham."

The shock must have shown on her face—and look more like the disapproval he was likely used to from her.

"Not that I excuse their poor judgment or condone their actions, but I've been in their shoes," he explained. "Sometimes it truly isn't easy to be the second son, or the fourth, or the low-hanging fruit on the extra branches of the family tree." He shook his head. "I never gave it a thought when my parents were alive, but after they were gone, my brother's trustees and guardians practically ripped him away. They were so concerned with turning him into the perfect duke—and they never gave a thought or a word to me. I felt extraneous, unimportant. And then I was shipped off to school and out of the way."

The thought of him as a lonely boy set off a twang in her chest. "But your brother cares for you. I've seen it."

"He does. But he was young, too. There was only so much he could do." He sighed and propped his chin on his hand. "I followed my peers into the usual 'young buck about Town' mischief for a while, but no one ever tells you that the drinking, gaming and wenching only fill the emptiness temporarily." His shoulder lifted. "I tried other ways to fill my days. I had quite a cricket obsession at one point. But it was never enough."

"And then you heard a girl in a garden call for help." She of all people understood the temptation to respond.

"And like a fool, I rushed in," he said bitterly.

"Not foolish, but brave and good-hearted," she conceded. "And by all accounts, you acquitted yourself well that night. The rumors all had you mightily outnumbered."

"Yes, I reveled in the attention and praise. I was quite proud of myself, until Marstoke came to call. I'd made a colossal mistake, he told me. He never quite used the word 'spy' but he made me understand that the girl was under suspicion and that I had ruined a long, expensive scheme to catch her at her mischief." He shook his head. "Sometimes I still can't believe how stupid I was. Why didn't I see through him?"

"You don't have to tell me how convincing the man is. He has the tongue of a serpent and a sharp, quick, clever mind. I've met girls he's deceived. My best friend was once engaged to him. No one at Half Moon House would ever blame you for mistaking his lies for truth."

"He's damned clever," Tru agreed. "He baits his lies with enough truth to make them utterly convincing. When he set me to rewriting the old Love List, I really did believe the money it earned would help offset the losses I'd caused with my interference. And when he said I was charged with keeping watch for subversive influences, for men and women who meant to work to undermine the government and the crown, I believed that too. I didn't realize that *he* was the villain, until it was almost too late."

"You did realize it, though. Your actions kept him from creating the international scandal he'd planned for, in the end."

He heaved a sigh and eyed her carefully. "I know you and Hestia despised me for it—and I was initially disgusted when I was first told how I would have to make amends—but actually, after I'd been at it a while, I was glad the task of rewriting the List had been handed to me."

"I remember how the girls vied for your attention, trying to secure a place on the List." Callie fought off an entirely inappropriate surge of jealousy.

"I was shocked to find how many girls *wished* to be included."

"Everyone has heard tales of the old List, and how it increased the custom for those who were featured."

"Yes, but the older versions could be biting, and more than a little demeaning. After I had spent some time in that world and got to know so many of the women, I wished to do better for them. I was glad of the chance to treat them more gently."

There it was again. The soft melting of her insides. The more she saw past his brittle shell of relentless determination, the more she actually liked him—and the more she wished to see. "I saw a copy of your manuscript. You did do a kind job of it, even if it never made it to print. And you refused to write those horrible lies about Hestia and the rest of us at Half Moon House. Not one of us will ever forget that."

He started to speak, but she cut him off. "Please. This isn't easy for me, but I'm trying to find the courage to say something to you. I know that all you want to do is to go back—back to your life the way it was before any of this happened. I know, also, that I gave you a lot of trouble right after Marstoke fled, but I want to say that, even though I'm sorry it's been difficult for you, I'm glad it was you."

He made a sound of protest, but she hurried on. "I am. I'm glad for that Russian girl. Glad for the girls in Covent Garden you befriended, for Stoneacre and the Prince Regent and the whole country—everyone you helped when you helped to foil Marstoke's plans." She sucked in a breath. "But I'm glad for me, too."

Good heavens, but this was hard. She'd spent a lifetime learning to protect herself, developing her defensive instincts. Battling them now was far more difficult than facing down a pair of thugs in an alley. She glanced away. It was easier if she didn't have to see the conflicting emotions crossing the chiseled fields of his face. "This trip, these last few days, they've been good for me. I've settled some things in my mind. Hestia is right. I do have to begin to trust someone sometime. I have to stop closing myself off. I need to learn how to share pieces of myself—and I've begun. With you."

She heard him shift back away from the table, but she refused to look at him, afraid she would see rejection or worse—pity—in his eyes. "You've been up close and immersed in the world I live in. You've seen the contrast of the horror and beauty that live there." Her shoulders hunched a little. "You understand. It's a small thing. Yet, it's vast, too. You've been kind with me when I perhaps didn't deserve it." She swallowed, then forced herself to forge on. "I don't think I could have shared my history with anyone else."

She pressed her lips into a grim smile and turned at last to look at him. "For all of that, I thank you."

He stared at her with an entirely new expression on his face. She couldn't quite decipher it. Before she had more than a moment to try—she froze.

There it was once more. The quiet creak of a footstep on the stairs. Victoire again? Or Marie? It didn't really matter. Thinking quickly, she stood and slid the small plate away from Tru. "Now that you've eaten," she purred. "Why don't you finish with something sweet?"

He gaped at her, but she did not hesitate. Moving sinuously, she slid into his lap.

He sat frozen, blinking up at her. She touched the spot where his fake sideburns hid his scar and inclined her head toward the passageway. "On the stairs," she whispered.

Comprehension dawned. The rigid swell of his chest relaxed beneath her hands. Fighting back a grin, he settled his hands around her waist. "That tart was enough to satisfy any man's sweet cravings."

She rolled her eyes but kept her tone light and breathless. "Then let me tempt you with something with a bit more spice."

There was not a sound from the stairs. They were surrounded by shadows and silence. The dying fire sparked quick highlights in his hair and along the curve of his cheek. It illuminated the shift in his expression.

They were moving fast, thanks to their unseen

visitor, but it was still right where she wished to go. Heat washed over her, but didn't come from the fire. It surged to life inside of her, hovered on her skin and at her fingertips, and tingled at the tips of her breasts. Leaning in she latched her fingers behind his neck. With her heart thumping, she ducked down and kissed him.

Yes. There it was again. Sweet warmth. Firm demand—and yet he gave too—gave her passion and strength and a blunt approval that pricked all along her limbs and set up an ache in her chest.

He deepened the kiss. She parted her lips and he swept in, hot and slick. His hands moved from her waist and began to slide up her spine.

She was in his lap, looming over him, and yet she felt surrounded, protected by dense muscle and tender care. Need rose inside her. She made a sound she didn't recognize and tightened her grip.

Abruptly he stilled. His mouth pulled away.

"What is it?" She had to strain not to pull him back. "Is Victoire still on the stair?" she whispered.

"She left ages ago." He shook his head. His hands slid away and that small retreat felt like a great chasm. Running a finger along her cheek, he held her jaw and looked into her eyes. "What are we doing here, Callie?"

Chapter Eleven

I asked why the inn, so far from any shore, had been named The Oyster? She laughed and said the locals jokingly called it that because it contained a Pearl. I knew how right they were.

--from the Journal of the infamous Miss Hestia Wright

Tru watched the color bloom at Callie's neckline and creep up to her face—the exact opposite trail that his hands longed to take.

Calling an erotic encounter to a screeching halt—this was not how he would usually handle the pretty girl sitting in his lap. But Callie Grant was so much more—more complicated, more interesting, more dangerous—than a mere pretty girl. And Stoneacre's words hung in the back of his mind. *You'll be responsible for maintaining your disguises and new identities.*

He was glad enough to put his mouth and hands on her infinitely tempting body, all in the name of their mission. But there was more than that going on here.

She kept her hands locked around his neck. "I thought we might be . . . having fun." Her fingers began to play with the ends of his hair.

He stiffened in his seat. She had to feel the hard press of his cock against her. "Fun?" The word emerged on a croak. Her incredible bosom hovered right before his eyes. He could think of nothing he'd like better than to bury his face in her lushness. But, fun? Entirely too tame a word for the situation.

"You've made it clear that I've been lacking fun in my life, and Hestia has urged me to seize something for myself on this adventure. I thought that . . . this might serve both purposes."

He yanked his brain past the images she called forth

and tried hard to concentrate on what she was really saying.

"I'm taking the good advice I've been offered. No matter what happens with Letty, I'm taking this chance to set her—and myself—free." She pressed her lips together and wiggled just a little. "I'd rather like to do the selfish and impractical thing and take you, too."

His cock surged higher and shifted with her, eager to agree. But Tru hesitated. "Take me?"

She laughed. "Is that what worries you? Are you afraid I'm setting a snare for you?"

"It doesn't sound like you," he admitted.

"You may understand my world, but that doesn't mean you belong in it. No more than I belong in yours."

He couldn't stand for that. "Callie Grant, you are beautiful, intelligent and ferocious. You could make yourself at home in any world you choose."

"Careful, if you keep puffing me up, I might change my mind." Fondness transformed her face—and struck a blow through his chest. How long had it been since anyone looked at him with such an intimate mix of frank admiration and exasperation?

"I've no designs on you past tonight, Tru. I promise." She closed her eyes a moment and breathed deeply. Her caressing fingers fell still. When she opened again, she wore a naked vulnerability that he'd never seen in her.

"Just this once," she whispered. "I want something just for myself. As I told you, I'm tired of not knowing. Tired of not having something that is only mine." She shook her head slightly. "No one needs to know. This is private. Something to fill in the gaps of my knowledge. Something I can think about and look back at later. Something just for me."

He stared and she met his gaze steadily. Allowed him to look without deflection or resistance. He let the beauty of her strike him, sink into his skin, touch his heart. And he acknowledged her permission as the victory that it was.

He could not help but recall his brother's wedding, when they'd stood toe to toe, snarling at each other. They'd been adversaries then. And now they were . . . what? Co-conspirators. Friends, perhaps. But he knew that glimpse into the utter truth of her meant that he'd gained her trust—and that left him riding a rising surge of triumph.

Reaching up, he took her face in his hands, gently cradled her jaw. A single curl, auburn in the firelight, brushed his hand. "That's the thing, Callie. There's the two of us here. For this to be worth doing, we must share the experience. Completely engaged, the two of us together."

Was that fear that flashed behind her eyes? His respect for her flared as he watched her struggle, and then cast it away.

"It will always be here, afterwards," he warned, "hovering between us. Are you willing to put it there, knowing you'll always have to look past it?"

"For how long?" she asked simply. "If all goes according to plan, we've only days left here. You are going back. And I—I think I am going forward. We will not be seeing each other when this is done."

She was wrong. Their paths would cross again. His brother was married to his best friend. His burning desire to run his hands over her curves and breathe in the sweet, comforting smell of her, warred with that certainty.

He reined himself in, determined to curb his old impetuousness, to slow down and weigh his options.

He'd kept his focus so far and refused to let her beauty and his growing admiration distract him from the job at hand, and it had paid off. Their identities were—mostly—established, their plans were advancing. With

Edgar's help he had the perfect hiding spot in reserve.

And therein lay the rub. They had nothing to do now but wait. What was to stop them from enjoying each other? They both wanted it. He could spend the next hours . . . perhaps days . . . exploring every luscious inch of her, indulging his fantasies and savoring every taste.

If ever it was to happen, the time was now. In the future, when they saw each other at christenings or house parties—well, the future would take care of itself. In all likelihood he would be otherwise entangled, or she would be.

Or neither would be, and they might choose to enjoy each other again.

"Let me be clear in what I'm asking." She'd used the time to capture her thoughts as well, it seemed. "Just here. Just now. No consequences." Her color deepened. "I've heard the girls talk. There are ways . . ."

He took a deep breath. "Ways and ways." Want plucked at his nerves as if they were harp strings. His body tightened with need. "If we . . . proceed, we'll explore every one of them."

She arched her back the smallest bit. The movement opened her thighs a fraction, settled him more comfortably between them. He bit back a moan, but she cupped his face in her hands, as he'd done to her. "Then by all means, let's proceed."

It was as if her words tore a veneer of civilization and restraint from him. He surged to his feet, swinging her up into his arms. She was still making breathy sounds of surprise when he carried her through their bedroom door.

There it was, that damned big, mocking bed. The one he passed in the morning with his fists clenched and his gaze averted. The one that cradled her at night, where she lay looking soft and tousled and tempting. He saw it through a haze, he was so hot, so impatient.

Slow down.

He must. He'd given her her first kiss not long ago, for God's sake. She deserved tenderness and care. He set her down at the edge of the bed, let her slide down his inflamed body, then leaned down to kiss her again.

He did a thorough, leisurely job of it, coaxing her passion to rise again—and she responded with enthusiasm. Her eagerness fanned his higher yet. He shifted closer, captured her mouth. Something primitive prowled through him as he penetrated her with his swift, sweeping tongue and ground his hips against her.

He didn't let up. He teased and demanded until she made a sound in the back of her throat. At once, he pulled back, hoping like hell he hadn't frightened her. But her gaze was unfocused, her expression dazed and then impatient as she reached to pull him back.

Thank God. He was impatient, too—mad to see more of her at last. On fire to feel her skin next to his.

He did *not* start tearing at her clothes like a lunatic—a heroic effort for which he awarded himself a dozen accolades. Instead he placed a kiss upon her pert nose. And one on each cheek. And one for that stubborn chin. Soon he was raining small kisses over her face and along the sweet stretch of her neck. And all the while he poured sweetness over her as she poured ganache over a cream cake, he worked the high buttons at the back of her dress. He kissed and kissed her while he made his way to the end, then he stood back and tugged on both of her long, tight sleeves until they came off and her bodice sagged. Without hesitation he knelt to grasp the hem of her gown and lifted the dress over her head, letting it fall unheeded to the floor.

She stood, uncertain. But he suffered no such affliction. He was certainly on fire at the sight of her generous curves still layered with corset, shift, garters and stockings. Definitely suffering the whip hand of greed as he surveyed all of the parts left exposed.

Skin. Alabaster white and soft pink.

Touch her, his passion-fogged brain demanded.

He took a step back instead. *Tender*, he reminded himself. *No hurry. Let her catch up.*

"Will you take down your hair?" It came out on a rasp, his voice gone rough with need. "I want to see those curls against your skin."

Flushing a little, she raised her hands to remove pins. The position did interesting and gratifying things to her bosom behind the corset, things that made his fingers twitch.

Her hair came down and lay softly along her shoulders, gathering at the top of her corset, looking dramatic everywhere it contrasted against her skin.

She stood still a moment, her exhalations audible and just a bit shaky—and then she reached down and began untying the laces of her corset.

He jerked to awareness. "Front laces?" he asked. He must have been randy indeed to have missed that.

"No ladies maids at Half Moon House," she answered wryly.

He stepped forward to help, but didn't hurry. Steadily he pulled and slowly the corset loosened. Her scent wafted up and over him. Rosemary and beeswax and something uniquely sweet. The corset loosened enough to fall and suddenly she reached up to catch it, holding it against her.

See? His heart gave a thump. She was stubborn, capable and strong—and innocent.

He stepped forward, tight against her so that the press of his body held the corset in place. Let her keep her armor. He buried his face in her nape, followed the lovely curve of her neck to her jaw, then moved around to take her mouth again. Her hands came away, lifted to his shoulders. The corset stayed in place while he kissed her deep and slow.

Eventually he left her mouth and kissed his way to the sensitive spot behind her ear. She shivered and the corset slid down. She let it go. Even wriggled a little so that it fell completely away. Her hands moved lower to trace a tentative path over his hips and lower back.

Yes. There she was, catching up with him. Thank God, for he burned with need. He put his hands on her waist and slid them up at last—at last!—to cup that wondrous bosom.

Her breath hitched—and he felt entirely sympathetic. Her skin glowed warm right through the fine linen of her shift. Her breasts were a wonder—full and firm and tipped with tantalizing, tiny peaks. He pinched one between his fingers and she gasped.

Such a small sound, but more than enough to push him over the edge into a lust-filled frenzy. He yanked her shift down, pulled the straps out of the way, all the easier to get her bare. He let his eyes feast just a moment, then he knelt and closed his mouth over her.

Callie could not hold back her moan. Tru was pulling strongly at her nipple, flicking it with teeth and tongue. The other he rolled between finger and thumb. The sensations were acute and amazing, a mix of pleasure and pain that set off a throbbing need between her legs and created an elemental shift in her inner landscape.

It had always been about constraint with her. Inherited directly from her mother and reinforced by countless examples of women undone by the excesses of their passions.

Far better to pull back, rein all of that in, stay in control. Safer, too. Remain the calm one in a volatile situation and you were almost guaranteed the helm—and the ability to steer it in the direction you wished.

A fine philosophy. One that she'd held tight to with both hands. And why not? It had proven effective time and again—until now.

Now she found she wanted nothing to do with constraint. Her back was arched. Wordlessly she offered herself and demanded more—and Tru was obliging her. He bit down on a nipple and lightning bolts of pleasure shot through her.

"Yes," she hissed.

He stood then, and pulled her shift away. "I've never seen such skin," he whispered. "So smooth, it almost doesn't look real."

She flushed with pleasure at the compliment—but she was bare and he was still fully clothed.

Now that required action.

"Now you," she whispered. Her hands were already pulling at his neckcloth.

He unbuttoned his waistcoat and tore off his coat along with it. She ran her hands up under the soft linen of his shirt. Dear heaven, but he was beautiful. She lifted it off and stood a moment in admiration.

Her hands roamed over him. His skin blazed hot. His manhood bulged. Curiosity and a desire for balance between them nudged her. She reached out and touched it, covered him with one hand.

Tru's groan was low, deep and heartfelt. He thrust toward her and she felt a surge of power. Of need. Of fear.

She closed her eyes. This. She thought again of the gin soaked shells of women she'd seen in the streets. How easy it would be to come to need this. Not only the incredible feelings he raised in her, but the heady knowledge that she could do the same to him. The satisfaction of being in tandem with him, of being wild with need and a little out of her mind with desire—and knowing there was trust and safety in the two of them exploring it together.

Abruptly he backed away from her touch. "No consequences," he reminded her. "Lay back on the bed."

He grinned suddenly and quoted her own words back to her. "I'm going to show you what it's all about."

She froze for a second. But no. There was no room for fear here. Tru was brilliantly balancing both of their needs. He was respecting the limit she'd placed on this—but she suspected he was going to careen recklessly out of control right up to the line. And she found she wanted to go with him.

"It's what you want, is it not?" he asked.

"Yes. I want it all," she breathed. "I want laughter and fun and your hands touching me beneath star-lit skies." She wanted exasperation and growing fondness and wild urges. "But I can't repeat my mother's mistakes."

"You won't." He said it easily, but she thought he understood all that lay beneath the simple words. "I won't let you."

So she did it. She let go.

She dropped the reins, abandoned the helm, let her empty hands reach for him and plunge them both into chaos.

Into heat. Into desire.

She lay back onto the bed.

He kicked off his boots and climbed over her clad only in his trousers. The fire behind him left his face in shadow, but she didn't need to see. She was feeling now. Utterly absorbed in the weight of his hand and the brush of his fingertips as he traveled to all the sensitive spots on her body. Oddly thrilled as he buried his face against her skin and inhaled as if he could not get enough of her.

The force of his desire ran as wide as a river. She let it carry her along with him.

He touched her breasts once more, tarried there a bit when she made encouraging sounds all over again. Then he slid his hand down and over her belly, to the place that pulsed for him, regular as the tide. For long moments he explored, his fingers roaming through silken, wet folds, until she could only breathe in ragged, little gasps. Over and over he stroked, a slick, continuous caress, until he slid a finger up and over her stiff bud of pleasure—and she cried out.

Before she could think, he'd moved away to stand at the edge of the bed. Her thoughts had gone wild, her body on fire for more. She stared, and then he knelt, pushed her legs wide and put his mouth where his fingers had been.

She was lost. Constraint? Laughable. There was only the feel of his tongue, the arch and twist of her body, the incredible pleasure building inside of her. It grew, pushing her higher. She went willingly, reaching, reaching, until finally she grabbed his head, let out a moan and dug her fingers into his hair, holding tight to keep from losing herself completely, from falling away and fading into pure bliss.

She came back to herself several minutes later, boneless, sated—and with him peering down at her with a smug smile. "That's what it is all about."

She summoned a smile. "That explains so much."

He didn't budge, didn't change expressions—and at last a bit of urgency nudged her. She had no wish to move, but neither could she leave him with that superior look.

Finding strength, she propped herself up on her elbows. "Your turn."

Arrogance faded. He shook his head. "This was about you."

"No. You said it earlier. It's about us. Together." She raised her brow at him. "Do you think I haven't been listening to all of those women at the House? Ways and ways, you said it yourself. I know the generalities. You can teach me the finer points."

She sat up and pushed him down in her place. "I'm quite looking forward to it, I find."

He looked like he would still protest—and also like a starving street urchin being offered an entire game pie.

"Take the rest of that off." She found she enjoyed giving the orders, and seeing him leap up to do as she bid. But when he lay back down on the bed, she started to doubt herself.

"Well." She cleared her throat. He was certainly . . . impressive.

He laughed. "Oh, don't worry. I'm hard as a pike. You've likely only to look at me and I'll go off."

She bit back a laugh. "The girls say that the gentlemen always exaggerate. Glad to know that you've no need to."

He started looking smug again, so she moved in close and ran a feather-light touch across his abdomen. His expression quickly changed, but after that she forgot to watch it. She was caught up in the heat and feel of him. His muscles tightened beneath her touch.

Abruptly she leaned down to kiss him. She invaded with her tongue, conquering his mouth just as he'd done hers. He relaxed into the kiss and after a moment she reached down and lightly grasped his jutting manhood.

Chapter Twelve

Word arrived from my parents. They were not interested in having a despoiled daughter in their home. Had I not been so headstrong, I would not be in this position. I was asked to break all ties and not contact them again.

--from the Journal of the infamous Miss Hestia Wright

Tru's mind splintered. She was so sweet, so brave. Unsure and yet determined. She lacked all the adept skill he'd known in partners before, yet he was glad of it. Her touch was all earnestness and it felt damned good.

Lightly, she explored him. Gentle fingers ran along the length of him, touched his sac and cupped it in curiosity. There was nothing practiced here, only honest curiosity and desire.

Nerves, too. He could see her eyeing the breadth of him—but as usual, she banished fear. Without warning, she dipped her head down and took him in her mouth.

Hot, wet, sweet. Her tongue tasted, learned. She experimented, seeing how much she could take of him. Ran an exploratory lap around him and then dipped into the crevice on the underside.

It was innocent—and so very damned hot. He made encouraging noises at the right times and she paid attention. Soon enough she was taking him deep, pulling back and plunging again. His hips pistoned. His blood roared.

Don't stop. Never stop. He tried to say it with his body. She heard. And he pulled her away just as he exploded, pouring himself out, spasming without end until he'd emptied everything he had.

"Hell and damnation." It was several long moments before he was able to summon even that much thought.

She nodded. "Yes." She looked a little dazed.

He pulled her close. Kissed her brow. Settled the both of them in under the covers.

She curled up against his side. "Is this how it always feels, after?"

He considered. He felt as if she'd hollowed out his insides and filled him with contentment. "No."

"Oh. That's too bad."

He should worry about that, he thought. But his eyes closed. She'd gone warm and boneless all along his side. Tomorrow, he would worry.

He was asleep before another thought could work free.

* * *

"Enormous! Rats as big as dogs, I swear! What do you Frenchies feed the vermin about here? I found one in my boot and another gnawing through my saddlebags . . ."

Rackham droned on and Tru let him, feigning a sympathetic ear. "I suppose you can only hope you don't get bitten," he said as Rackham paused for breath. "Before your host returns home to take care of the problem, I mean."

"Bitten? Good heavens, do you think they will *bite*?"

Tru shrugged. "It is what rats do, is it not?"

"Damn it all! And that's just it in any case, isn't it? We've been left in charge, you might say, instructed to care for . . . things." Rackham's frown must indicate a deeper level of thought than he was used to. "If we cannot handle a few vermin, will he not wonder if we are not to be trusted with the polit—" He paused. "With more important matters?"

"Ah, I see your dilemma." Tru waited a beat. "Well, if you wish to take care of the matter yourself, I hear there is a very good rat-catcher in this area. I have not met him myself, but my man of business used him to clear out the inn before we arrived to take possession. I can say that we've seen nary a whisker since we arrived—and the man does a clean job, for my wife will not have poison left near her food or her guests."

"Do you have his name?" Rackham asked eagerly.

"Surely I must have a bill about, somewhere." He clapped the man on the back. "Come. I see your nerves are shot. You shall rest in the private parlor for a bit while I search out the name. Have you had your luncheon?"

"No." Rackham shuddered. "I didn't dare eat at the house for fear of attack."

"Ah. Come, then. You shall have a meal and some wine and I'll send a boy out to find this man to come and attend you. You'll have the matter settled before the sun begins to set."

"Thank you, Chaput. That sounds exactly right," Rackham said on a sigh.

Not quite an hour later, Tru presented Nardes to the man. Rackham poured out his story.

Nardes nodded. "It sounds like quite a bad infestation, sir. Still, I can clear your home in just a day or two, I should think."

"So quickly?"

"Indeed. My methods are speedy. We can begin as soon as the house is empty."

"Wait—empty? Of people?"

"Yes, sir. Everyone must be gone for the day. I work quick and I don't contaminate the place with poison, but that means I need space and quiet for my animals to do their work. They don't do as well with people about, distracting them."

Rackham looked dazed. "You don't want us to distract your animals?"

"Aye, sir. Folks usually prefer to be gone, too. The

rat terriers are effective, but no one truly likes to see their little dead trophies all laid out. And my ferrets are shy. Too many people in the house and they won't come out of the holes—and that leads to another whole mess of problems." Nardes looked a little sheepish. "They been known to bite before, too." He shook his head. "No, it's best to evacuate for a day or two."

"But . . . but . . ." Rackham sputtered.

Nardes drew himself up. "There's no need to worry that I'll rifle through your silver, if that's what's worrying you, sir. I got a good reputation. I'm an honest tradesman and I get paid well for my work."

"No, no, of course not," Rackham began.

"There should be no problem," Tru interjected. "The staff likely has family hereabout, and you and Mr. Penrith should stay with us. You are fine, regular customers and I'll give you a rate that reflects it."

"But Penrith and I are not the only guests at the house," Rackham said desperately. "There is a young lady—" He abruptly bit off anything else he had to say.

"Ah, I see." Tru paused. "Discretion is called for?"

"Yes," Rackham answered miserably.

"Well, we've just the thing. We've only just converted the Crescent Room into a bright and airy lady's bedroom, with a well-appointed parlor attached. We can set up your young lady there and put her under my wife's protection. It faces the kitchen garden and is quite private. Nobody will know she's up there, should you wish it."

"You definitely don't want a lady about while the killin's going on," Nardes said with a shake of his head.

"Well, then I suppose we shall have to take you up on your offer, Chaput." Rackham clasped his hand. "Thank you. You've been good to us."

Tru ignored the twinge of his conscience and poured him another drink.

* * *

"I'm *so* sorry, *Madame*! I forgot the time!"

Callie ignored Victoire's wail and bent over the smoking oven. "Do stop sniffling, dear. It doesn't help and it is just burned bread, after all." She made a face as she pulled the blackened rolls out. "I should have been watching as well, but I got caught up in my menu planning." She sighed. "Oh, well, we'll start again. Run out to the garden for more rosemary, will you, Victoire?"

"No need."

They both jumped, then turned to see Tru standing in the doorway.

"There is," she contradicted, feeling testy again. "I've made the stew you requested, *husband*, but there must be bread to serve with it."

He merely reached into his pocket and withdrew some coins, which he gave over to Victoire. "Run around the corner to Monsieur Dufour's bakery and buy what we'll need for tonight, will you?"

The girl looked to Callie, who gave him a long, searching look before she nodded her head.

"I do believe the baker was becoming jealous of your growing acclaim in any case," Tru said. "Perhaps this will appease him. In the meantime, you and I have plans for the evening, *wife*."

She blinked, wondering what he was up to now. "We do?"

"Indeed. Business is about to pick up for us in the next few days, so I am giving you an evening off while I may." He glanced over at the girl. "Is that basket prepared?"

"It is, sir!" With a conspiratorial grin, the scullery maid went to the pantry and returned with a large, covered basket. "All ready."

"Thank you, Victoire." He took it from her.

Callie looked from one of them to the other, then broke out into a smile and began to unwrap herself from her apron. "Well, if it is to be our last chance, how could I refuse?"

"You've met Young Tom, our new errand boy, haven't you?" Tru asked the girl. "He'll help you here if you need it."

She looked to Victoire. "Just make sure Young Tom washes his hands, will you?"

'Indeed, *Madame.*"

Callie took Tru's arm and let him lead her out to the courtyard, where Edgar waited with a tiny curricle and a hired horse.

"Thank you, Edgar." Tru helped her into the high seat. "I'm leaving you to watch over the inn. You know right where to find us, should you need us."

"I'll watch," Edgar agreed. "It's seven hundred and thirty nine wagon lengths to that spot. That's four thousand, four hundred and thirty-four steps."

"How precise you are," Callie told him. "There's something comforting about knowing that, isn't there?"

The man nodded. She looked past him to where his mare was hitched to a pole. Half of her mane had lovely purple heather blooms woven in. A pile of them waited nearby. "Your mare looks to be in fine shape."

He nodded agreement. "Rose likes it here."

So do I. They pulled out into the square. The cobblestone streets were busy, so she kept quiet to allow Tru to concentrate on the traffic. A few people nodded or waved. She returned the gestures, but as they moved farther away, she recognized fewer faces. The inactivity freed her mind and she went back to the fretting that had led to the burnt rolls earlier. Traffic grew sparser as they reached the edge of town, but she barely noticed when they joined the south road toward Combourg.

Tru tried a few conversational sallies, but after a few short, distracted replies, he left off. For a time.

She jumped a few minutes later when he reached over and laid a big hand over her clutched fingers.

"Great gamboling garters! Your knuckles have gone white from all the hand wringing you're up to. What has set you off?" He grew serious. "Are you going to be nervous with me now? Are you already regretting our . . . last night?"

Callie pulled her hands away and clutched the seat while she rounded on him. "Lord Truitt Russell!" she scolded.

He shushed her, but she brushed the reprimand aside. "There is no one to hear me save for the squirrels. Truly, I thought you knew me better than that. I asked for last night—and you fulfilled my wishes in spectacular fashion. There is nothing to regret." She gave him her most ferocious frown. "And why must you continually expect me to act in so pudding-hearted a fashion? I defy you to name one time when I have been so missish!"

A corner of his mouth twitched while he thought, clearly taking up the challenge.

"You cannot!" she declared.

"A moment! I am thinking."

She folded her arms now, although it was a feat to maintain her balance as they moved over the rutted road.

"Ha! I know!" The horse twitched at his shout and he lowered his volume. "You cried at my brother's wedding! Don't try to deny it. I saw."

She scoffed. "I can't deny it. It's true. But they were tears of happiness. How could I not shed them when they are so in love and it seems such a miracle that they not only found each other, but found a way to keep each other?"

He relented. 'You're right. I should not have

teased you. And yes, their happiness does seem miraculous."

Mollified, she teased him back a bit. "I'm sure you will feel quite the same at your own wedding."

"Wedding?" He snorted. "Society's matrons will not even let their chicks in the same parlour with me these days. You would be amazed at all the forgotten appointments, sick relatives and other manufactured excuses that pop up when I enter a room."

She sobered. "No wonder you are in such a hurry to get Marstoke back and your name cleared."

"Is that what you think?" He glanced askance at her. "That I am frothing at the mouth to jump back into the marriage mart?"

"Well, it hadn't yet occurred to me."

"As well it should not."

Before she could inquire as to the real reason, he hurried on. "Truthfully? Aldmere shocked me, falling so hard and fast. I can't imagine a day in which I'm *marrying* someone." He quieted, his expression gone contemplative. "Even less can I imagine anyone crying over it."

"They will, if they care for you—and if you are marrying wisely and happily, like your brother."

This time his gaze rested heavily upon her, almost tangibly. "And if I'm marrying for other reasons—unwise reasons?"

"If you are marrying unwisely, then I hope that someone who cares for you will make a fuss over it."

"What? Make a scene?" He shook his head. "Like crying over someone else's happiness, it takes a higher plane of intimacy for such a thing. A certain level of care. There is no one like that in my life."

"I'll do it," she said stoutly. "In fact, I will make a vow to you now. Lord Truitt Russell," she whispered his name this time, "I promise I will come and cry happy tears on your wedding day." She raised a brow at him. "So don't forget my invitation."

"And if I am being unwise?"

She snorted. "I trust the idea of me raising a ruckus during the ceremony should be enough of a deterrent to keep you from being unwise."

"By God, you are right. It is," he declared.

He pulled the horse in as they approached a turn onto a narrow, wooded lane. Here she had to hold onto the seat in earnest.

"Not far," he promised.

She didn't answer for fear of biting her tongue.

They broke out of the shadowed lane next to a pretty little meadow. The entire cleared space was carpeted in soft, purple heather blooms.

"Oooh, how lovely," she breathed. "How did you—" She stopped. "Oh. Edgar's horse was wearing these blooms."

"Yes. He told me about this place. I thought we could rest a bit here and talk business." He pulled the break and climbed down, then moved around to assist her. "Pick a spot while I care for the horse?"

She wandered amidst the gorgeous blooms, picking some to take back. "I'm gathering some to take ho—. She stopped, blushing furiously. "To take back with us."

He didn't seem to notice her slip. "Where to?" He hoisted the basket. "There's a blanket in here, I believe."

They spread it out in a spot where the blooms grew thinly. While the sky blazed with a vivid orange sunset, they enjoyed the bread, cheese and local, hard-cured sausages Victoire had packed for them. Tru told her all about the encounter with Rackham and Nardes.

And just like that, her appetite vanished.

He stopped after a moment, to look at her. "You

are doing it again."

"Doing what?"

He nodded toward her napkin she twisted in her lap. "Whitening your knuckles. I thought I was the one frustrated with the smallness of my role, but you seem utterly intent on strangling that napkin. What did it do to you?"

She gave him a feeble smile and kept twisting.

He threw the leftover cheese in the basket and then set it aside so that he could move closer to her. "I know something's bothering you." He thought a moment. "Is it the thought of Rackham hanging about? Are you worried that he'll—"

"No!" Callie forgot her worries in the face of her rising irritation. "As if I could not handle a lordling like Rackham?" She huffed. "If you do not stop subscribing all of these weak-kneed reactions to me . . ." She flushed. "I'm going to do something drastic!"

"Drastic?" He sounded intrigued.

"Yes!" She scrabbled for something suitably threatening. "One more time and I shall . . . pinch you."

"You do tempt me." Instead of picking up the thread and turning it into innuendo, he laid a hand over hers. "What is it, Callie?"

She merely looked at him, waiting and trying not to appear like she was pleading.

"You did ask me to watch for when you start a storm to brewing."

She didn't appreciate the reminder.

"Something tells me there is a tempest forming in that pretty little head—and you are trying to distract me from it."

He was right, damn him. She sighed. "It's Letty."

"Ah. Still worried that she'll kick up a fuss?"

"Oh, I know she will. She'll spit piss and vinegar. She always does when I ride in to rescue her from trouble." She rubbed her temples. "The things I've helped her out of over the years . . . Just once you'd think she would thank me, instead of pitching a fit." She sighed. "But I learned a long time ago that I cannot make her decisions for her. Even if she consistently makes the wrong ones."

"Would you like me to talk to her, when she arrives?"

'No!" She narrowed her gaze at him. "I warned you once and I'll remind you again to leave her to me."

"Fine, fine."

"I'm deadly serious, Tru."

Hands raised in capitulation, he asked. "Then that's not what's troubling you, is it?"

"No." Callie tucked her feet up under her gown and leaned back to look up into the sky. The sunset's colors were fading. Evening was setting in. "I suppose I should have said it's *me*, not Letty."

He leaned back on his elbows beside her and waited.

"The whole notion of cutting the bonds between us. It is freeing, as Hestia said. But it's frightening, too."

He still waited.

"You won't understand," she complained. "No one can."

He shrugged. "Then explain it."

She heaved a great sigh and watched a bat wing its way about the open sky overhead while she gathered her thoughts. "Letty learned how to get into trouble practically with her first step. I've been saving her skin just as long. Scalded fingertips, skinned knees, broken hearts, thwarted prospects—I've hauled her out of it all."

"Her mother was an actress—isn't that what you

said?"

The light was fading fast. A star winked awake right above them. Callie felt a certain gratitude for the growing dark. It made it easier to share the things she'd always thought she'd keep to herself.

"Yes. My father took her mother for a paramour, but he moved on from her, just as he always did. She'd heard the story of my mother, either from him or perhaps in their fast circles. After he left, some sort of fever made its way through the theatre she worked in. It was closed down and when she found herself without a position, seriously ill and with a newborn babe, she must have had nowhere else to go. She showed up on our doorstep, with Letty in tow."

"Your mother took her in?"

"Yes. She took them both. You could see the beauty that Letty's mother had once been, but the fever had ravaged her. She didn't last a week. Letty was such a tiny thing, so pink and adorable."

"And you kept her."

"What else could we do?" Her mother's words still echoed in her head, along with all the worry, love and resentment. *She's alone now, save for us. We're all she has.*

"She was just over a year old when my mother gave her mostly into my charge." *Watch over her, Callie, and keep her safe.*

"How old were you?"

She frowned. "Six, perhaps?" She stared bleakly upward. "And now I'm going to just let her go."

He made as if to speak, but she interrupted him. "Yes. I know. It's better for both of us. But it's going to be so hard! My mother sacrificed so much. She gave me everything, taught me all she knew—and this was the only thing she ever asked of me."

Abruptly, without precedence or warning, she burst

into tears. She was horrified. Never had she meant to show such weakness. But part of her was glad, so glad that he was there to gather her up and hold her tight.

He said something against her hair, but she couldn't hear it. It was all right, though. She didn't need to. She clung to his chest and buried her face in his shirt. He smelled like sunshine and hay. He was as solid and strong as a wall, yet he held her with tenderness. And she might never have the chance to be held by him again.

His thumb brushed her cheek, wiped away a tear. "It does sound difficult, but you'll get through it, Callie. I've yet to find an obstacle you can't breach." His tone lowered. "And setting Letty free does not mean you are letting your mother go."

Tears welled fresh and so did the old instinct to pull away, to avert her eyes and throw up the barriers that came so naturally to her.

But no. It was too late for that—and she didn't truly wish to, in any case. They had such a short time left, so few chances for honesty and she wanted more of it—from both of them.

So she drew a deep breath. She'd been bare before him last night, but now she was going to make herself truly vulnerable.

"It feels like I'm letting her go. And that's not the worst of it." Her chin dropped. "I know you want to go back, but I shy away from the thought of it. I can't picture it, can't imagine myself alone. And if I'm not Letty's keeper, then who am I?"

Chapter Thirteen

It was as hard a blow as any Lord M— had ever struck me. I was despondent, lost, alone.

--from the Journal of the infamous Miss Hestia Wright

That aching little whisper sent Tru's every feeling into revolt. "You are who you've made yourself, Callie Grant. And you will stop being ridiculous right now. Alone? I do not believe so. You have Hestia. The girls in Half Moon House. Your closest friend is now the Duchess of Aldmere." His heart raced a little as he gathered her in. "And you have me."

Her grip on his shirt tightened. "I think Brynne is part of the problem. She's so happy—not just with your brother, but with her new foundling enterprise. It makes me wonder if I've stayed put too long, gone stagnant." Her voice grew muffled as she buried her face. "I don't know. I just feel . . . adrift. I'm not the same Callie. I'm certainly not Chloe Chaput. I feel as if I'm losing my moorings with the past and can't quite see where I'm drifting into the future." She leaned back and he could almost feel her straining to see his face in the dark. "Do you remember what you said about Penrith and Rackham and those like them? Suddenly I feel the sort of empathy you spoke of."

Bitterness choked off some of his softer feelings. "Don't waste too much emotion on those men. You've seen enough of the ugliness and truly terrible things that life can bring. There are horrors out there—and people rise above them every day. These are men of privilege—and they've let envy and disappointments tempt them onto a path towards treachery, villainy and treason."

"Is that the reason for all of your urgency, then? You don't want people to think the same of you?"

Her quick insight pierced him. He stiffened, his first thought to fend off such a clear view into the heart of him. But there was only curiosity in her voice and encouragement in the soft brush of her hands. Understanding, not judgment. Slowly, all of his tightly clenched muscles began to loosen.

She nodded and gave a little smile. "I know. It's nerve-wracking, isn't it? Letting someone peek through the cracks?" She traced her finger over his false sideburns, right where his scar normally showed.

"Yet I'm oddly comforted too," she continued. "When this is over, I think I will like knowing that you are out there, carrying it around with you."

"It?"

"The truth of me. The image of who I really am, tucked away somewhere safe inside you. The picture of all the contrasting bits of me—struggles and foibles, goals and dreams and follies."

"When this is over," he said quietly. "That's the crux of it, isn't it?"

She sighed and bent to lay her head against his shoulder. "It's no wonder we've got along so well," she whispered. "We are cut off from the world, from our old selves, and we're seeing all the bits and pieces that might normally be hiding away. We're both contemplating, sorting, deciding, trying to discover which version of ourselves will be going back."

Good Lord, she was right. Right about every damned thing. Worry and panic lurked somewhere at the realization. She couldn't know how close she'd hit to the core of his misery. He'd harbored so many doubts about himself over the years, suffered so much uncertainty about his place and purpose in the world—but no one had ever known of it. He'd used everything at his disposal to craft his facade. The world looked at him and saw only privilege and wit, his skill at sport, his charm and his easy way of making friends—and he worked hard to keep it that way. Society's doubts about him, Prinny's hesitation, they had driven him into a frenzy because he didn't ever want anyone else to see his flaws and uncertainties—and now she was staring right at them.

He pulled in a breath. But she wasn't recoiling in shock or horror. Perhaps she didn't see all the cracks and inadequacies. She must not, in fact.

He would agonize about the why of it later. Because right now she was pressed all along his side. Right now the heat of them lying together was warming the night.

He let worry go and allowed desire to move in, swift and unsubtle. "I want only to contemplate you."

He rolled up beside her and laid his hand on her waist. *She's not your lifeline.* It was a timely reminder. The safety she offered was only temporary. But he wanted it anyway.

"My hands on you under the starlit sky. That's what you said last night. Is it still what you want?"

Her head shifted so that she could look up at the night. She breathed a sigh. It sounded happy to him. Anticipatory. He hoped to God he was right.

"Yes," she whispered. "It's what I want."

He shivered as all of the small hairs on the back of his neck rose. In gratitude, perhaps.

He sent his hand drifting upwards, over the long, graceful sweep of her arm. Paused for a moment at the collar of her dress, where he could feel her pulse beating as swiftly as his own. And up further still, to rub a thumb over soft lips.

She reached up to bury her fingers in his hair and trace slow, tortuously sweet circles on his scalp. Why did that feel so damned good? It made him want to arch like a cat.

He breathed in her scent. Rosemary again, and the flowers she'd collected, and just the faintest whiff of starch. It called to him, tugging at his cock. God, she should bottle that smell. She could sway armies with it.

Slowly, with all the gravity and care that she deserved, he bent down to press a kiss to her mouth.

Almost a kiss. The slightest, sweetest promise of one.

She moaned. Her fingers trailed along his neck and across his shoulder. She lit tiny fires of desire everywhere she touched. Her palm slid under his arm and urged him down to her.

He went, scoring her lips, branding her mouth. Restraint disappeared. He abandoned subtlety. *Mine. Mine.*

His hand crept unerringly to her breast. He wanted to touch her all over. Mark her. He erect nipples teased him through her gown and he began to work all of her layers loose.

His fingers fumbled and he stopped. He would not act the randy, impatient boy today, no matter that his entire being was on fire, remembering the utter completion of last night's climax.

At last he had her dress draped open, her stays undone. "No corset," he said against her nape.

"Just in case."

He heard the smile in her voice.

Practically afloat with lust, he gripped her shoulders and rolled, landing on his back with her astraddle him—and those magnificent breasts right there, just waiting for his touch.

"If they were making a list today," he vowed, "your breasts would be declared one of the wonders of the world."

She laughed. He filled his hands with her, then settled in to bestow upon her the worship she deserved. With fingers and thumbs and lips and teeth he pleasured her, while she gasped and moaned and threw her head back, giving every evidence of her approval.

"Tru," she said at last, urgent.

"I know." He sat up. "Take off your drawers." The whisper sounded harsh in the dark.

She scrambled off of him to comply and he took the opportunity to shrug out of his coat and waistcoat.

"Oof." She was back, pushing his shoulders, climbing right back over him. He pulled at her skirts until they were hiked up high.

He stared. Her form looked dark and shapely against a backdrop of stars. That porcelain skin had been gilded with faint moonlight, just a sheen tracing the curve of her cheek, the slope of her shoulder and the beautiful mounds of her bosom. "You are beyond compare. I could stare at you all night."

"I can barely see you," she answered. Bracing one hand on his chest, she reached behind her to run a swift caress along his thigh. "I can feel you just fine, though."

"I want to watch you ride me," he whispered.

She stilled. "Ride you?" For the first time he heard uncertainty in her voice.

He answered by burrowing a hand under her skirts. She flinched when he brushed the soft, bare skin above her garter, then sucked in a breath when he slicked a finger through her wet folds.

She melted against him. Both hands came back to clutch his shoulders. Her skin was satin and she was helpless against the slow exploration of his fingers. Gently. Softly. Long, slow strokes. Her hips moved with him and his cock strained against the confines of his breeches, aching to be where his hand roamed.

Deliberately, he let a finger slide up, to lightly brush her swollen, straining nub.

Her moan was instantaneous, low and guttural.

Her began to stroke her in earnest.

Her hips were rocking now. Her movements grew wilder—and then she stopped.

"What?" He couldn't even form a coherent question.

She was too busy fumbling at the fall of his trousers to answer. In a moment his cock sprang free.

She grasped him. Firmly.

He made a noise. "Easy."

She made a sound of apology and gentled her grip. Soon she began to stroke him with a steady, gentle rhythm. The tip of him rubbed the soft skin of her thigh with each pass of her hand.

Every article of his being focused on that spot, that soft caress. His cock hardened again, his belly tightened in anticipation.

Her hips nudged him.

He was lost. Only the pump of her hand existed, the next soft brush of skin.

"Tru," she said urgently, rocking again.

"Oh, yes." He reached for her once more, slid his fingers to her warm and welcoming center.

"Ahhh." Her back arched on the sigh. Tru gazed at her in wonder. She looked otherworldly, shadowed desire and exquisite wanting come to life. He'd felt so uncertain for so long, yet now he felt as if he must have done something right, sometime. Why else would fate give him the gift—even temporarily—of Callie Grant?

She began to move faster, her breath catching on a hitch. The pace of her stroking matched the rocking of her hips. His own breath began to sound like a bellows. My God. She'd coaxed him into a towering cockstand.

Quickly now, they moved together. His fingers teased, her hand stroked. Her hips rocked.

Suddenly she stiffened, her head thrown back. She was a gloriously erotic image of passion—and he followed her over, pumping endlessly as his hips bucked and their cries mingled before piercing the quiet night.

Chapter Fourteen

It was Pearl who told me that I was not lost, but free. Free to choose. Free to be whomever I wished, whatever I wished. I could take a new name. Go anywhere.

--from the Journal of the infamous Miss Hestia Wright

Letty climbed into the carriage, her spine straight and her gaze averted from the unrelenting glare of the stout housekeeper. On no account was she going to show her nervous excitement at leaving the villa.

Rackham and Penrith climbed in after her, still bickering, as they had been all morning.

"Of course you think all will be well," Penrith complained. "It's not you who has fallen on his bad side. And all over a few waistcoats! Who could imagine such fury over the shipment of a few waistcoats?"

"*No* outside communication," Rackham replied. You know that's what we agreed to and you know why we—" He stopped and gave Letty a wan smile, then directed a pointed look at his friend.

Penrith sat back, straightening his coat. "It was only my valet," he muttered. "A man who has shown his loyalty and discretion a hundred times." He crossed his arms. "You say it was not you who tipped me out, but who else would know? And who else would ascribe a moment's importance to such a small thing?"

Letty knew. Frau Bosch, that's who. The sour old woman claimed the title of housekeeper, but the villa had come with a Frenchwoman in that position. Frau Bosch had arrived with Marstoke and Letty knew she was more than that to the marquess—something far more menacing.

Letty had first run afoul of her at that cottage in the woods. Once Marstoke had gone, the knowledge of the place, the certainty that that screaming girl was likely still trapped there, had haunted her. She'd finally worked up the nerve to investigate. She'd plotted and planned, found a time when she could escape the villa unnoticed, and had been searching for a back way into the cottage when she'd been caught by Frau Bosch. The hateful old relic had marched her back to the villa and taken up residence with them there as well—the better to keep an eye on Letty. The woman kept her distance as long as Penrith or Rackham were about, but on more than one occasion, Letty had found herself locked in her room when both gentlemen were away.

She shivered. Those rats had been disgusting—and huge—but they just might be her salvation. She looked out the window at the villa as they pulled away and vowed not to come back.

Rackham called for the carriage to halt at the end of the drive. He put down the window and had words with the arriving rat catcher before they moved on.

"Are all of the estate buildings infested?" she asked. "Or is it just the main house?"

"I don't know," Rackham admitted. "I didn't think to ask." Frowning, he looked back. "Once we arrive in town, I'll send a note back instructing the man to check the outbuildings."

He wouldn't gain access to the cottage, Letty knew. Frau Bosch hadn't let any of the chaos affect her. Sour milk, spoiled meat, insects crawling from gravy boats and wine glasses—none of it had made her so much as twitch. She wouldn't care if that poor girl was buried in rats the size of cats.

As they rumbled toward their new, temporary home, Letty weighed her options. She had a bit of money, a couple of pieces of silver to pawn—and utter determination to escape Marstoke's clutches. But her mind kept wandering back to that unknown girl . . .

She was still thinking when they arrived at the inn,

and already tired of hearing the gentlemen sing praise over the place. She cared only for the opportunity to escape. She glanced around as they entered, noting layout and exits as she was presented to the innkeeper.

"It is a pleasure to welcome you to our establishment." The man bowed low. She took a second look when he rose. Was there something familiar about him? She ran a quick gaze over him, noted the painful looking scar on his hand and dismissed the notion. She didn't know any of these Frenchmen.

Turning away, she looked up, following the line of the stairs, and realized suddenly that it was the smell of the place that was familiar. Something about the homey scent made her think of her childhood.

"We have a lovely room with a private parlour all ready for you, mademoiselle." The innkeeper led the way up the stairs. "And my wife is happy to assist you in any fashion you require."

"Thank you." Letty followed him up to the next floor, noting the maid exiting the servant's stairs a bit of a way down the hall.

Her room was lovely, all done in shades of blue. The familiar scent hovered heavier in the air here. She drifted into the room, then went to the window, leaned against it and shut her eyes. Maybe it was just her mind playing tricks on her.

"I hope it is to your satisfaction."

Longing welled up inside of her. What made that smell? It forced her back, to the days when she was young and restless and impatient—and utterly safe.

"Mademoiselle?"

She summoned the fine words she was supposed to use now. "It is lovely, thank you." She focused on the kitchen garden and cobbled yard outside. Truly, the strain must be affecting her mind. She thought she could now detect a whiff of butter cake, her old favorite, from long ago.

"Mademoiselle," the man's voice had gone soft and gentle. "I think you will want to meet my wife."

The smell of butter cake grew stronger. She straightened. Perhaps this was all a dream.

But somehow she already knew. Impossible hope and the fear of disappointment made her shake as she turned.

And then she was moving across the floor, sobbing and falling over her own feet. "Callie? Callie!" She fell into her half-sister's arms. "I'm afraid I must be dreaming. How can you be real?"

She dissolved into a flood of grateful tears.

* * *

Callie looked at Tru over Letty's shoulder, her eyebrows raised in shock, her heart filled with unexpected joy.

He'd done such a wonderful job of distracting her while they waited for this moment. He'd sneaked quick kisses for Victoire's sake and he'd teased her for having nerves now when she'd faced down two criminals so easily that first night in Dover. She'd laughed at his antics and blushed at his praise, and tried not to come apart as Letty's arrival drew near.

She'd come into this room prepared for a fight—and brought Letty's favorite cake as a bribe and peace offering. An unnecessary gesture, it turned out, as Letty was in over her head and, for the first time, cognizant of it. Marstoke must have thoroughly frightened her. She cried over Callie in gratitude and relief—and then sat down and ate three pieces of butter cake while she talked and answered questions.

Callie's heart sank when Letty confirmed their worst fears. She was indeed being groomed as a doppelganger for the Princess Charlotte. She spoke of her training, of learning how to walk and talk and sit. Every day she'd been drilled on what the royal princess liked to eat and drink and do, as well as what she didn't like. Over and over again she'd reviewed the relationship that Charlotte had with her staff, her companions, her few friends.

Tru sat with them for a while, taking notes and asking questions.

"But how did he plan to use you?" he asked Letty at last. "Were you to act outrageously and destroy her character? To frighten her?" He watched Letty closely. "To take her place?"

Tears welled in Letty's eyes. "All of those, I believe. But I do not know specifics. Marstoke doesn't trust me. He told me nothing ahead of time."

A shudder ran through her and Callie reached over to grasp her hand. She recalled the time that Letty had lived with a notorious madam in London, despite Callie's best efforts to draw her away. Letty had sworn that she wasn't being used as a prostitute, but trained for a large and important role. Now, here was the confirmation of what that role was meant to be.

"I can't go back," Letty whispered. "Please. You are here. Somehow you've come, Callie. Will you take me back home? Get me away?"

"Yes, of course," Callie soothed. "We're here to help you. Plans are in place. You're safe now, Letty."

Her sister dissolved into tears again and Callie nodded when Tru rose, gathering up his notes. He nodded at her as he left, presumably to contact Stoneacre.

"I don't know why you came," Letty said, sniffling, after he'd gone. "I've lied to you, thwarted your efforts and Hestia's, made a fool of myself and almost committed treason. Why would you risk yourself to help me like this?"

"You are my sister," Callie began.

"Half-sister," she interrupted.

She sat back and met Letty's stare dead on. "There is no such distinction in my heart. Just as there was none in Mother's. I love you, Letty. She took a deep breath and narrowed my gaze. "But this is the last time."

Letty's expression went blank.

"I'm changing, Letty. Moving on. This pattern is damaging to both of us. It's time you were in charge of your own life, of making your own mistakes, and living with the consequences. And it's time I let you."

Callie was shocked to see relief flooding her sister's features.

"Yes. You are right. It will be better for both of us." Letty's head nodded as she spoke. "But I'm not going to make these mistakes anymore, Callie. I promise. I've had a lot of time to think since I got here. While I was so busy learning to be someone else, I was thinking for once, about the person I would like to be."

She drew a long, shuddering sigh. "I'm finished looking for adventure and fame. I want to go away. To America, perhaps. I'll get a position in a theater, if I can. I don't care if I only have small parts or if I'm sewing the wardrobe. I'll be happy enough just to be a part of that world."

So far away. Callie summoned a smile. "That sounds like it would suit you very well. You've talked of the theatre for so long." She tilted her head, thinking. "It should not take so long for you to answer Lord Stoneacre's questions. Your testimony should be over quickly if—"

She stopped as Letty's eyes widened and she began to shake her head.

"Letty," she said firmly. "There will no getting around doing your part. Do you know how livid the Prince Regent is after that stunt Marstoke pulled? The marquess tried to make him into a fool in front of his own people, all of those visiting dignitaries—the whole world, essentially."

Letty had begun to look frantic. Callie reached out and gripped her hand. "There have been considerable resources dedicated to getting you free, Letty. You will do your part in return." She tried to smile. "Think of it this way—the Prince Regent might be so thrilled with you for helping to bring Marstoke to his just rewards, he's sure to offer *you* some sort of reward. You might just be able to go to America and *buy* your own theatre."

That calmed her a little. "Truly?"

"Well, it might be a slight exaggeration, but this is more than just your duty. It's your responsibility. You do want to see Marstoke punished, do you not? He must be stopped before he causes more chaos or hurts someone else."

Letty's eyes unfocused for a moment. "Yes. That is true." She appeared to be lost in thought.

Callie waited. "Letty?" she said at last.

"Yes?" Her sister started. "Oh, yes. You are right." The corner of her mouth twitched. "And it would be better to travel with a nest egg than without one."

Callie stood to gather up the dishes onto the tea tray, but stopped when Letty stood and gave her a quick embrace. "Thank you," she whispered. "For everything."

She smiled and nodded and left with her spirits as high as she could ever remember them. Letty was going to be fine—and at last she *understood*.

It truly did feel as if a weight was lifted from her. She felt free in a way that she hadn't realized she'd been missing. Taking the tray to the kitchen, she went on then to the bedroom, where she opened a bedside drawer and lifted out the small packet she'd found there.

A French letter, the prophylactic still sealed tight in its original envelope. She'd hidden it away, but it had been haunting her.

At last she felt as if she could focus on her future—

and yet . . .

There was still likely to be a night or two before the future truly began.

She tucked the small envelope in her bodice and returned to the kitchens.

Chapter Fifteen

Because she was truly a Pearl, she offered to let me stay. To help her run The Oyster and to take it over one day.

--from the Journal of the infamous Miss Hestia Wright

The hour grew late. The dining customers had mostly gone. Only a few farmers nursing their ales were left in the taproom—and Penrith and Rackham, of course.

That pair had slipped well below the mahogany hours ago. They had been tightly strung and nervous since they'd arrived yesterday. Something bothered them. Something about a waistcoat was all that Tru could decipher, for all of his listening. Whatever the reason, they had finally succumbed to the call of his brandy this afternoon.

He left them to it, slipping silently through the inn, making his rounds, checking rooms, doors and windows as he did every evening. He neared the back of the building as his normal route drew to a close, turning a corner just in time to see a cloaked figure slip silently up the servant's stairs.

Not one of his servants, he knew. His new boy-of-all-work was currently in the kitchens, being stuffed to the gills courtesy of Callie and Victoire. He'd seen Marie upstairs, laying fires, freshening water pitchers and turning back beds. He glanced toward the nearby door, leading to the herb garden and back courtyard. No, too small to be Edgar.

He followed on silent feet. At the first floor he peered through the green baize door and caught the brief flash of light and the slight click as Letty's door closed, several feet away.

So. Letty had been all cooperation and gratitude

yesterday. Her nerves had re-emerged today. Several times she'd asked if the rat catcher had finished the job at the villa. She'd also caught him alone to ask if the man had found anything unusual as he cleared the estate.

In fact, he hadn't heard anything from Nardes since the man went out to the villa. They hadn't made specific plans to communicate, so he was not overly concerned, but still . . .

What was the girl up to? He slipped back down the stairs and exited the rear door. Glancing up at her window, he made sure she wasn't watching, then crossed to the stables.

Edgar was there, hanging tackle, wearing a smile.

"Good evening, Edgar. Has young Tom come out to bed yet or is he still in the kitchen, eating his weight?"

The big man looked around. "He's not here."

"Ah." Tru picked up a polishing cloth and perched on a hay bale. "Well, let the boy eat. I shall finish cleaning his fittings before I retire myself." It had been a long time since he'd taken up such a homey job. He tossed a glance at his stable manager. "You are looking well pleased, if I may say so."

"I am," Edgar enthused. "I have a job. A delivery."

Tru stilled. "Do you? And before you've got your new cart, even. Congratulations to you."

"Yes, thank you. No cart needed for this. I'm to deliver a note and a parcel and I can do that just with Rose and me." He crossed over to stroke the mare's soft nose.

"That truly is good news. When will you make your delivery? I'll be sure that young Tom is free to watch over the stables."

"Early," Edgar answered. "Before dawn. I'll wake him when I leave."

"So soon? Have you the note, then?"

"No." Edgar looked briefly confused. "The lady has just gone to write it."

The lady. It was Letty, then. Callie was not going to like this. "And the parcel?" Tru asked very gently.

Edgar grinned. "The lady is the parcel. That is funny."

"It is indeed." And very interesting. "Well, no one could be happier for you than I, Edgar. I know how much you miss your deliveries. How long shall I keep young Tom free?" He smiled at the other man. "How many steps will you be taking?"

"Seven thousand, nine hundred and fifty."

"Soon I shall learn enough from you to know where you are going, just by the number of steps you predict."

"Yes, it isn't hard." Edgar was all earnestness. "That is the number to the villa where you sent the rat catcher. It does not take long to go there and back."

Tru paused in his polishing. Letty was going back to the villa?

He should tell Callie. First thing. He knew he should.

He started in on the brass fittings again.

She deserved to know that Letty was lying to her once again.

She would hate to be left out of whatever he decided to do about it.

The trust and honesty they had shared was the thing she valued most about their brief affair.

And she had warned him to leave Letty to her. More than once.

And yet, he hesitated.

What if it were something simple? Some trinket Letty had forgotten? What if she only meant to say goodbye to someone on the estate? He would have riled Callie up and possibly damaged their newly cordial relationship for nothing.

And what if it was indeed something more sinister? What if Letty meant to leave Marstoke a message? Or to destroy evidence of his whereabouts? It would be smartest to let her play her hand, follow and catch her in the act of making her move.

It could be something altogether more dangerous. What if there was another, unknown player hereabouts? Letty might be meeting him, making an attempt at an escape.

Callie had reached the end of her tolerance for her sister's shenanigans. She might refuse to wait and see what the girl had in mind. She'd likely lose her temper and confront her sister head on. Prevent the girl from carrying out her plans.

There was no guarantee that Letty, once caught, would tell the truth about what she meant to get up to. And if this was a scheduled rendezvous, and she didn't show up, they could alert Marstoke and his people to their presence.

He could not lose *any* advantage over Marstoke, no matter how small. The man was intelligent, wily and always two steps ahead. It had had been a long, difficult job, even for a man with Stoneacre's resources, to discover the marquess at this bolt hole. Who knew how long it would take to track him to another? All of Tru's anger and impatience returned at the thought of losing to the bastard once again. Marstoke must *not* win.

It was a long list of perfectly plausible reasons he'd come up with, yet he knew keeping Callie in the dark was the wrong decision.

And still he meant to make it.

He pasted a concerned expression on his face. "I do feel as if I need to warn you, Edgar. You know I am very happy at the thought of you making deliveries again, but I am afraid that there are worse things than rats out at that villa."

"I heard they were big ones. Worse than that, even?"

"Far worse."

Edgar thought a moment. "Snakes?"

"Worse still. There have been some very dangerous men tracked to that estate. And it would not do," Tru said with sudden inspiration, "to place either the lady or Rose in danger."

Edgar's caressing hand stilled. "No."

"We must make preparations, then, must we not? Prepare for all eventualities? It might be best if I follow along, just in case."

Edgar nodded agreement.

"And there's no need to inform the lady. We don't want to frighten her unnecessarily. Between the two of us, we should keep them safe." He thought a moment. "Here's what we'll do. I'll need the silver gelding from the livery . . ."

* * *

Nerves taut, Callie prepared a tea tray. She fiddled with dish and saucer, napkins and spoons until everything was just so—and then she straightened resolutely and dropped a small vial of laudanum in her apron pocket.

Letty was up to something.

Marie had come to her this evening, worried.

"I'm not one to tell tales, Madame, but you should know that the lady up in the Crescent rooms has been sneaking about the halls all day, turning corners and ducking in rooms to avoid bein' seen. I am not accusing her of anything, but I thought you should know, especially as when something goes missing in an inn, it's usually the maids what get questioned first."

"Thank you, Marie. I'll keep that in mind. Did the lady enter any of the occupied rooms?"

"Not that I saw. I believe she just hid in the empty ones to avoid being spotted." The maid nodded wisely. "But I see things, I do."

"I'm sure you do. Thank you for informing me."

"She's been out at the stables too. You don't think she'll steal one of the horses, do you?"

"I doubt it, but I'll talk to Monsieur Chaput and we will keep an eye on the lady."

"Thank you, *Madame*." Marie bobbed a curtsy and left.

Callie had seen for herself that Letty had been wearing her old look—the one she always displayed just before she bought a gown she could not afford, ran out with an inappropriate gentleman—or bolted.

Not this time. This time Callie had come prepared—and she meant what she'd said about handling her sister herself. She would head Letty off before she could cause further trouble, if she had to.

She knocked on the door and entered at a muffled call. Her sister sat in the bedroom, writing at the small table in the corner.

"I brought some tea. I thought it might calm your nerves and help you sleep."

"Thank you. Though I'm not sure my nerves will be calm until we are on board ship and headed for England. Has there been no word on an earlier passage?"

"No. Still tomorrow evening. If something changes, I'll be sure to let you know." Callie hefted the tray. "Can I set this down there?"

Letty's arm shifted slightly, blocking her papers. "Would you mind placing it at the bedside? I'd like to finish these notes."

"What are you writing?" Callie asked as she made room for the tray. She'd caught a quick glimpse and could see that it looked like letters.

"Just a few notes. Things that I don't want to forget when I have to answer questions."

Callie heard the lie as loud as a bell. Just as she had when Letty was five, with icing smeared on her face and dribbled down her pinafore, and she swore that she had not touched the cakes.

Heart sinking, she fussed with the dishes a bit, then turned to see Letty standing—and no sign on the table of the papers she'd been working on.

Fear and doubt chilled her. Letty had a history of returning to an abusive situation. She'd lived with Hatch, that unstable madam, for months. Callie hoped it was true that she'd never been hired out, but she knew her sister had been abused. She'd even come to them at Half Moon House once, badly beaten. Callie had been devastated when, after she'd healed, Letty had gone back. The thought that she might be repeating such a mistake now filled her determination.

She turned back to the tray, careful to block her sister's view as she poured—and added a healthy dose of the laudanum to one cup. "If you don't mind, I'll pour a cup and join you. I could use a few moments off of my feet."

"Of course." Letty dropped onto the bed, while Callie dragged a chair over. "I know this was all a scheme to get close to me and Marstoke—and quite a brilliant one—but I must say, you play this role brilliantly."

"Psssht. I've merely been pretending to be Mother." She handed Callie her cup and silently asked for her mother's forgiveness.

But were those tears welling in the girl's eyes?

"She would be so proud of you," Letty whispered. Suddenly, her chin lifted. "And I swear, I will do something to make her proud of me, as well."

"She would be proud of your plans to turn everything around," Callie told her. "She loved you dearly." She raised her cup and took a long draught. Letty followed suit.

"Yes, she did," her sister answered after a few moments. "I wish I'd been wise enough to appreciate it."

Callie sat silently as they both drank. After a bit, she began to speak quietly, telling Letty about the cleaning solution receipts that she'd used here, and talking of the dishes her mother had taught her that had been put to such good use in the kitchens downstairs. As she'd hoped, Letty's attention wandered and her eyes grew heavy.

"Oh, how tired you must be, with all of the anxiety," she said quietly. "Let's get you ready for bed."

"Yes. I should sleep early." Letty's words blurred a bit. She allowed Callie to assist her into her nightrail. By the time she's been tucked into bed, she was nearly asleep. "Don't let me sleep late. I have to get up early," she mumbled.

"Of course," Callie hedged.

When she was sure Letty was dead to the world, Callie crossed over to the small table. A quick search and she found the notes her sister had been writing tucked underneath the cushion of the chair.

"Madame? Are you here?" Marie tapped the door from the attached sitting room and peeked in. "I beg pardon for the interruption, but could you unlock the linen cupboard? That new gentleman what just checked in—he came in cupshot and just cast up his accounts all over the bed."

Casually, Callie slid the papers under the dishes on the tray. She sighed heavily. "How rude he is—he didn't even have the decency to get drunk on our ale. Yes, of course I'll come."

Marie indicated the tray. "Would you like me to run that down to the kitchens?"

"What? And leave me with the linens?" Callie laughed quietly, came through to the sitting room and shut the door. She placed the tray on the low table next to the settee. "No, I'll just leave it here and fetch it later." She left the room with the maid, carefully locking it behind her.

She fretted the entire time she was helping Marie, and then just swallowed her impatience when young Tom came and asked for help getting Penrith and Rackham to their rooms.

"They're three sheets to the wind and fair on their way to passin' out over the table," he told her.

"Where is my husband?" she asked as she, Tom and Victoire stood in the doorway and stared across the taproom at the soused pair.

"Edgar says he had an errand."

"Very well," she sighed. "Victoire, you stay here and watch the taproom and the kitchens. Tom, we'll get these ones upstairs, but all we are going to do is get their boots off and get them onto the bed."

"Yes, *Madame*," they chorused.

She approached the table. "Monsieur Penrith?" she called in a lilting voice. "I believe you are ready to retire, yes?"

The man raised himself up. Beside him, Rackham merely opened one eye and shut it again.

"Ah, Madame Chaput, well met! You'll tell me, won't you?" He sat up and leaned back in his chair, running his hands across his belly. "It is a magnificent waistcoat, is it not?"

She nodded and got an arm around his shoulders. "Lovely, sir. Now, let's get you upstairs."

"Can't be schpected to abandon such artistry? Can I? I ask you!"

"No, of course not," she soothed. "On your feet, sir."

It took some time, but they got them both settled in. Callie sent Tom off to his own bed in the stables and headed at last for Letty's room.

She met Tru on the landing of the main stairway.

He looked . . . angry. As he used to in London.

"What is it?" Sudden panic knifed through her. "Word from Nardes? Is there trouble?"

"No, I haven't heard a peep from him, and I'm not sure that's a good thing or bad."

"There's not is a problem with our passage?"

He shook his head. "No. The packet leaves tomorrow evening. Unless Stoneacre shows up sooner with a ship of his own. I wouldn't put it past him."

Part of her longed for it. She was tempted to keep Letty groggy until they were bound for England—which she should hope to be as soon as was possible. But she dreaded it too. He hadn't said, but she doubted Tru meant to travel back with them. He would stay here and join Stoneacre in the chase for Marstoke. Even if the earl showed up with the marquess bound in chains, still their . . . association . . . would be at an end.

She should tell him her suspicions about Letty. About what she'd done to her sister. But what did she know, really except that the girl had been skulking about and had written some letters and lied about it?

Her shoulders slumped. It wasn't benign, whatever Letty was up to. She knew it. It never was, with Letty. But she didn't have any details yet. She had to read those notes, first.

But Letty was sound asleep and like to stay that way until late morning tomorrow. And this was their last night together.

"What is it?" His expression had changed to

concern and he stepped closer to wrap her in his arms. "What's bothering you?"

"Her. Them." She gestured from one end of the inn to the other. "All of it." She frowned. "It's nearly over. My part in this adventure, at least." She pressed her lips together in a grim smile. "This is our last night as a married couple."

He laughed, but there was no humor in it. "Believe me, I know. It's been weighing on me." He tightened his grip—and the forgotten package in her bodice crackled.

"What's this?" he asked.

"It's . . ." The words trailed away and she merely shrugged.

Frowning, he swept a finger into her bodice and fished it out. Holding it up, his face cleared. "A French letter?"

She blushed furiously. "I found it yesterday morning in the back of a drawer when we were cleaning a room. The seal on the envelope is still intact. I'd thought . . ."

He opened her hand, placed it back there, and folded his own over it all. "I'm honored that you would consider me."

"We were so busy in the dining room last night and you were asleep by the time I finished with Letty . . ."

Defiance and sudden determination rose up her breast. Want flared high. Letty wasn't going anywhere tonight. Neither was that tea tray.

There would be no more shared laughter, no exchange of confidences or healing acceptances. No more cooking for him or kissing him. No more tender impatience in bed or secret caresses under the night sky. This was it. Her last chance to snatch a bit of him for herself.

And by God, she meant to have it.

She pressed into his embrace. "Will you, Tru?"

He didn't answer. She could see the conflict in his face.

She moved against him. It wasn't a matter of wanting. She could feel him hardening against her. "I said, not so long ago on that ship, that I wanted to understand everything. And you were the one to tell that what we were doing was not everything. Well, now I want it. All of it. But only with you, Tru."

"Callie, I really should talk to Letty . . ."

"You can't. She's sound asleep. And I am right here."

"I'm not—"

She didn't let him finish. She held up the French letter and pressed the packet to his chest. "This will protect us, will it not? Keep us from . . . complications?"

"It will help," he admitted. "But Callie I'm not sure you are going to want me—"

Again, she cut him off. "I'm sure. You are the only man I will consider. Either you show me—or I'll likely never know."

He made a sound of protest. He was rock hard against her. She moved against him and he let out an anguished groan. Before he could protest again, she pulled his head down and kissed him.

"Now, Tru," she whispered. "Before anything else happens to keep you from me."

He buried his face in her hair and held still for a long moment.

Then, like their first night together, he swept her up and carried her to their room.

Without words, in perfect unison of thought and motion, they kissed and touched and removed their clothes. When they were both bare, he lifted her and placed her in the center of the bed. It was familiar now, and felt almost safe, coming alive in his arms. They each knew where to touch, how to please.

The difference this time was that Callie deliberately opened herself up. She allowed herself to be completely present and available, in a way that she had not done before. She showed him what he did to her, and let him see her own feelings of power and pleasure when he responded to her.

Never had she been so vulnerable with another person. Never had she wanted to. It was frightening . . and glorious.

The old instincts tried to kick in, shouted at her to cover up, deflect, protect herself. She locked them away. *Insanity!* they screamed as she closed the door upon them.

Perhaps. No, certainly. She was a little insane and more than a little drunk on desire. And he was beautiful and caring and she couldn't wait for him to take her.

When they were both in a frenzy, he paused to retrieve the French letter, smoothed it over his erection and tied the tiny ribbons in place. She lay back and took him in her arms, twisted and gasped as he readied her—and threw her head back as he pressed home.

It was . . . strange. A tiny bit uncomfortable.

Clearly he was in thrall to the experience. And as her body stretched and accommodated him, he began to move—and she understood. It *was* different. So much more. Together they moved and climbed. The barriers between them faded. They had one goal and together they reached for it.

Her breath hitched as he filled her more deeply than before. "I didn't know," she whispered. "I didn't know I could fly so high."

Something tender and fierce warred on his face. "I'll go with you," he answered.

So she let go and they soared together. And she knew that all would be well, because he had become her safe place to land.

Chapter Sixteen

I considered the generous offer. I was comfortable there. But a man came around one day when I'd gone to the local village for supplies. He was Lord M—'s lackey. He asked questions about me. It was clear he was trying to track where I'd gone after I'd been dumped.

--from the Journal of the infamous Miss Hestia Wright

Tru was quiet afterwards. Solicitous, to be sure, but he threw an arm across his brow and was quickly asleep. Callie curled up against him, reveling in his warmth and letting loose a few tears at the idea that this most beautiful encounter must be their last.

Anxiety pricked at her, however, and soon she eased from the bed to dress and slip down the hall to Letty's room.

She gathered up the tea tray, the notes still tucked underneath the dishes, and retreated to the privacy of her kitchen. Lighting a lamp, she took up the papers.

The first note came close to breaking her heart.

Frau Bosch,

This inn is not all that our gentlemen friends have purported it to be. They are spending all of their time here eating and drinking themselves into oblivion, while I feel as if I am receiving too much curious attention from the staff and other guests. As the villa is currently uninhabitable, I will journey to join his lordship. I am not so unwise as to state the destination in this missive, but I know the high regard he has for you and I feel sure that he has confided his location to you, as well. I ask that you meet me in the second town upon the road to that destination, where I will take a room in the largest inn and await you. From there we may travel together.

It bore no signature. Callie's hands shook as she sat at the scarred oak table. Biting her lip, she smoothed open the next note.

Callie,

Forgive me for telling you yet another lie, but this time I hope you will agree it is for a good cause. You see, I believe that there is a girl trapped on Marstoke's estate, locked in a small cottage in the woods. I haven't seen her, but I have heard the sound of her suffering. I cannot make my own escape without at least attempting to help her—and I refuse to let my folly place you in further danger. A dragon guards the girl, but I have a plan to lure her away. If I succeed, as you have done so many times, I will hide away with her and meet you tonight at the docks. If I fail, then know that I learned something at the last and I am happy to fail trying to be a fraction as good as you.

Now the sobs came in earnest. How terrible she felt, misjudging her sister. It was true that she had a lifetime of precedent, but this time Letty had indeed changed. It was Callie who was holding on to old prejudices.

Wiping her tears, she read both notes again. What were Letty's plans to rescue this unknown girl? She'd mumbled something about rising early, but Callie knew that the dose of laudanum she'd given her would keep her out cold until mid-morning at least.

They couldn't abandon another of Marstoke's victims. Callie would have to take her sister's place. She stood, intent on waking Tru and making plans.

But she nearly jumped out of her skin when the

pantry/passage door opened and Edgar stepped in.

"Oh, good heavens!" She clutched her chest. "You scared the wits out of me, Edgar."

"Excuse me, Madame. I did not mean it. I saw the light and I thought that perhaps the lady was up and about. We're to make deliveries today, but she never did come back with the note. Is she ready? The pretty lady with the room over the kitchen garden?"

Callie's mind was awhirl. "I'm afraid the lady has been detained. It seems that I will have to take her place."

He frowned. "Are you sure?"

"Yes."

"But what of the note?"

"I have it here." She raised her hand to show him the papers.

"Oh." Clearly that relieved his mind. "Well then, it must be fine."

"I'll just get dressed." She paused and asked casually. "How long shall we be gone, Edgar? How far is our destination?"

"Not far. I told the master that. We're to take the note to the villa where the lady stayed before. The one with the rats. But we must be careful, he says, as there are bad men there. Will he be leaving with us, since you go? Or is he still planning to follow?"

Callie paused mid-stride. Her gut clenched. "What was that you said, Edgar? About the master? Do you mean to say that Monsieur Chaput knows about this?"

"Aye." The big man nodded. "But he says the lady doesn't need to know he knows." He tilted his head. "Do *you* know if I should saddle the gelding for him?"

Tru knew. He knew Letty was headed back to Marstoke's villa this morning.

Did he know what she meant to do there?

Did it matter?

He'd kept it from her. He'd meant to let her sister walk back into that serpent's nest—and he wasn't going to stop her or give Callie the chance to dissuade her.

And she'd warned him. She'd told him more than once that Letty was her responsibility and hers alone.

Why? Her heart cried out the question. She'd just shared the most beautifully intimate moments of her life with him—and he'd been keeping this secret the whole time. All along he'd been meaning to shut her out of something so important—

And that must be the why of it, she realized. Because it all came back to Marstoke for him. He must believe that Letty was going to lead him to something that would be useful in the hunt for the marquess.

He'd put his own goals ahead of hers—and ahead of Letty's safety. He'd gone right back to his stance in London—find and capture Marstoke, no matter the harm or consequences to anyone else.

So much had happened between them—*everything* had happened between them—and yet it had changed nothing for him.

It broke her heart. Filled her with fury. Forged the fiercest determination to thwart him.

Except that she couldn't. Not entirely. She had changed, even if he had not. She understood now how important it was that Marstoke be stopped. But her calling was the same—she could not abandon this girl who needed help.

She would take up Letty's plan, find the captive girl and discover what she could. But she would be damned if she did it with Tru.

"No," she told Edgar. "Monsieur Chaput will not be joining us now. Let him follow later, if he wishes to."

While she did what she'd known she was going to

have to do all along—pick up the reins of her life again and move forward.

Alone.

* * *

The morning mist turned to tiny droplets on Callie's hair and on the borrowed gown and cloak she'd taken from Letty's room. She ignored the damp, and the cold, too. The first rays of the sun struck the haze, lighting it from within. She could just barely see Edgar's form as he knocked at the villa's front door. He waited patiently, and she did too, crouched behind one of the stone gateposts.

At last he gave in and returned to his waiting mare, note still in hand. He followed directions perfectly, never looking her way or indicating that he knew she was there as he rode away.

Callie scrambled back up the lane the way they had come. She crouched low, keeping close to the bushes. She stopped when she crossed over the lip of a rise and couldn't be seen from the house.

Edgar looked desolate, waiting for her. "No one answered," he mourned. "I couldn't deliver the note."

"Don't despair yet. The note mentions a cottage here on the estate, somewhere in the woods. Do you know it?"

'Yes." He frowned. "I delivered furniture there not long ago. But I wasn't allowed to carry it in. They had me leave it on the drive." He sounded disapproving. "Do you think I should try to make the delivery there?"

"The woman the note is meant for could well be there. It's worth a try."

He led them back along the lane, bordered by vineyards and fields. He took a turn just before an apple orchard bright and alive with blossoms. The road meandered, eventually passing the back side of the stables.

"No horses," Callie remarked. "But look." She

gestured toward a small building with one half of the door standing open. "See that little gig? We could make use of that. Could Rose pull it?"

"Easily." He sounded slightly insulted at the question.

"Good. Remember, there's a chance the lady the message is meant for will need you to take her into town. She'll likely want to head for a livery to hire transportation to take her further. Now, instead, you can suggest that you use the gig and take her where she needs to go."

"She would pay more, then, wouldn't she? More than just for a delivery."

"She should. And you can report back on her destination, which may be valuable information."

He nodded. "Fine, then."

They continued along the narrow road until Callie glimpsed a chimney through the trees. "You go on from here. I'll follow along and find a spot to hide and watch."

It was a much easier task here, with the small wood surrounding the place. The cottage was small and charming, made of timber and stone. Callie peeked between the split trunks of a tree and waited while Edgar repeated his performance.

Except this time, someone answered the door. A stout, middle-aged woman in a plain gown. She read the note and then stuck out a finger, shaking it at Edgar while she barked orders. She quickly moved to close the door, but Edgar stopped her, speaking for a moment.

The woman paused, her head turned back over her shoulder, as if contemplating something inside the house. She spoke sharply, then abruptly she nodded and went inside. Edgar turned away to lead Rose away.

Callie watched him come and regarded the cottage with a thoughtful eye.

That woman had certainly looked like someone that

Letty might label a dragon. She'd spoken to someone in the house. If her job was to guard the girl that Letty had heard, then it was doubtful that she'd been speaking to her—or planned to leave her alone.

So. Someone else was likely in there. But who?

Her lips pressed tight, she stared at the house a few more seconds, then spun on her heel to follow Edgar and his mare as they headed back toward the stables. She stamped her displeasure into the ground with every step.

The whole way out here, she'd thought of nothing but beating Tru at his own game. She'd fetch this girl out of harm's way and have her sitting in her kitchen, drinking tea before Tru even hauled himself out of bed. Now, however, things were looking a little more complicated.

Edgar was already hitching Rose to the gig when she trailed into the stable yard after him. "Edgar, could I have the heather blooms from Rose's mane?"

He looked up. "Why?"

"They'll make a good marker."

He thought a second, then nodded.

When he'd gently unbraided an armful, she thanked him, and clasped his hand when he would have turned away. "Do be careful. This woman is working with the dangerous men that Monsieur Chaput spoke of. Try not to anger her."

"I'll be careful." He frowned a little. "What will you do?"

She sighed. "I'll be careful too."

She was still utterly furious with Tru, but she'd been dealing with situations like these for a long time. She knew when to be cautious.

Bidding Edgar farewell, she headed back towards the corner where this lane met the main road through the estate. A quarter of an hour later, she stood back, examining the carefully placed and anchored pile of heather blooms with a critical eye.

If Tru came this way, he should notice it. Whether he would catch the significance of it and stop—well, that was still to be seen.

She left her marker and headed back to the cottage, ducking into the woods when Edgar came by with Letty's dragon in the gig. When they had passed, she returned to the spot by the split tree—and waited.

She knew how to be patient. Near a quarter hour she watched and listened, but there was no change in the quiet surrounding the place. She moved then, keeping to the trees and circling around to the back of the house.

Quietly now.

The back of the cottage was not nearly so picturesque as the front. A few chickens scratched in an untended garden bed. Empty kegs and boxes were stacked in a corner. As she drew slowly closer, she noticed the butts of cigarillos scattered near the kitchen door.

Any activity this early would likely be centered there, around the kitchen. She studied the windows, imagining the layout. The windows on the third floor were long and deep, likely affording a pretty view of the forest. Those were probably the main bedrooms. A small balcony graced the room on the corner, furthest from the kitchens. The master bedroom, in all likelihood.

Would the girl be ensconced there? Was she a prisoner or a guest? There was no way for Callie to know, but she surely must be in one of the bedrooms.

She approached the windows on the ground beneath that room and peered in to see a desk and bookshelves. A study. The window slid up without noise or protest and she slipped inside.

A wraith, she moved through the house, knife in hand, entering the main passage and taking the main stairway up and away from the faint noises drifting from the kitchen.

She climbed steadily, quietly, keeping to the wall and testing each step as she went. The slam of a door below made her jump and she began to hurry. On the third floor she crossed to the largest bedroom she'd selected from outside.

The door was not locked. She turned the knob slowly and peeked inside.

A fire, burning low. A table set with last night's dinner. A glass door onto the balcony behind it and across the room, a closed door to an adjoining room. A rumpled bed and a slight figure in it, fast asleep.

Her heart sank as her brain registered what she'd seen and her gaze went back to the table. It had been set for two.

Her heart rate ratcheted. She eased inside and followed the sound of soft, easy breathing to the bed. A spill of golden hair lay across the pillows.

A woman, barely more than a girl. Pretty and innocent looking, she slept wrapped around a pillow pulled tight to her chest.

Callie listened carefully for the sound of anyone else nearby, then stashed her knife in her cloak pocket. She reached for the girl. In one motion she placed one hand over her mouth and gently shook her shoulder with the other.

The girl came alert instantly, her eyes wide. They stared at each other. Callie pursed her lips and pressed a finger to them. The girl nodded. She removed the hand over her mouth.

The girl raised her head.

Callie recoiled. The other side of her face was bruised and swollen. Her right eye was a horrid shade of red. She mouthed one, silent but urgent word.

Run!

Behind Callie came a soft click from the adjoining

doorway. She straightened. A high-pitched hum sent a shiver down her spine. And then a horribly familiar voice broke the silence.

"Well, well. What have we here?"

Chapter Seventeen

I knew then I could not stay. I was vulnerable.
Lord M— could take me again, at any time, lock me up
again and who would stop him? Not gentle Pearl.

--from the Journal of the infamous Miss Hestia Wright

True awoke with a start. Rolling over, he reached for Callie and surged upright when he found her gone.

What time was it?

The sky still wore that faint grey that comes before the dawn. Not too late, then. He braced his hands on the window frame and peered out towards the stables.

All lay still and dark. If Callie was up and in the kitchens, surely Edgar should be astir in the stables?

Dressing quickly, he hurried downstairs. His gut clenched when he found the kitchen dark and empty. With rising alarm, he raced outside.

Gone. No sign of Edgar, his mare, or Callie. Young Tom slept peacefully in his bunk and the gelding he'd brought back from the livery last night was in its stall.

He turned on his heel and raced back into the inn and upstairs.

Letty's door was locked. After a frustrating search, he found Callie's keys and let himself in to find Letty asleep as well. Soundly. Try as he might, he could not get her completely awake.

Drugged.

And the others gone. Sick dread washed over him.

Callie knew. Somehow she'd discovered Letty's intent. She'd gone in her sister's place. He knew it in his bones. It sounded exactly like something Callie would do.

The question was—did she know Tru's part in it?

Heading back to the stables at a run, he sincerely hoped not. In the raw early light, he understood anew what a betrayal that would feel like to her.

His own impulses didn't hold up well to a second viewing, either. Especially stark was the one he hadn't even yet acknowledged—his burning need to play a major part in taking Marstoke back.

He'd tried to bury it. Worked to ignore the relentless pricking of his frustration. He'd told himself that it didn't matter who brought the villain to justice, as long as it happened.

But it was true, some deeply dark part of himself needed the distinction. Needed to show the world that he may once have been naive and foolish, but he'd won in the end.

He'd placed that selfish need ahead of Callie's— and ahead of Letty Robbins' safety.

Damnation! He had no time for guilt and self-flagellation. He had to get out to that villa. Hurriedly saddling his mount, he rushed out of the courtyard and into the nearly empty city streets at a gallop.

He pushed the horse hard and they made good time, but the animal was winded by the time they reached the estate. He had to slow down as they traveled the road that led through the estate fields to the villa.

It was likely the only reason he noticed the clump of blooming purple heather beneath an apple tree.

It immediately sent him back to that night beneath the stars, when Callie had responded to his touch so sweetly, and peered so dangerously close to the worst part of him.

But there was no heather in any other spot along this road. And that hadn't looked like a natural configuration. He reined in and turned back.

Beneath the mound of fragrant blossoms he found a

note anchored by a rock. Letty had written it to Callie. He read it quickly, looked down the narrow lane that branched off from the road—and set off as quick as his mount could take him.

* * *

Callie turned. The Marquess of Marstoke, wearing only breeches and a loose linen shirt, cast a benevolent smile upon her and wiped his face with a towel.

Marstoke was back. And they'd had neither word nor warning. Callie sent up silent thanks that it hadn't been Letty to find him here—but her own situation did not look good.

The younger man beside him held a razor. One finger absently trailed along the flat part of the blade as he looked Callie over. "The clothes are right," he drawled. "But it's the wrong girl."

Handing him the towel, Marstoke stepped into the room. "Do you not know who our unexpected guest is, Anselm?"

"Should I?"

Annoyance flashed across Marstoke's face for the briefest of moments. "Indeed you should."

Callie stood rigid while the marquess stepped close and took her hand. Oh, God in Heaven, but she'd made a colossal mistake leaving that marker for Tru. She had to get away from here, and quickly. She didn't want to think about Tru arriving in this secluded spot, facing the man he so despised. They were outnumbered and without reinforcements. Nothing good could come of that scenario.

Bowing low, Marstoke kept his gaze fastened on her bosom. "This is Miss Grant, Hestia's right-hand whore. Now, what she is doing here? That does seem to be the question." He glanced from Callie to the girl in the bed and back again.

Neither answered him.

"I'd like to know to what we owe the pleasure of this intrusion, Miss Grant." He hitched his head in the direction of the younger girl. "I know that this one did not send word to Half Moon House, looking for help."

"No, my lord!" The girl's words were slurred due to the swelling in her face.

"Neither did Hestia send you alone into my den." Marstoke folded his arms. "Who has come with you?"

Still, Callie said nothing. Her mind was racing, trying out one option after another, looking for one that ended up with her alive, the girl free and all before Tru came charging in after them.

The marquess eyed her thoughtfully. "This smells of Stoneacre. Is that interfering wretch of an earl with you?" He walked around her, thinking, then reached out to pat her sides, smiling evilly as he found the knife in her pocket. Pulling it out, he handed it to the other man, then snapped his fingers. "Go. Search the house."

The man turned on his heel and left at once.

"Come, now." The marquess wore a deep scowl now. He was thinking as fast as she was. Callie could almost see the gears in his brain spinning. "What has brought this on? It could not be Penrith's damned valet—it's too soon for you to have made it here, surely, had you gained your information from him."

Both girls jumped as he suddenly exploded into motion, striking the bedpost a massive blow with both hands and rocking the bed back a foot or so. "Damn the fool and his blasted waistcoats!"

The girl scrambled down and retreated to the far corner of the room.

The marquess paced to the balcony door and back, growing quieter with each step. "No. Here you are, in borrowed plumes, no less. This reeks of something else entirely. But what?" He ended up before her again. "Tell me what it is. I bought those clothes for another girl. You fill them out admirably, but how did you come by them? What do you know of her?"

Callie looked down. This was as bad a spot as she'd ever been in. Marstoke was a violent, dangerous man. She still had a knife tucked in her garter and a few minutes to face him alone, but defeating him would not be easy. Still, she had to try.

He must have seen it in her face. "It would be best not to consider it," the marquess said with a snort. He grabbed her arm, gripping it painfully. "Bring that chair over here." He barked the order to the other girl. "And fetch me several of your stockings."

The blonde scrambled to do his bidding, but she'd only just got the chair into position when the young man returned.

"The house is clear, but someone is coming in. I was checking the attics and caught sight of them at the top of the far rise."

"Penrith and Rockham with the traveling carriage?"

"No, sir. A single rider."

Cursing, Marstoke pulled her close. "Come on. Let us go see who else is arriving without an invitation."

He pulled her from the room and down the hall toward the stairway. Beyond the landing was an empty space facing the front of the house. Light streamed in through a large window.

Not Tru. Please, let it be anyone else.

They all stared out. Callie could see nothing at first, but after a moment she saw a horse and rider emerge from the covering canopy of the wood. Her heart sank. It was him. She stiffened her knees. Kept her spine rigid. She could not, must not, allow Marstoke to see her anxiety.

Below, Tru rode right up to the cottage, as brazen as you please, as if he'd been invited to tea. He didn't know Marstoke was here, but he must have found the letter she'd left. He'd know that something was not right. What was he planning?

"Who is that?" Marstoke pressed closer to the window, watching as Tru rode closer.

"I don't know," his flunkie answered.

"Of course you don't," the marquess spat back. "He looks familiar." He yanked Callie closer to the glass. "Who is it?"

Her mind spun. What could he be thinking? He wore his slouched hat, which helped to obscure his features a little, and he moved casually, as if he'd not a care in the world and no clue he was being observed. Dismounting, he hitched his horse.

"Has he come for you?" Marstoke demanded. "Who is he?"

"I think . . ." Callie paused. "I think . . . at least . . . He looks like Monsieur Chaput, an innkeeper in town."

"No. No, that's not it." He peered down, eyes narrowed in concentration, while Callie tried desperately to come up with a plan to avert the coming disaster.

Tru disappeared beneath them as he stepped up to the door.

Suddenly Marstoke's head flew back. Revelation shone on his face. "The innkeeper? Is that who he looks like, indeed?"

A knock sounded below.

The marquess stared ahead until another pounding sounded on the door. "Come. We must prepare for our visitor. Here is what we will do . . ."

* * *

Tru knocked several times, with no result. The place lay deadly still. He'd left the horse a ways back and circled the place on foot before riding in, so he knew the back was just as quiet. It might have been a pretty little spot, were it not for the atmosphere. It felt as if the structure itself breathed silently, waiting.

Enough foolishness. Pulling out his pistol, he turned the latch.

The door opened on silent hinges. The small entry hall lay empty. A quick check through the public rooms on this floor revealed the same state of things. He stood at the foot of the stairway and debated—kitchen or top floors?

Up.

The second floor was as empty as the first. He'd just finished scouting when something sounded above him. A thud, slight and muffled.

He took to the stairs again, pistol at the ready. He hadn't reached the next landing yet when someone spoke.

"I've another one ready, sir. Would you like me to tie it this time?" A male voice, coming from behind a slightly open door on the left.

He waited, but couldn't hear a distinct answer.

"The scarlet waistcoat, my lord? Or the embroidered grey?"

Tru froze. *My lord?* The words rang repeatedly in his head. Had Marstoke returned? He straightened, riding a fierce wave of triumph. This was it. The end of his exile. Fate had given him another chance. He could capture Marstoke and end this nightmare at last.

He gripped the pistol tighter with one hand and eased his knife from his boot with the other—only to pause when another noise came from the room on the opposite side of the landing above. A quiet moan. A thump, then a short, sharp cry.

Oh, hell and damnation. It was a woman's cry. Was it Callie being held in there? Or the young girl Letty had wanted to help?

He crouched down, right where he was. His temple

started to throb. Triumph drained, turning quickly to dread reality.

Had he forgotten? This was Marstoke he faced. The man who orchestrated violence and upheaval, small and large, in the name of the *game* to which he'd dedicated his life.

Tru felt suddenly ill with the force of his fury. This wasn't the end. Nothing could be taken at face value when he dealt with the marquess. He'd been presented with a choice. It was his turn to make a move in Marstoke's bloody, benighted game.

He began to back down the stairs. He'd be damned if he chose either option presented to him. Did Marstoke think he'd learned nothing in their dealings so far? Damn it all to hell and back, but he was going to forge his own path through this mess.

When he reached the landing, he turned down the right passage, heading straight for the room on the end. A small, private parlor, it had a window that opened onto the back of the house. He eased it open and looked up.

Yes. The struts supporting the balcony above were there, not quite in reach. He climbed onto the window frame, balanced for a second, and jumped.

* * *

Her arm was going to break.

They stood behind the slightly open door, she and Marstoke. He twisted her arm higher behind her back. Callie clenched her teeth, but did as he wished and let loose a quiet whimper. It did no good to resist. She'd done so a minute ago, refusing to make a sound, and he'd merely called the other girl over. The vile man had been satisfied with the cry of pain that one had let out when he struck her hard across her already injured face.

The girl had been knocked to the ground, but she'd scrambled back up and retreated to the bed, where she sat with the covers pulled up to her chin.

Callie gasped when Marstoke pulled her arm high again.

"Louder," he whispered. "We must make sure your *innkeeper* knows you are here."

They waited in silence for a few moments, but there no sound came from outside.

"Which choice will he make?" Marstoke whispered in her ear. "Not charging to your rescue, is he? Perhaps I was mistaken, after all."

They waited some more, all of them alive with tension and watching the door with anxiety, even the girl in the bed.

"No signal from Anselm, either," Marstoke mused. "Perhaps I did see something that wasn't there." He put his face close to Callie's and sent a wash of slightly sour breath over her. "Or perhaps he just doesn't care what happens to you."

"Or perhaps he merely changed the rules of the game to suit himself."

Callie's heart sank.

Tru stood in the balcony doorway, striking and tall, a heroic shadow against the bright morning sun. He had a pistol in his hand and an almost pained smile of pure determination on his face. "Let go of the girl."

Marstoke came abruptly alive. There was no other way to describe it. Held as she was against him, she could feel it. His posture shifted along with his focus. She felt his breath quicken, just the smallest bit. All along her back she felt his muscles tighten. She looked up, and then away from the light of anticipation and enjoyment in his face. His game was afoot. "I knew it was you," he breathed.

Tru merely waved the pistol, encouraging the marquess to move away from Callie.

"We've played against each other long enough for you to know that I am not a fool. I'm keeping this one."

Marstoke let Callie's arm fall and she gasped at the pain as the blood rushed back in. "She'll be incredibly valuable as I take the level of play to the next phase." He gripped her upper arm with one hand and casually reached out for the razor Anselm had left behind with the other.

Tru stepped into the room. "You know, I'd far prefer to take you back in chains. It fair warms my gullet to think of you in Newgate. And imagining you facing a trial of your peers lulls me to sleep at night. Think of the broadsheets that will coat London. They'll denude entire forests, printing all the caricatures of you and your nefarious crimes. How many women will line the halls of Parliament, gather in the streets outside, waiting for you to pay for your crimes?" He sighed. "It would pain me to give all of that up, I tell you." He shrugged, then raised the pistol. "But I won't mourn overmuch, I suppose, if I get to carry you back to England in a pine box."

He'd touched a nerve. Callie felt it in the tension all along Marstoke's tightening frame. But the marquess kept his tone light. "You fascinate me, Lord Truitt. You always have. Even more than usual, in the last months. Because you're intelligent enough to understand what a colossal fool you've been. How do you bear that burden, when you wake up to it every morning?"

Tru was still advancing into the room. "Let her go."

"No. You had potential, I'll give you that. But you've proven that you'll never be a worthy player. And you have been a constant irritant, I'll admit. So I won't be letting you live, I'm afraid." He stepped backwards, tugging Callie with him. "It's time we were going."

"Wait. My lord! Wait!" The girl cast aside her covers and scrambled to the end of the bed.

He didn't even look her way.

Callie's attention was locked on Tru. He stood in the middle of the room, a pillar of resolution. She didn't know how Marstoke was not shaking in fear.

She was. Because she had the sudden certain feeling that there was no scenario in which all three of them could survive.

Tru had not once looked her way. It was the smart, strategic move. She knew it was true. And yet, she wished she could tell him somehow, without words, how sorry she was. Sorry she wasn't more help. Sorry she'd left that marker pointing him here. Sorry she'd let herself get so entangled with him that she'd let hurt and betrayal dictate her actions and put them both in danger.

Marstoke reached behind him to open the door.

It all happened so quickly then.

The marquess pulled Callie in front of him, a human shield to guard him as he left the room. Tru stepped forward, his pistol braced to take the shot. The girl perched on the end of the bed launched herself, crashing into Tru just as the pistol discharged.

Callie flinched away as the doorframe beside her exploded. The door swung open and Anselm appeared, just outside, a pistol of his own held out in shaking hands. "Sir. The carriage is here."

Marstoke reached out and shoved the man forward, toward Tru, who struggled to extract himself from the girl.

"Kill him," he ordered.

The pistol shook even harder. "But sir," the other man whispered. "He's the brother of a Duke."

"And you are the bastard son of a marquess! Now *shoot* him!"

The pistol lowered. "This is not the same. He's not even standing. His brother would hunt me down and kill me like a dog."

"You are a disappointment, Anselm." Marstoke shoved Callie at the man and snatched the pistol himself. "What good are you to me if you can only hurt a defenseless girl? Now get that one down to the carriage."

He spun around and aimed at Tru just as he climbed to this feet. "I wish I had the time to enjoy this, but I'll be satisfied with just removing the thorn from my side."

"No!" Callie gasped. Anselm had a hold of both of her arms, but an image flashed in her head suddenly. Tru's patient lessons on the ship. She braced herself on her captor, bent her leg and kicked out with all her strength, rage and determination, striking Marstoke squarely on the back of his knee.

He toppled forward. The gun roared. And inside the room, Tru jerked back, then sank slowly to the floor once more.

Chapter Eighteen

I needed status, notoriety. I needed Power. But how to obtain it? Ruined as I was, no Great Man would marry me. What could I do? I moaned to Pearl that I was fit now to be nothing but a whore.

--from the Journal of the infamous Miss Hestia Wright

Chaos reigned on the small gravel courtyard in front of the cottage. A large, well-appointed traveling carriage was parked there. The dragon was back, barking out orders to Penrith and Rackham as they strapped luggage to the top. Anselm was talking, explaining himself endlessly, though no one was listening.

Callie, too numb to fight his continued hold on her, saw it all through a blur of tears.

Was Tru dead? Had Marstoke killed him with that shot? Was he finishing him off even now? The marquess hadn't come down with them. Neither had the blonde. She stared listlessly up at the house, unable to do more than wipe at the tears streaming down her face.

The bickering continued. None of it penetrated the cloak of shock and grief wrapped around her like a bubble.

"Madame? Madame Chaput?" Penrith's surprised voice finally struck her.

"That is not her name," Anselm spat. "You idiots let those innkeepers make fools of you."

Rackham paused to listen now.

"They are working with Stoneacre."

The pair of lordlings exchanged worried looks.

Marstoke exited the cottage, now immaculately dressed. "Stop standing about and finish quickly. Who knows who else will show up, or when. Let's get on the road." He stopped suddenly. "Where is the girl?"

"Inside," Penrith answered. "She is still drowsy. It appears she was drugged."

"Was she?" Marstoke turned to look Callie over, brow raised. "Get this one in the carriage with her."

"But sir," Rackham protested. "There is no room. As it is, Anselm will have to be left behind."

"I, left behind?" Anselm demanded, outraged. "Do not think you can replace me, sir, just because you have a set of semi-valuable breeding stones." In his excitement, he let one of Callie's arms go.

She came awake, suddenly. Pushed the fog of grief and uncertainty away, though she took care to continue to hang limp and listless. He held her only by her left arm now, and beneath her right garter was tucked her knife. And Letty was in that carriage.

They all stilled as a shout rang out. It echoed strangely, until she realized it was coming from the back of the house.

"My lord! Don't leave me!" The poor, deluded blonde girl must be standing on the balcony, yelling for all she was worth. "Let me out! Take me with you! Don't leave me here, locked in with this dead man!"

Dead man. Dead man. Dead man. The words echoed, pinging about Callie's chest, breaking her heart, loosening her fear and fury, setting her free from all normal conventions and constraints.

They'd all turned toward the house to listen as the shouting continued. Anselm's grip was slack. Marstoke stood mere steps away.

It would be so easy. He was vulnerable and it would only take one simple thrust. One strike and she'd rid the world of a great evil. Letty would be free. Hestia would be free. The Prince Regent and the country would be safe from his machinations. No more young girls would be abused, abandoned or twisted like that sad girl upstairs.

She did not stop to consider it any further. She pulled up her skirts, grabbed her knife, yanked away from Anselm and swung.

Time stood still and sunlight flashed off the blade.

At the last second, just before the knife plunged into his back, Penrith pulled Marstoke clear. Her former guest stared at her in shock. She glared back in frustrated fury.

"*Madame Chaput*," he said in disapproval and disbelief.

Ignoring him, she raced for the carriage door. Pulling it open, she found Letty curled on a bench.

"Letty," she whispered. She shook her sister, trying to wake her.

Letty's eyes fluttered.

"I love you, Letty." She had to tell her one last time, before they killed her.

Letty roused, barely. "Callie?"

Rough hands pulled away from the coach. Marstoke stared down at her, his towering glower of rage fading into interest.

"You see?" Rackham stabbed a finger at her. "You cannot bring her along. She nearly stabbed you in the back! We would all have to watch ourselves without ceasing, be on our guard every minute of the day until we reached London."

Callie looked up. They were going back to England?

"That is enough out of you, you fool," Marstoke snapped.

The dragon spoke up from the back of the coach. "You only need one girl," she said calmly. "The other one knows more."

"And might still be useful," Marstoke said. He growled in frustration. "Damn it, but I want this one, too.

So many uses for her . . ." He shook his head. "She's wily. I'm afraid she might be too much for you alone," he said to the woman.

Glancing from one of the men to the other, he struck the coach with a fisted hand. "She puts you all to shame. Not one of you to be completely trusted! How has this come to pass? Why am I surrounded by weaklings and hindered by something so simple as a lack of traveling space!"

He stared upward for long moments, not moving, but holding her tight.

Suddenly he exploded into motion. "Anselm, you will ride up with the driver. Penrith, you will stand up in the back where the footman should ride. Get it ready to go. Now." He strode toward the house, dragging Callie with him. When they reached the front stoop, he turned her to face him.

"Lord Truitt Russell is dead."

She started to shiver. How was she to survive the jagged pain tearing a path through her chest?

"I want you to tell the Duke of Aldmere that I killed his brother."

She bowed her head to hide the hate that blazed in her. It quivered under her skin, making her shiver even more violently. When she looked back up, he was glancing in contemplation between her and the coach.

"Do you know what I like?" he said casually.

She bit back several caustic, likely unwise, responses.

"I like secrets. Other people's secrets. Most people never know what real power is, do you realize that? It's far less to do with armies and artillery than it is to do with knowledge. It's standing in a crowded room of diplomats and dignitaries and seeing the truth beneath the glittering surface. It's truly knowing the people around you, and the people who command. Understanding all the hidden currents and connections." He sucked in a deep breath. "I'm going to let you live, Miss Grant—and I am going to learn all of your secrets." He smiled then, and Callie knew that it was possible for true malice to exist in the world. "And you are going to wish that I hadn't."

Over at the carriage, the luggage had been tied on. Everyone was aboard, save for Penrith, who waved the marquess over.

Marstoke leaned close. "One last thing. I want you to tell Hestia Wright that I know *her* secret." He placed his hands on both of Callie's shoulders and pushed. She went sprawling over the step and into the gravel. "And she, too, is going to wish I didn't," he said, walking away.

As the carriage pulled out, she sat up and watched it go. She started to call out after it, but only a gasp emerged. She choked on it. And then the first sob caught her, squeezing her chest.

She sat, palms stinging, in the gravel. And she cried.

* * *

Tru woke to stabbing pain in his chest and sobbing in his ear.

"He said you were dead. He said you were dead."

He swam up through a haze, trying to reach the surface, where Callie bent over him, tears streaming down her face.

"Am I dead?" he asked thickly. Why couldn't he remember?

That stopped the tears. She stopped doing whatever she'd been doing to his chest, which was a relief, because it hurt. She gave him a dark look. "Not yet."

That was good. It must not be so serious, if she could resort to bitter irony.

She bent close again and the pain returned.

Eventually he came awake enough to realize she was trying to rip the shirt from him. He groaned louder than the tearing sound as she succeeded.

She shook her head. "You have the damndest luck. The way you bled, it looked like you'd been shot through the heart." It felt like she stabbed him with a hot poker when she lifted his arm, even though she was being careful. "The bullet went wide and passed through your muscle and out underneath your arm." She tsked. "It's going to hurt like the devil while it heals."

It hurt like the devil now. Yet he felt strangely . . . disconnected. He watched her sit back with her hands on her knees. Vaguely, he thought about summoning the strength to sit up.

He took a sudden leap a little closer to reality. "Where's Marstoke?"

Her face closed. "Gone."

"And the girl?"

"The blonde, you mean?" Her expression didn't change. "She's sobbing her heart out in the dressing room. I locked her in there. She needs more help than I can give her right now." She stood and headed for the door.

"Wait." He pushed himself up on an elbow and instantly regretted it. "Where are you going?"

"For supplies." She detoured suddenly and stopped at the bedside table to pour a glass of water. "Drink that. You've lost a lot of blood."

He wanted something stronger than water, damn it all. He struggled to sit up while she was gone, using his good arm to prop himself up against the bed. He heaved a sigh as he leaned back, and then another as he started to bleed again.

Callie came back, her arms full, but he focused on the bottle of brandy dangling from her fingers. "Yes, I'll take that, if you please."

"Take a good swig or two. There's another, but I couldn't carry both." She busied herself setting out her supplies. After a moment she took the brandy back and gave him a leather strap in its place. "Here. You'll want to bite on this."

He eyed it with trepidation. "What are you going to do?"

"What needs done." Grimly, she tore a strip from a linen sheet. "It's not going to be pleasant."

It wasn't. But near an hour later he'd had both sides of his wound doused in fine French brandy and his left side wrapped as tight as an Egyptian mummy. The whole side burned, like he was a haunch left unturned over a high fire, but he had the start of a fine drunk going, so he hoped to care less for it, very soon.

Heaving a tired sigh, Callie shoved all of her materials out of the way and leaned back against the bed beside him. She didn't say a word, but sat breathing deeply.

She felt warm against him. He closed his eyes and savored the feel of her. He knew there was much to discuss and more to worry about, but he thought he'd give himself a few minutes before he tackled it.

"It's the look of him that fools you at first, isn't it? He looks like someone's favorite uncle. Almost affable, when he smiles and the heavy lines on his face shift. You think he's going to be kind to you. Friendly. And then something happens and you see the truth of it in his eyes."

He knew exactly what she was talking about.

She heaved a great sigh. "Now, my father is the opposite. He wears his sour, mean-hearted disposition all over him." She shrugged. "At least he did, the one time I've seen him face to face as an adult."

Tru got his mouth to work. "What happened?"

He didn't think she was going to answer, she took

so long about it. "My mother had passed away. Letty and I no longer had a place in the house where we'd grown up. She was working as an understudy and opera dancer and I had already begun my work with Hestia." She closed her eyes. "I had a grand idea. I wanted to run my own house, a companion to Half Moon House. In honor of my mother, I wanted to help the girls who found themselves with child and nowhere to turn. Crescent House, I was going to call it."

"You told him about it?"

"Yes. My mother kept that house immaculately for years. She waited on him and his guests when he was in residence. He never paid her a sou, past our room and board. Never bought me so much as a pair of shoes. My mother never stopped working. She wouldn't use the household money to provide for us. She sold her simples and solutions to get us what we needed." She looked at him. "Other royal by blows move in Society or they are given a position or a living. I didn't think that a little, out of the way house was too much to ask for."

"It wasn't." He thought he might have slurred his answer. But she must have understood.

"Apparently it was. He laughed at me. Told me I was a fool to think I could change anything. That he wasn't going to let me wait hand and foot on a bunch of pregnant harlots. I was pretty enough, he said, that he might be able to find me a husband. And that would be the end of it."

"Bloody bastard."

"I agree. I've heard similar taunts over the years. Men telling me to find my place. To stop interfering in the natural order of things." She turned away. "I thought you were different."

That hurt nearly as much as getting shot. The edges of his vision faded and went a bit grey. He couldn't answer. His tongue was huge and he was thirsty again, and even his good arm didn't seem inclined to obey him.

Beside him, Callie sniffed. He turned and realized she was quietly crying again. With Herculean effort, he lifted his good hand and let it fall over hers.

Quickly, she pulled away and wiped her face. Rolling away from him, she got to her knees, and then her feet.

"Goodbye, Tru." Just a breath, really, more than words. He wondered if he had been supposed to hear it.

"Goodbye?" he repeated dumbly.

"I'll send Edgar back for you. I assume he's fine, although I thought I'd sent him and that dragon-lady halfway to Rennes. She turned back up here, though." She wiped her hands on a leftover piece of linen. "Drink the water, if you please, not the brandy. At least until Edgar gets you safely back to the inn."

He marshaled his thoughts, pushed the grey away and pushed himself straighter. "Where are you going? And what are you talking about? Dragon-lady?" He stared at her stricken face. "What did I miss?"

"I almost killed him. Marstoke." Her lip began to quiver. "But I missed."

She shocked him right into clarity. "Good God, Callie. Tell me. All of it."

She did, sitting again and growing more agitated as she talked. He listened in horror.

"And now here we are," she said, wiping her face. "And you are *not* dead."

"Here we are," he repeated, still absorbing the blow he'd deserved and all the implications of what she'd told him. "And you can't seem to stop crying."

"I'll stop now that I'm able to do something." She spoke shortly. She started to rise again. "Which is why I'm leaving."

"Leaving?" He struggled to his feet, made awkward by booze and blood loss. "You're going without me?"

"Yes. I'm going after Letty. If I hurry I could still make that packet tonight." She paused. "And you? You have an advantage. Marstoke believes you dead. Use it, if you can."

"But, you can't mean to leave me here?"

"I *am* leaving you here, Tru. It's time. Time we went our separate ways." She headed for the door.

"Wait. Callie." The anger on her face stunned him, along with the resentment showing in the stiff lines of her body. "What exactly is happening here?"

She turned. "This was a mistake." She gestured between them. "It's over now, though. I wish you luck in the your pursuit of Marstoke."

"A mistake?" he asked quietly. Pain, exhaustion and brandy had loosened his tongue. "What we did together, created together—was not a mistake."

She pulled herself straight. "It was for me."

He'd never known her to be cruel before. There was something deep going on here.

"Then I failed you."

"Failed me?" Her laughter rang out, at home with the bitter mood of the room, before she turned and walked to the balcony door. She didn't stare out at the woods for long. She turned to face him squarely, safe from a distance. "You didn't fail me. You ruined me."

Perhaps he'd gone fuzzier than he thought. "Ruined you? Nobody here knows your real name. Nobody from England knows anything of what we got up to. Not Stoneacre, not Hestia, not even—"

"Pssht." She cut him off. "Did you ever listen to me? As if I give two damns for what people think." She snapped her fingers. "I'm talking about what you did to *me*."

At a loss, he merely stared at her.

"What am I supposed to do with myself now? With this—" She pointed to her head. "Or this—" She cupped her breasts. "Or worst of all, this?" She made a fist and thumped her chest, where her heart beat. "You've ruined me because you changed me. And it's as much my fault as yours, for I allowed it. I *asked* for it, thinking it wouldn't touch me. And yet, I let it happen."

Shaking her head, she started to pace. "I shouldn't have asked. I was fine before."

"You were alone before." The words came out as soft as a butterfly's wings, and he felt as fragile.

"I'm alone now," she snapped. "Don't let half a bottle of French brandy tell you anything different, Lord Truitt Russell! We both knew it was at an end. And you never planned to take it any further. You know you did not, or you would have told me about Letty's plans when you discovered them. You would not have cut me out of the only reason I came here and took part in this mess!" She opened her mouth to say more, but cut herself off and turned away.

He was grateful. There were plenty more words she could throw at him, more than enough blame to share between them. He held out a hand. "Callie, I'm sorry. It was wrong. And worse, I knew it was wrong, even as I planned it."

Another tear slipped down her cheek. Such a small, shining drop—and yet the weight of it crushed him.

He shook his head. "I don't know how to explain it. My feelings for you have been such a whirlwind."

She made a harsh noise of agitation.

"When I first learned you were coming along on this mission, I was irritated. All I wanted to do was to find Marstoke, to put away my mistakes, hide from them and make them disappear, just as I've been doing forever. And I thought you would stand in the way. That I might never be able to look in the mirror again."

She looked as if she might say something, but thought better of it.

"Then I got to know you a bit. I learned to respect you, to like you. And I thought, even as I feared I might never change the world's opinion of me, that I would feel better, that it might go easier, if I started with you."

She closed her eyes.

"And then we . . . grew closer. We shared our stories, bits of ourselves. You began to look clear-eyed and close—to really see my flaws and foibles, as you put it. I panicked. How long could it be before you discovered the awful truth? That there's really nothing to me." He hung his head. "Little more than doubt and uncertainty behind the shell of flippant charm, money and a good family name. I couldn't let it happen. If you saw the truth, then everyone might."

He swallowed and raised his head. The least he could do was to meet her gaze as he told her the sad truth. "I had to choose quickly—and I chose the path that led me closer to Marstoke—and away from you."

"You chose poorly." Blunt to the end. And the amusing thing was, he liked her that way. "For it led you straight to the man—and look at the result." She waved a hand.

Wiping her eyes once more, she walked to the door, pausing to look at the splintered spot where his bullet had hit. "I wish you luck, for we've made things worse." She looked back at him. "I *will* find Letty and free her—and then we will both find a way to start over." She sighed. "I hope you do find Marstoke. I hope you kill him." Her chin fell. "And I hope you find the man behind your facade—and I hope you can live with him."

Trailing a finger along the shattered wood, she walked away.

Chapter Nineteen

I'd never seen Pearl even remotely angry before. She'd been a whore, she informed me. And her life had been a hard one, but a good one, too. She'd been careful. She'd kept control of her own destiny. Chose her protectors with care. A regular customer had set her up here and when the place closed, he'd bought it for her outright. There is a certain power, she told me, to being a whore.

--from the Journal of the infamous Miss Hestia Wright

Two days passed before Tru got aboard a packet bound for home. Two days in which he spent his time cleaning up the mess they'd made in St. Malo and cursing himself for a fool.

The inn had been in an uproar when he finally made it back, with Edgar's help. Letty's dragon-lady had roared in, hauled the still-cup-shot Penrith and Rackham out of their beds, forced them to kick in Letty's door, and bundled the whole company of them away in a rented traveling carriage. Hours later Callie had returned, but offered no explanation. She'd only packed a few things, asked Victoire if she'd like to learn to cook in an English kitchen, taken the girl and sailed for home.

Tru was left to make explanations and calm nerves. He'd told the truth, mostly. He'd assured each of them that there would be continued employment in some capacity or another. He'd sent men looking for Nardes, and the man had been found locked in the basement of Marstoke's main villa.

"That squat toad of a woman found me riffling through Marstoke's papers," the erstwhile rat catcher said with regret. "My own fault." He shook his head and pitched in, helping Tru calm the uproar. He knew a gentle, quiet couple in the area, and he took the unhappy blonde girl to stay with them until Stoneacre could work out who she was and what to do with her. He proved a dab hand at keeping Tru's wounds clean and bandaged too.

"You're not really a rat catcher, are you?" Tru asked, while he was being rebound after another fiery dose of spirits to his inner and outer layers.

"I am, occasionally, among other things," Nardes said with a shrug. "I do what Stoneacre needs done."

Tru had found a missive from the earl waiting for him. Stoneacre had discovered that Marstoke meant to return to England and had departed right away, intent on beating the marquess there. He hadn't been aware of the man's detour to St. Malo.

He found out quickly, though, and both Tru and Nardes received further instructions before the sun had set on the new day. Nardes was to stay and take over the inn for the time being, and to watch for the return of any of Marstoke's people. Tru was to get himself home as quickly as he could.

He already had tickets on the first packet to Portsmouth, and he walked a rut on the deck, according to the captain, as he paced his way across the English Channel. He smiled at the joke, ignored the pain in his side and went back to ferociously plotting the many things he was going to do and say to Callie Grant.

He was first off the slip, striding through the docks. They'd put up in the east end, amongst coastal huggers and other channel packets. He'd have to walk a ways to find transportation. He hoped like hell he could find something well sprung, because he didn't relish the thought of being jostled in a bumpy coach all the way to London.

The crowds grew thicker as her neared the main docks. He pushed through the throng, then paused to make way for a crested coach to pass.

It didn't. Instead it pulled up next to him. The window went down and a hand beckoned him. He looked down to find his brother's crest on the door, and opened it to find Hestia Wright inside.

"Come along, Lord Truitt. We've no time to lose."

He had to admit to a certain amount of nerves, but he heaved a sigh of resignation and climbed in.

She knocked on the ceiling and the coach began to move. Silence reigned for a bit while the two of them sat and observed each other.

"I'm disappointed, sir," she said at last. Her voice lilted even when she admonished him.

"No more than I, I assure you."

She gestured to the bench beside him. "I don't expect the ride to be easy on your injury. Please use the pillows and blankets to make yourself comfortable."

"You are all thoughtfulness." He was sore—and likely to be worse if he did not take her up on her offer. With her help, a rolled blanket and a pillow propped in the corner looked to do very well, though.

"Let's get the worst of it out of the way first, shall we?" She sat back on her bench. "I have to ask you not to present yourself at Half Moon House. She's not ready to see you."

"I hadn't meant to show up on your doorstep, actually. I'm not ready, either. I have some work to do before I should see her."

"Well, that does sound promising." Sighing, Hestia shook her head at him. "You've wounded her."

"I know."

"The most interesting thing is, I don't know whether to make you pay for it or to applaud you."

"Oh, I'm paying for it," he assured her.

She smiled. "I've watched them try, over the years. No one else has budged her an inch, let alone cracked her open far enough to get in a blow."

"It was a blow," he acknowledged. Hell, if there was anyone to confess the whole ugly truth to, it was Hestia Wright. She might just help him, for Callie's sake. If she didn't knock him senseless and drop him back into the Channel. "But I intend to make it up to her—every day, for all of her days."

She tilted her head, considering. "If she'll have you."

"If she'll have me," he sighed.

"Why should she?"

"Because it only took about a minute's thought to realize that she was right."

"Well, that is a promising start." She laughed. "Please continue."

"What she said to me, at the last. It shook me." He shot her a pleading look. "She sees me so clearly—far better than I saw myself. And she liked me still."

"More than that, I believe," Hestia said softly.

"And I threw it back at her. The greatest gift I've ever been given." He closed his eyes, though, and drank in hope along with her words. "It makes no sense, I know. Our acquaintance looks short from the outside, but it was . . . deep. True. It scared me, from the inside out. She saw what I'd been hiding from the world and laid it bare in just a few words."

"It does sound terrifying." It sounded like real sympathy. "My Callie has always been terribly blunt."

"It's one of her best qualities." He laughed. "Because, don't you know, she tossed out the solution for my problem just as casually."

Should he go further? He gave a mental shrug. He was already playing fast and deep with parts of himself that had never seen the light of day. "At first, I thought there was no use pursuing it. Why bother, if I didn't have her? And then I heard myself—and thought of what she'd say to that. And I knew."

He didn't have to explain further. Hestia was nodding understanding. "What will you do?"

"First thing—I'm going to get Letty away from Marstoke and turn her over to her sister. Again. And forever, this time."

"A very good start." She smiled. "I should be able to help you, there."

He forgot and leaned in, wincing when his chest and shoulder reminded him of his mistake. "What do you know?"

"Now that Marstoke's plans for Letty are known, they are impossible to carry out. But the wicked man has finally worked out just why she so closely resembles the Princess Charlotte. He's offering Letty as a trade."

"What does he want?"

"A chance to come home. He wants free passage through England, unmolested."

Tru couldn't block the cynicism that rose up, bitter in his mouth. "The royal family hasn't done a thing for those girls. Why should they start now? The Prince Regent wants Marstoke jailed. He'll never agree."

"He already has. He doesn't want the girl used against him, now or in the future. He wants to be the one shaping her destiny." She looked out at the dreary, busy street. "Lord Stoneacre put the fear of God into them all, outlining what Marstoke might have accomplished with her. Also, the Regent endures so much criticism about how he treats the Princess Charlotte, about his excesses and the hypocrisy of his behavior and that of his siblings. He doesn't want to hand Marstoke or his other enemies a martyr."

"He'll never just trade her outright."

"You're right about that. Marstoke never makes a move that doesn't have three levels of play in it."

"He's here?" His mind began to roil. So many possibilities for mischief.

"Yes. We're trying to discover what he's up to. And we want your help."

He nodded.

"There's much to do. This is turning into a large enterprise, a concerted effort to put a stop to the marquess. Stoneacre and his men are working to discover where he's run to ground. My own contacts are trying to discern why it was so important for him to come back, and what he's planning next. Your brother is looking into leads from the papers we found in that secret office."

"But he's safe, if you intend to keep to the Prince Regent's word."

"He's safe until we have Letty. After that . . ." She raised a brow. "As you said, he'll never just turn her over as he's promised. We want you to take point on getting her out of his clutches."

"How?"

"Marstoke thinks you are dead. He won't be wasting resources worrying about you. He's also not wasting much effort on Penrith any longer. He's left him in London and is using him as an errand and messenger boy. He's acted as the go-between with Stoneacre's men, setting up the truce. He also seems to be making arrangements for Lady Pilgren, one of Marstoke's known co-conspirators, to throw a ball."

Tru scowled. "Penrith should get out while he can. It's a dangerous position to be in, having failed Marstoke."

"And he's done it more than once."

"Even worse. He needs to come over. Offer him protection for whatever information he can get—although it won't be much. His days are numbered if he stays. Marstoke doesn't tolerate mistakes."

"I know. Penrith is acting like a man who knows

his end is near." She paused. "Callie seems to think he'll respond to you."

Tru considered. "She might be right. I've been in a similar position. But he might also hold my lies against me."

"Either way, you might learn something useful just in asking." Her fingers tapped the bench beside her. "He's at the Pulteney. What we need is a way to get you close to him, without anyone realizing . . ."

* * *

Tru had turned invisible. All it took was donning the uniform of a hotel porter—and it was as if he'd ceased to exist. A glance here or there fell upon the expensive bottle of wine he carried, but not one person glanced up at his face. He walked through the hotel without any questions and went straight to Penrith's room.

The man grumbled through the door when Tru knocked, until he told him that he'd come bearing gifts of wine. Then Penrith let him in and went back to collapse upon the sofa and pick up the drink he'd already poured.

It wasn't his first, Tru judged. He went to the sidebar, popped the cork and poured two glasses. Crossing to the sofa, he offered one to Penrith.

The other man looked up and sneered. "You're a cheeky—" Sudden bright color flooded his face. "You!" Shock warred with fury. "You're alive?"

"I am." Tru thrust the drink at him. "But I don't like your odds over the next weeks."

Penrith ignored the offered glass. "Do you think I don't know that?" He stood, anger emanating from him, and pushed Tru.

Tru didn't retaliate or resist. He only winced and clutched the drinks wide as Penrith put his hands on his chest and pushed again.

"Oh, hell." Penrith slumped. He took one of the

glasses and drained it. "I'm sorry." He poked at a red bloom on Tru's white shirt. "I see you were wounded at least."

"A right nasty one, too."

"No more than you deserve, lying to us like that."

Tru merely raised a brow.

Penrith had the grace to flush. "Oh, all right. We're both despicable."

They clicked glasses.

Penrith drank again and frowned at the wine in surprise. "This is far better than the swill I've been drinking."

Tru shrugged. "I figured Marstoke was paying the bill. We might as well have the best."

"Why are you here?" Penrith asked suddenly. "Did anyone see you? You're going to make things worse!"

Tru set down his glass. Calm and steady, that was how he needed to present himself. "I'm here to get you out."

"There's no escape." Penrith waved a glum hand. "Look at you, right back into the spider web."

Tru couldn't deny it. He was still caught up in the war. "At least I'm out of the line of fire—and I have a chance to get in a shot of my own. What do you intend to do? Do you think you can make penance by staying? Win back his favor with service? He doesn't work like that. He chews people up and spits them out. And once you've failed him . . ." He shook his head. "Marstoke will have an *accident* lined up for you within weeks."

Penrith shrugged. "There's no escaping it."

"Why not leave? Start over? Do something worthwhile with your life and let that serve as your penance. Stoneacre can get you a fresh start."

"In exchange for what?" he asked bitterly.

"Letty Robbins."

The other man slumped back onto the sofa. "Even if I wanted to, I couldn't give you the girl. I'm just a messenger boy now." He reached for the bottle and poured another glass of wine. "You must know he's not going to turn her over."

"It's what we suspect and fear. And it's why we need you. Help us save her."

Penrith shook his head. "Can't. Marstoke's planning something big. Something . . . unpleasant. I know it's all to happen at that infernal ball he's wrangled Lady Pilgren into throwing, but I know little else. They tell me nothing now." He sighed and tossed back the good wine like water. "There goes my chance at a German princess."

"Come on, man. There's more important things than your dreams of marriage. That girl's life is at stake." And Callie's heart. And his own future. "You must at least try."

"Why? So I can spend what's left of my life looking over my shoulder for Marstoke's assassin? You don't understand him at all if you think he'll just let me go." He threw up his hands. "The girl is the least part of it, in any case."

"Not to everyone." He had to find a way to convince the man to help them—and himself.

"He's planning several moves in that damned endless game of his. Whatever he's working on right now, it's something political and far-reaching. And there's something about Hestia Wright, too. And that's all on top of whatever he's planning with that pretty little girl."

"There are a lot of people working against him, in various ways. I'm to help the girl—and you." Tru's mind was turning. "But there's nothing to say that we cannot overlap. Penrith—what if I gave you the opportunity to earn Marstoke's favor—maybe even put him in *your* debt?"

The other man snorted. "I'd have to take a bullet for him."

"I may be able to arrange that—or at least the appearance of it. Or something equally as significant. Marstoke has no idea just how eventful that ball is going to be—and this might just be what you need in order to break ties with the man."

Penrith set his glass down. "Do you think it could work?"

"Who has been put in charge of Letty?"

The other man stilled. "Rackham."

Tru clapped his shoulder. "Get me the information I need to save the girl and I'll make sure you do Marstoke a good turn."

"How? When? The ball is tomorrow . . ." He checked his watch. "Tonight."

"Make your arrangements. I'll make mine. We'll meet before the ball—in the garden square outside Lady Penrith's home." Tru squeezed the man's shoulder. "We can do this."

The man shook his head. "I hope you're right."

Chapter Twenty

Pearl pulled out a stack of London papers and broadsheets. She'd had her Town friends send them. To my shock, they were all about me. About how I'd run away and left my family and all that was decent behind. About how I'd deliberately chosen a life of debauchery and sin.

--from the Journal of the infamous Miss Hestia Wright

Callie had dressed as a doxy more times than she could count, in the course of her work with Hestia Wright. She'd masqueraded as a governess a time or two. Once she'd even dressed as a nun.

Never had she looked like this.

Staring at her reflection, it was as if someone else looked back. Of significant note—her hair had been tamed. It taken two of the girls from the House well over an hour, and about a hundred hair pins, but her unruly hair had been swept up into a tidy mass at the back of her neck that somehow looked as if it had been crafted of rippling chestnut waves. A soft brush of powder had smoothed her complexion and just the hint of rose colored her lips.

She stood and crossed to the long mirror that the girls had dragged in. Now this—this was beyond anything of her experience. The dress was magnificent—and it was all hers—a gift from Hestia.

"I've had the fabric for an age. I saw it in Paris, and I knew I had to buy it, even though it is all wrong for my coloring." Hestia had caressed the orange-red silk net when she'd come to deliver it. "I knew I was saving it for something special, and once I met you, I knew it was yours."

"It picks out the colors of her hair like a treat," Peggy, one of the girls, had sighed.

"It was made for you, no doubt." Hestia smiled, but Callie saw the damp in her eyes.

"But how did you get it made so quickly?" Callie loved the simplicity of it. High waisted and low necked, it highlighted her bosom with a pleated, V-shaped fan. The skirt fell straight to a slightly flared hem. An embroidered border of rosebuds and garland decorated the bodice and was repeated at the bottom.

Hestia bit her lip. "I had it made to your measurements months ago," she'd confessed. "I knew the day was coming when we would have need of it."

Now Callie could only be grateful that she had. Alone at last, she watched herself in the mirror and twisted once to set the hem swirling. Outside the door she could hear feet hurrying up and down the stairs, hushed voices, slamming doors. Half Moon House was preparing for war.

And she was wondering what Lord Truitt Russell would think of her now.

Idiot that she was, she missed him. She missed his smile, the secret one that was for her alone, that meant they were sharing something hidden. She missed laughing with him, plotting with him, bouncing strategic ideas off him and watching him scoff—or occasionally raise his eyebrows in pleased respect.

She missed the feel of his hands upon her.

A knock sounded upon the door.

"Come."

Victoire came in with a tray. "I thought you might like something before you go out, you hardly ate a thing today . . . Oh, *Madame*!" she breathed. "You are like a princess!"

Ah, irony. Callie smiled through it. "Thank you, Victoire. Perhaps just some tea."

"I hope you are not nervous," the girl said, pouring. "You look wonderful." The girl gave a sheepish smile.

"Everyone wants to see you and wish you luck."

"They'll get their chance. I'd like to ask you, though—are you happy in the kitchens here?"

"Oh, yes, Madame! Thank you. I'm learning so much from Mrs. Marepott."

"Good." She put down her cup and saucer. "Listen, Victoire. Likely nothing will happen here tonight, but if it does, do not venture out. Stay in the kitchens, or stay in your room and you'll be safe enough."

The girl nodded, her eyes wide. "You keep safe too, *Madame*."

Callie nodded. Breathing deeply, she smiled at the girl and opened the door.

A smattering of applause greeted her, along with a collective sigh. Women and girls lined the stairs and waited in the open spaces below. Their faces beamed with approval.

Callie flushed. This was not the sort of attention she was used to, around here.

Below, Hestia Wright emerged from the passage that led to her small suite of rooms—and utter silence fell upon the crowd. They'd often seen the beautiful woman dressed to go into society, but tonight she'd outdone herself. She shone, a vision of ethereal beauty made flesh. From her golden curls to her jewels to her exquisitely fitted gown, she looked a storybook queen come to life.

Hestia cast a smile upon them all. "I know you will all be watchful tonight. Be careful, please, and take care of each other." She beckoned Callie. "Come, my dear. There is much work to be done."

* * *

Letty bent her head, her heart pounding while Marstoke's hands hovered at the back of her neck. He finished with the clasp and she looked up to meet his gaze in the mirror. Her hand automatically rose to touch the rope of magnificent pearls.

"I've kept this piece a long time," he told her. Memories lived behind his eyes—and they were not happy. "Only one other woman has ever worn it—and she was someone . . . very special."

"Thank you, my lord."

"You've trained hard and done well."

"Thank you, my lord."

"This is the role you were born to play, my dear. Tonight you will help me to accomplish some of my most cherished dreams."

She nodded.

He touched her shoulder, and then turned and walked out.

Letty stared at her reflection.

She looked wondrous. Truly like a princess, from her tiara to her toes, in jeweled and embroidered slippers. Years. She'd been preparing for this part for years, since the exciting days of her first real performance. Since she was pulled from the common green room and told a *lord* wished to see her privately.

A maid opened the door. "Lord Rackham is ready, miss."

Letty stood. *The greatest role in the history of theatre and the stage.*

She took up her reticule.

Such a shame that she would never get the chance to truly play it.

Chapter Twenty-One

They've already labeled you a prostitute, Pearl told me. Why not be a good one?

--from the Journal of the infamous Miss Hestia Wright

Callie followed Hestia into the servant's entrance at the back of Lady Pilgren's home.

"Stoneacre has arranged for us to have full access to the service areas of the house," Hestia explained. "With so many things to plan for tonight, he's taken over the butler's office as his hub of operations."

"Does Lady Pilgren know? Will she betray us to Marstoke?" She looked in wonder at Lord Stoneacre's men, in formal dress and the occasional brightly colored uniform, bustling right beside the countess's busy servants.

"What great lady ever truly knows what goes on below stairs?" Hestia's mouth twitched. "In any case, she's on uneasy ground, as it's become known that she's acted as one of Marstoke's allies. Tonight she's treading a delicate balance between him and the royal family. She only knows what she must."

Privately, Callie thought the lady was lucky to be on any ground at all, rather than tossed in a traitor's cell.

"Ah," Hestia stopped and squeezed Callie's hand. "Look, there is Mr. Lawrence McConnell. His part is crucial tonight. I must be sure he is ready." They exchanged meaningful grins. There was a delicious taste of irony to this particular bit of the plan to thwart Marstoke. "Why don't you wander a bit back here and get acclimated? I'd especially like you to become familiar with the two servant's entrances close to the ballroom, just in case. One of them is just down there." She pointed.

"You get to have all the fun," she griped. But Callie dutifully went off where she'd been bid. She could see the green baize of the door she wanted ahead, past several other doors and a connecting passage or two.

Ahead, a gentleman turned a corner and headed in her direction.

Her step faltered. "Tru."

He looked as surprised as she.

Her chin went up. "Lord Truitt." She had the mad thought that she could push past and ignore him.

He was having none of it. He approached, never taking his eyes off of her for a second. Just before he reached her, he opened a nearby door and pulled her inside. A storage area, it had been packed with furniture removed to make room for tonight's guests. Sofas and settees were pushed against the walls. One open spot remained, between a pedestal and urn and a stack of chairs. Tru pushed her into it, against the wall. He looked her up and down. "My God. You are exquisite."

"And you are full of nerve!" She pushed against his chest. "What are you doing?"

The answer became obvious. He was kissing her. And fool that she was, she was kissing him back. So much between them and it was all there in the complex dance they were doing with lips, teeth, and tongues. Frustrated passion, accusation, hope, desire . . . and love. They said it all with panting breaths and wandering hands and insistent mouths.

But she wasn't going to let him off so easily. She pulled back. "Nothing has changed."

He disagreed, the message flaring hot and bright with the press of his body against hers. "Everything has changed. Everything."

He continued on, kissing her again, making her tremble with the force of their wanting. Her body knew. Knew that she was coming home when she burrowed deeper into his embrace. But she was who she was. Her mother's child. Hestia's friend. She knew what she deserved. He had to convince her heart.

He knew it too, thank heavens. He pulled back. "You are thinking," he accused.

"Worse than that," she informed him. "I'm waiting."

"We're both going to be waiting." He pulled her close and she felt him, hard and ready. "Because there's work to be done tonight. We'll do it together, too. But before anything else happens tonight—I have things to say to you."

"I'm all ears."

He ran an appreciative finger along the edge of her bodice. "Thank God that's not true."

She rolled her eyes, and couldn't help but laugh a little too. But she couldn't let herself slide back into that ease with him, as much as she craved it.

He'd grown sober. "There will be things that we both must get used to, moving forward. I'll grow used to the fact that you are occasionally going to scare me spitless, like you did when you saw past my carefully crafted facade and realized that only a hollow man lived there."

She frowned. "That's too harsh a—"

"It isn't." He silenced her with a finger brushing across her lips. Back and forth, as soft as the touch of a breeze. "You made me think, made me take a long look at myself. You were right. There is a lot of empty space back there, but there are a few bricks to my foundation. My love for my brother. A few friendships I treasure. A quick turn of phrase and a damned good bowling action." He made a face. "It's a piss poor showing for a man of my age and position."

She pressed her lips into a kiss for the end of his finger. "It sounds like a lovely start."

"I vow to you," he whispered, "that a hollow man is

not what you'll have to get used to. I mean to add to that foundation, Callie. The first brick comes tonight—when I ensure Letty's safety and freedom. I'm going to do what I should have done before. No matter what happens tonight, I'll move heaven and earth to return your sister to your side."

Tears tried to well up, but she blinked them back. She'd waited so long, hadn't known if the day would ever come that someone would want to put her needs ahead of his own. She should be thrilled. And yet . . .

"With you by my side," he assured her.

Some of the tightness eased from her shoulders. He did know. He understood. This time she let the tears come.

"The empty spaces will get filled every day, I hope, with you as my partner." He raised his brows. "You made me promise to challenge you, and I will. But I want you to be my tempest, Callie, and my port in a storm too. With you, only one will never do. I have to have them all."

She flushed. "I will—"

The door opened. "Russell? There you are." Stoneacre stood at the door. "Miss Grant, good. You must come at once, both of you."

"What is it?" Irritation bloomed in Tru's voice.

Everyone stopped as Penrith pushed in past the earl.

"I couldn't wait." The man's eyes were wild, his breath coming fast and urgent. "He means to kill her!"

Callie gasped. "Letty?"

Tru stepped forward. "We have men here. Greater numbers. Many eyes to watch and react. We won't let it happen."

"That's just it. It's not going to happen here." He glanced at Callie, then at Stoneacre. "He's sent them off to Half Moon House. Rackham is to slit her throat and leave her broken body out front for all to see."

"Oh, my God." Callie's heart pounded in panic and denial.

"Tru—head out there. Go!" Stoneacre barked the order. "I'll get Penrith ready for his part."

She was already moving forward when Tru reached for her hand.

"Miss Grant!" Stoneacre was still barking. "You stay here."

"She goes." Tru met her gaze. "She goes where I go."

Stoneacre didn't waste breath arguing. He started calling for carriages.

Together, they set off at a run.

Chapter Twenty-Two

I thought and thought about my options, my future. I looked at those broadsheets and I thought about my family and about Lord M--- and about the man he'd sent looking for me.

--from the Journal of the infamous Miss Hestia Wright

For once, London had been blessed with a clear night, with nary a drop of rain or wisp of fog. There might even be a star or two visible overhead in the darker areas.

But though the stars were clear, the streets were not. And Tru had no time for stargazing. He and Callie pressed through the streets in a delivery cart, as it had been the only vehicle rigged and ready to go when they emerged. Every turn, every haul on the reins sent fire tearing through his chest and side. He gritted his teeth and drove on.

"Cut through this alley and it will get us nearly to the Strand." Callie sat, tense and balanced upon the bench. Her fists were clenched over the edge and her knee bounced unceasingly.

He made the turn, praying that they would make it in time.

"Isaac knows everything that goes on in and around the House."

"The butler? The big one?"

"Yes. He'll never let anything happen to Letty."

Traffic on the Strand was crowded, but moving along. After just a few minutes, Tru pointed with his chin. "Isn't that Craven Street, ahead?"

"Yes. Almost there."

They drove quickly down the quiet street. Nothing else moved over the cobblestones, though the houses were brightly lit. As they drew closer, Tru saw a carriage pulled

to the side. It had been left a ways before Half Moon
House and turned to face the Strand, not the river at the end
of the street. In preparation for a quick departure?

Yes. Once they moved past it, he spotted them.
Rackham was pulling Letty along the pavement, toward the
House.

She wasn't making it easy for him. As they drew
closer, he could see that she was dressed as if for the ball.
Jewels in her hair caught the faint light as she struggled.
She dug her heels in and when Rackham forced her along,
she tangled her feet with his.

Callie was climbing down and out of the cart even
before he could get it parked. He pulled over.

"No! Not here!" Letty was cursing and crying.
"It's too cruel."

Tru sucked in a breath as he pulled the break.

"Letty!" Callie was in the street now, and heading
toward them.

He leaped down. His shirt grew damp as he started
to bleed through his bandages.

"Callie!" Letty struggled anew and began to smack
Rackham with her reticule.

Tru fished for his pistol, but he could barely hold it
with his shooting hand. "Let her go," he shouted.

"Chaput?" Rackham peered towards them. He
yanked Letty closer and Tru saw that he had a pistol too.
"Russell, I mean, don't I?" He shook his head. "Marstoke
is not going to be happy to hear that you are alive."

"I don't give a damn what Marstoke thinks." He
gestured toward Letty. "If this is what he asks of you, then
I'm not sure why you do."

"What choice do I have?"

"Don't do this. Make the right choice, at last,
Rackham. Easy enough not to blight your life. Let the rest

take care of itself."

Rackham laughed. "You don't even know. The duns are called in, the creditors at the door. My family cast me out rather than pay my debts again. Marstoke bought me some breathing room, but this German princess is my last, best chance. And I owe him."

"You don't owe him this," Callie said.

"I don't want to hear a word from you," Rackham sneered. "I watched you almost kill the old man."

"He deserves to die. He is a disease, spreading pain and turmoil. Letty is innocent." She was watching her sister closely. Some silent message was passing between the two of them.

Rackham kept going. They were nearly at the iron gate at Half Moon House.

Tru transferred the pistol to his other hand and stepped closer. "That's far enough. You are not going to do this."

"I am," Rackham spat. "And I'm going to reap the reward for loyalty that you and Penrith were too stupid and weak to claim." He waved his own pistol. "I'm supposed to cut her throat," he growled, "but I don't mind putting a bullet in her first. Now back away!"

He only laughed as Tru raised his pistol. "I just watched you switch hands." He gestured towards the blood seeping through Tru's linen shirt. "Your good hand is useless. Can you aim with the other?" He jerked Letty so that she stood between them. "Do you want to try?"

The bastard was right. He held his finger ready, but not on the trigger, thinking, searching for his next move.

"I do." Callie stepped forward. Her hands were at her side, but one of them held her knife.

Rackham sneered. "And just what do you think—"

"Letty—low!"

Tru held his breath as Letty jerked free and ducked down. Callie sent the knife spinning toward her. Just as he'd seen Callie do, mere weeks ago, Letty plucked the blade out of the air. In one smooth motion she stood and plunged it into Rackham's chest.

The man shrieked. His gun clattered to the pavement as his arm fell useless. Letty brandished the blade again and he fell back.

Tru could not find words. He stared at the spectacle before him and then back at Callie. "Under his clavicle?" he asked.

"I told you it worked," she said smugly.

"But you . . . But Letty . . ."

She shrugged. "Who do you think I practiced with?"

* * *

The next hour flew by. Callie let Isaac deal with Rackham and his wound. The man was currently bandaged and tied to a chair in the wide and spacious entry hall. Callie spent her time in tearful reunion with Letty, catching up and sharing stories.

And she watched Tru.

He was anxious. He started up every time the door opened, as if he could will the news of what was happening with Marstoke to come quickly. She finished drying Letty's tears, tucked her up in her own bed, left Peggy to sit with her, and searched him out.

He was pacing and watching Rackham exchange sneers with the girls of the house. The bravest of them were gathered in groups in the two parlors off of each end of the main hall, whispering and shaking their heads.

Callie slipped into his arms and held him tight.

"There, but for the grace of God, go I," he said quietly, indicating Rackham.

Giving him her most ferocious stare, she gripped his arms. "Enough of that. You are entirely too hard on yourself."

"I rather think it is the opposite—"

"Nonsense. You faced the same test he did—and you passed yours in flying colors when you stole away that manuscript of the Love List rather than let it spark an international incident—and ruin all of us here. You've proven yourself again and again since then too, so no more of that."

She ran her hands along his arms and took up his. "Again and again, I've met men who wish to ignore me, conquer me, or treat me like a soap bubble. None of them could take the time to pay attention, to believe and trust in me. And trust leads to trust. You are the first man who ever tempted me into letting go, who allowed me to loose the reins and still feel safe and accepted."

"Until I made the huge mistake of being like all the rest."

"Yes." She tilted her head. "But I expect you to see the error of your ways."

"Yes, *Madame*." He looked so beautifully meek.

She stepped in close and ran a finger over his scar, creased again by that wrinkle of tension. "I never gave you an answer to your question."

He frowned.

"Yes—I will be your tempest and your port—if you will be my anchor?"

He took her face in his hands. The look he gave her—it made her clutch his wrists. They stood a moment, sharing breath and space and want, and then he leaned in—

And Stoneacre burst through the door. "Is everyone all right?"

Several men poured in after him.

Girls shrieked. A few looked interested.

"No!" Rackham groused loudly. "That jumped-up whore might as well have put that knife in my heart. I'm a dead man anyway—"

Callie gave Isaac a look and the big man stuffed a kerchief in Rackham's mouth before he just tilted the man's chair and began to drag it away.

"Marstoke?"

Callie hated hearing the strangled note of tension in Tru's tone.

Stoneacre shook his head and the whole room deflated. The earl approached and took Callie and Tru aside.

"What the hell happened?" Tru demanded.

"Mr. Lawrence McConnell performed beautifully. Marstoke was struck with true fear, at least for a few moments."

"Penrith?" asked Tru.

"He did well, too. Wherever Marstoke is now, I'm sure he believes that Penrith saved his life."

"But how could he slip your net? All of those men?" Tru's bleakness was growing.

"He was prepared," sighed Stoneacre. "He was in the midst of the presentation he meant to make when McConnell interrupted."

"What was it?" Callie interrupted. "We knew it wasn't to be Letty. Was it something dangerous, as we feared?"

The earl shook his head. "It was . . . art. A sculpture." He sounded disbelieving. "A piece of art that he meant to present to the hostess."

Callie knew how he felt. "*Sculpture?*"

"Did you examine it closely?" Tru sounded

skeptical. "Check for a poison coating or a hidden compartment?"

"I called in an antiquities expert and left it in his hands. Jack Alden has only had a quick look at it but he says it appears to be only a piece of art." Stoneacre faced Callie. "Whatever the message it was meant to deliver, Hestia Wright understood it. She is there still, asking questions of Lady Pilgren, her staff and those of Marstoke's cronies who we detained."

Callie's heart fell. She didn't know the particulars, but only one subject could have kept Hestia away from Half Moon House on this night.

"Marstoke never made the presentation, but slipped away in the chaos after the McConnell's shooting."

"And who knows where or when we'll ever find him again," Tru bit out. "Likely not until he's ready to hit us with his next bit of mischief."

"We might still get him. We were prepared, too. There are troops at the city gates and along the port roads."

"He'll know that. Odds are that he's found a hiding hole in Town. He'll wait for the attention to wane—and then he'll likely head straight for that cursed maze of chalk tunnels in Dover. He'll be untouchable then, damn it all."

"Chalk tunnels?"

"Under the Castle, in the cliffs." Tru told her how close he'd come to catching Penrith and Rackham before they'd joined Marstoke. "Smuggling gangs and ruffians control parts of those tunnels now. Even Stoneacre couldn't get me in."

"He has contacts with them, obviously. We've made no headway. I don't even know anyone to go to for information." The earl looked tired and sounded worse.

"Chalk," Callie said. "Chalk tunnels." Her mind had gone away, back to that night in Dover. Birch and Cobb, with white dust in their hair and on their shoulders, turning into streaks in the rain. She looked wildly at Tru and then at Stoneacre. "I know who to ask. And I think I know where Marstoke has gone to ground!"

Chapter Twenty-Three

I decided that if the world wished for me to be a whore, then I would be the best, most dazzling, most influential whore that England—and the world—had ever seen.

--from the Journal of the infamous Miss Hestia Wright

A different city with a different sort of sky, but many things were similar to that fateful night in Dover. The lanes were just as narrow, the alleys just as filthy. The soft sound of small feet scurrying away ahead of them was the same, as was the feeling of helplessness hanging in the air.

This time, though, Tru and Stoneacre walked at her side and a gaggle of Prinny's troops trailed behind.

The house in Cock Pit Alley was small and looked to be crumbling under the weight of its own misery. Callie had never been inside, but she knew where Birch lived. Everyone knew—and knew to stay away.

After a short consultation, the men all melted into the darkness. Only Callie stepped up to knock on the door.

It took several attempts before someone answered. A dirty boy, rail thin, and perhaps twelve years old, yanked it open with impatience. "Wot ye want?"

"I want to talk to Birch."

The boy eyed her up and down. "He's busy."

She pulled her cloak tighter about her. "He'll want to see me."

"Look, he's already got company. So, git."

A querulous call sounded from within. The boy turned to shout over his shoulder. "Some doxy to see Birch!"

"I don't need to come in," Callie told him. "Just tell him to step out here." Suddenly inspired, she added, "Tell him it's about a job."

The boy sighed, then spat in the corner. "Wait here."

She did, looking neither to the right nor the left, but only at the weathered door before her. No telling whose eyes might be trained on her right now.

At last the door swung open again. Birch motioned her back and stepped out to join her. "Who's that?" he asked roughly.

She tossed back her hood.

He groaned. "Callie Grant, I have no time for your foolishness."

"No, you don't," she agreed.

"You did not come here about a job."

"I did. I want to ask about the job in which you were hired to take Letty Robbins to Dover."

"Goodnight, Miss Callie. I'm busy tonight and I've no time to tell you again to let that girl go."

"I know who hired you for that job," she said quietly. "And I know he's inside right now."

That got his attention. "Turn around and head right back to Half Moon House, girl, before you get yourself hurt."

"I can't, Birch. It's over. Lord Stoneacre is with me, and a mess of soldiers too. Your place is surrounded even now. They won't let Marstoke get away again. But you've been kind to me, in your own way. I don't want you to go down with him." She pursed her lips. "I also know you would never live in a place without a way out— one that most don't know about. Tell me where it is and where it leads and you can walk away right now."

He frowned. "My boy . . ."

"Will be released into your custody. Think, Birch. If you shout now or run back in there to warn him, there might be shooting. Your boy could be hurt. Marstoke might escape, but you'll hang in his place."

"Damn it, Callie Grant. I always did hate to go up against you."

The secret passage was a cobwebbed stairway, leading from Birch's parlor to the basement next door. Tru and Callie and a dozen ready rifles were waiting when Marstoke and Anselm burst through it, fleeing Stoneacre and his men.

The marquess froze when he saw the tableau—and reached for a pocket.

"Please, do," Tru urged him. "You will save the government the expense of your trial."

Marstoke's hands went up. Murder lived in his face. Two soldiers rushed forward to take him and chain his hands behind his back. He merely continued to glare, a temple to cold fury and the promise of revenge. And then he and a still-protesting Anselm were marched out.

Callie turned to one of the torch bearers. "Tell Stoneacre to send a message to Hestia Wright right away." She looked at Tru, tears starting to form. "It's over. It's finally over."

Tru was staring after the departed men. Now he heaved a huge sigh. Smiling, he beckoned her over and wrapped her in his arms. He kissed her, swift and fierce. "No. Now it's just beginning."

* * *

They were married at Half Moon House, at Callie's insistence. As she'd hoped, many of the women there entered into the spirit of the thing with zeal, making the place sparkle and arranging an abundance of gauze and garland. Victoire was thrilled, as she got to learn how to make salmon mousse shaped like a fish and a dozen types of little cakes.

The Duchess of Aldmere made a gift of the bride's gown, an exquisite dress of ivory, embroidered with sparkling gems and a trim of deep red blooms. Callie had never felt more beautiful than when she came down the stairs to where Letty stood poised to escort her to the makeshift altar in the blue parlor.

Tru waited for her there. He smiled hugely when she appeared and she caught her breath. The old restlessness was gone, the perpetual frown that creased his scar had disappeared. Constant tension had given way to purpose and confidence. Her chest tightened. So much joy, so much promise for the future. She teared up at the shining happiness of it all.

"What's this?" He welcomed her with a smile and wiped a tear with a thumb.

She gave him a watery grin. "I did promise to cry at your wedding."

He laughed and leaned in. "I believe you promised to cause a ruckus, too?"

"Only if you married inappropriately," she whispered in pretend outrage. She cast a jaundiced eye over the happy gathering and down the front of her gown. "I'll get to the ruckus later," she conceded. "In private."

He raised a brow. "Promise?"

Her mouth twitched. "I do."

Epilogue

They took a bridal trip to St. Malo, driving up to the inn in a colorfully painted delivery wagon, which they presented to Edgar even before setting foot inside.

"It's larger than my other cart," he said happily. "I'll have to redo all of the figures. It might be as much as six wagon lengths less from the docks!"

A new innkeeper had been appointed, as Nardes had been recalled. This one was a subordinate of Stoneacre's as well, tasked with keeping the inn in trade and watching the area for a few months, at least.

Tru shook his hand and apologized for arriving with the sole purpose of stealing away some of his staff.

"We are truly innkeepers now," Callie told Marie. "We have need of good help, if you would ever consider leaving Brittany."

The Oyster had been Hestia's bridal gift. She'd given it to Callie in exchange for her promise to use it as the Crescent House, as she'd once planned.

"This place was left to me by a woman with a soft heart and a generous nature. I promised to honor her and vowed to find someone with the same qualities. You have them, Callie, and so many more strengths to go with them."

Callie had cried and laughed and promised, and when their bridal trip was over, she and Tru traveled to inspect their new prospect.

It had stood empty for quite some time.

"It's going to need a lot of work," Tru warned as they went through the rooms hand in hand.

"I know," she answered happily.

They spent the first months of their marriage working together to restore the place and turn it into someplace welcoming and safe. An auspicious beginning for any couple, Callie thought. And when Hestia came for a visit, bringing the Duke and Duchess of Aldmere along, her happiness was complete.

They'd also brought her first special guest.

"She's had a hard time of it," Hestia warned. "She needs a gentle touch. I know you'll treat her well."

"She was a dresser to Lady Ashe, but was treated roughly by her son. Stoneacre has put the fear of God into the young man, and I hired her away," Brynne said. "I put it about that I'm sending her to Paris to be specially trained in the art of the *coiffure*."

"We'll take care of her," Callie assured them, "and by the time the baby comes, I'm sure we'll all have several options to offer her. Now come, you two. I want Hestia to see the parlor upstairs."

"You've done well," Hestia said as they sat down to tea. "Thank you for restoring it so beautifully. Your mother would be proud."

"We have plans for further improvements," Callie began.

"Don't get too caught up in them right away," Brynne warned. "Aldmere didn't ask Tru to go riding on a whim. He is even now asking your husband to take up the reigns on some of the ducal business ventures. He needs someone organized and easy to work with, and most importantly, someone he can trust."

Callie blinked.

"Don't look so dismayed. With a good courier system, he should be able to do a vast amount of work from here. And this way we can tempt you back to London for regular visits, too."

"You are sneaky," Callie accused her with a grin. Looking to Hestia, she asked, "And speaking of sneaky, what is the news of Marstoke?"

"He's still being held in Newgate, despite pestering for release. Preparations for his trial have begun.

Stoneacre is at work on the political side. I've offered up quite a few accounts of his abuse of women and several witnesses eager to testify against him. The barristers are working around the clock, trying to catalogue his misdeeds."

"No one speaks of anything else," Brynne told her. "London is plastered with caricatures and broadsheets mocking the Wicked Marquess."

"And I've taken great pleasure in commissioning a few of them," Hestia said with a smile. "He despises being mocked, so I make sure he has a new one delivered every morning with his gruel."

They all grinned.

Hestia set down her tea. "Aldmere mentioned something about some training sessions with Tru. When our visit is finished, Tru may take my place in the carriage back to London."

Brynne looked surprised. "And what will you do?"

"I am going on to Rennes. I must find out what's happened to Rhys. There may be clues there that will help me find him."

Callie choked on her tea.

"It's fine, dear. I've spoken to Brynne and told her the truth."

"I'm sorry, it's just . . . I've never heard you speak openly of . . ."

"My son? No. It has never been safe to do so. But I was hiding him from Marstoke, not the world. Even before he was born, I knew I could *never* let that monster near my child. So I did the hardest thing I've ever been called to do—I gave him up. I made the world think he'd never been born. It's been an ache in my heart every day since."

"I do think Marstoke was searching for him. Although how he found out you'd left him in Brittany . . ."

There was no telling how such information got out. "Somehow he learned of him, but are we sure that he found him? How can you know if he's ever telling the truth, Hestia? He would say anything to hurt you."

"He knows. I've failed." Hestia's complexion had paled. It put Callie right on edge. She'd never seen her friend and mentor look anything but serene. "That sculpture at Lady Pilgren's ball. It was a message to me. And my son created it."

Callie reached out to grip her hand. Brynne took the other.

They all jumped at a knock on the door.

"Sorry to disturb, Madame." Marie poked her head in. "There's a message and the boy says it's urgent."

Callie rose to take the note. "It's for you, Hestia." She handed it over and closed the door. While Hestia opened it, she set about to refresh everyone's tea. She looked up to hand over a fresh cup, and instead slowly set it down.

The note had fluttered to the floor. Gone was the forlorn expression. Hestia's entire body had tightened. She looked hard, angry and unforgiving.

"What is it?" she whispered.

Hestia did not whisper. She spoke in a tone that Callie had never heard before. "It's Marstoke. He's escaped

HALF MOON HOUSE

Author's Note:

Thank you for reading *The Leading Lady!* I sincerely hope you enjoyed it.

If you would like to read about what happened at Lady Pilgren's ball, between Marstoke, Penrith and the mysterious Mr. Lawrence McConnell, you can find the scene included in *Beyond a Reasonable Duke*, a short story in the *50 Ways to Kill Your Larry* anthology.

Would you like to know when my next book is released? Sign up for my newsletter at my website: http://www.DebMarlowe.com

You can also connect with me on:

On Facebook

On Twitter

On Pinterest

or at

http://www.RedDoorReads.com

And don't miss the other books in the Half Moon House Series

The Love List

An Unexpected Encounter

A Slight Miscalculation

Liberty and the Pursuit of Happiness

A Waltz in the Park

Beyond a Reasonable Duke: a short story in the 50 Ways to Kill Your Larry anthology

and

Coming Soon:

The Lady's Legacy

About the Author

USA Today Bestselling Author Deb Marlowe adores History, England and Men in Boots. Clearly she was destined to write Historical Romance.

A Golden Heart winner and Rita nominee, Deb grew up in Pennsylvania with her nose in a book. Luckily, she'd read enough Romances to recognize the true modern hero she met at a college Halloween party--even though he wasn't wearing breeches and boots. They married, settled in North Carolina and produced two handsome, intelligent and genuinely amusing sons. Though she spends most of her time with her nose in her laptop, for the sake of her family she does occasionally abandon her inner world for the domestic adventures of laundry, dinner and carpool. Despite her sacrifice, none of the men in her family is yet willing to don breeches or tall boots. She's working on it.

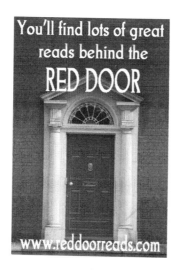

53550949R00150

Made in the USA
Charleston, SC
13 March 2016